STEFANO BLACKWOOD

THE CUBE OF DOMINIUM SERIES

BENEATH *the* VEILS *of* POWER

First paperback edition March 2025

Copy Editing by Sydney Weinberg
Book design by Stefano Schintu

www.stefanoblackwood.com

to Jadon and Rowan, my very first supporters

———

PROLOGUE

BODRUM VILLAGE – 2500 BC

The small Anatolian village of Bodrum was settling into the stillness of early morning. Most fishermen had already set sail, hoping to find enough fish to feed their families. Halina and her two younger sisters Ayça and Esma were playing in the warm sand, building makeshift castles with stones and twigs while their father, Morrat, repaired nets nearby. He paused his work to admire their innocence and joy, which he vowed to protect at all costs.

"Halina, I need to get something from the workshop," he called out gently. "Take care of your sisters, don't let them near the water."

"Yes, Papa!" she replied.

Morrat smiled before turning towards the village, glancing back one last time to ensure his daughters were safe.

"Halina! Spin me around fast!" shouted Ayça, the littlest sister.

Halina grabbed Ayça's hands and started spinning round and round until they both stumbled, dizzy with laughter. Just then, their other sister Esma began walking towards the shoreline. Halina quickly yelled for her to come back. The little girl's curiosity overrode her sister's command, and she paused at the water's edge. Turning back towards Halina, Esma extended her small arm skyward, her finger pointing. Halina's eyes widened as she spotted a peculiar sight in the sky.

A light, unlike any shooting star she had ever seen, flickered and pulsed with an otherworldly energy. It moved with purpose, growing larger and brighter with each passing second.

"Get away from the water!" Halina commanded, her protective instincts kicking into overdrive. She rushed towards her middle sister, her feet kicking up sand as she ran. Esma, still transfixed by the approaching light, remained rooted to spot. Halina yanked her back from the shoreline. The two stumbled backward to where Ayça lay cowering on the sand, their eyes never leaving the mesmerizing spectacle above them.

The light grew impossibly bright and descended rapidly. Halina instinctively shielded both sisters with her body, her heart pounding as she braced for impact. The light crashed into the sea, and an enormous plume of water erupted skyward, glowing with an inner light that defied explanation.

Halina, Ayça and Esma stood frozen in awe and terror as water rained down around them. The once-calm sea now churned and frothed, waves lapping frantically at the shore as if trying to expel the foreign object that had invaded its depths. An unnatural silence fell over the beach. The usual sounds of lapping waves and keening seabirds were conspicuously absent, as if nature was holding her breath. Halina tightened her grip on both sisters' hands, her eyes fixed to the glowing spot in the water.

Tentatively, Halina approached the shore, though Ayça begged her to stay back. She was shocked by what she saw: some sort of grey, humanoid creature was bobbing over the rough waves. She jumped back as the creature washed upon the sand and slowly turned its face towards her, mumbling something unintelligible.

"Go call Papa. Quickly!" Halina yelled.

Both her sisters turned to run, but just then, they heard the sound of footsteps. Their father and mother came sprinting down the path through the dunes, followed by a small crowd.

"Halina! What happened? Are you alright?" Morrat yelled, his voice thick with worry.

"Look, Papa!"

Halina pointed towards the greyish creature, lying on its side in the shallow water. Though it had four limbs and a head like a human, its body was shimmering, iridescent skin that changed colors with every movement, ranging from deep purples to electric blues. It was smaller than a grown human, and its eyes were three times larger than human eyes, lacking defined pupils or irises. Instead, they resembled swirling pools of bioluminescent liquid, continuously changing color and brightness. The mouth was a small, perfectly round opening surrounded by minute, crystalline structures in place of lips or teeth as he attempted to communicate in its peculiar language. An ominous symbol resembling a serpent had been branded into its forehead. She noticed its breathing was labored and it coughed raggedly.

Morrat stepped forward fearlessly, ignoring the warnings of those around him. He gripped the knife he used to gut fish tightly in his fist. As he moved closer, he saw that the creature was dying.

"*Onu koru,*" it rasped.

"*Onu koru?*" echoed Morrat uncertainly, taking another step closer.

Suddenly, the creature grabbed Morrat's arm with unearthly strength, making everyone press backward in terror. Morrat couldn't move. He was connected to the creature's thoughts for what seemed like an eternity. Suddenly, the connection broke. The creature's head fell back, its eyes wide and staring, and its hand slowly opened, revealing a small cube glowing brightly with a kaleidoscope of swirling colors inside – almost as if it was alive! Morrat thought he could see strange symbols appear in the cube's depths, and felt a pang deep within his soul.

Inexorably drawn to the cube's unknown power, Morrat reached for the cube with trembling fingers.

"Morrat, NO!" the girls' mother shouted desperately.

He didn't listen. Instead, he quickly slipped off his keffiyeh and wrapped it carefully around the cube, obscuring it from view. As Morrat took hold of the cube, the enigmatic dead creature broke apart into a million specks of shimmering dust and vanished into thin air.

1

NEAR TOULOUSE, OCTOBER 1793

The tavern door creaked open, and Napoleon stepped inside, the tension of the recent battle etched into his youthful face. As he settled into a quiet corner, a palpable silence fell upon the room. Every eye watched with awe, but Napoleon pretended not to care.

His entourage soon descended upon the other tables, drank, ate, and made merry. Laughter erupted like sporadic gunfire at night, punctuating the steady rhythm of clinking glasses. Patrons, emboldened by drink and the camaraderie forged in dim, warm rooms, shared stories and jests. The walls, lined with bottles whose contents promised both solace and oblivion, absorbed the symphony of human joy and sorrow that played this night as it did every night. Napoleon remained still, scanning the room.

A young maiden emerged from the shadows. Her hand was shaking as she lifted a mug of local wine off her tray and placed it on Napoleon's table. His reputation as a fierce warrior had spread far and wide across France; the very mention of his name was enough to strike fear into any who might oppose him. Although the maiden didn't dream of defying Napoleon, being near him stirred up a strange mixture of excitement and unease within her.

"Would you like something to eat?" she asked tremulously.

Napoleon scrutinized her, almost enjoying her apparent uneasiness.

"What's your name?" he asked.

"Anne," she replied, struggling to keep her composure.

"Do I scare you?"

"I'm not sure," she said, swallowing.

"Well," he said, in an almost tender voice, "only enemies should fear me."

Anne's heart raced as her eyes met his. He didn't look as menacing as everyone had said; there was something else in his gaze. Something that Anne couldn't quite place. Heat began to rise in her cheeks, and she felt drawn to him. It was a feeling she'd never had for any other man before. Almost frightened, she spun around as if to return to the kitchen.

"Wait,' Napoleon called, with a little chuckle. 'You forgot my order."

Anne stopped. She was flushed, acutely conscious of the desire to flee while at the same time fearful of shirking her duty as a waitress.

"What can I bring you?" she finally replied, approaching meekly.

"Your best dish!" he declared.

Anne tucked a strand of hair behind her ear, nervously avoiding eye contact, and smiled to herself as she hurried to the kitchen. Napoleon watched her leave. Grinning cheekily, he took a deep swig from the mug. The wine's fruity sweetness enveloped his palate, prompting a smile. "This is surprisingly delightful."

In the kitchen, Anne's mama gripping her arm tightly.

"What in the world were you thinking?!' she shrieked, the words flying from her mouth like bullets. 'I've told you time and time again not to get familiar with customers, especially that fellow. Do you even know who he is?"

Anne tried to explain that Napoleon had been nothing but kind to her, but it was no use–her mother knew best.

Violet Blanchet was in her mid-forties, but she still remembered the joyful days of her marriage, followed all too soon by tragedy when the war took her young husband. Left with no one but herself to rely on, she had worked hard in the family tavern to raise Anne, now almost full-grown. She dreamed of nothing more than to protect her daughter from the pain of life. To love a man and to be left alone with a young child was the fate Violet most feared might befall the lovely Anne.

"Oh, I could tell you stories, Anne, but you should stay away from him—he's a soldier and not to be trusted. Now take this! Quickly, quickly! Bring him his dinner, and then get back here!"

Anne gripped the steaming stew in the cleanest cloth she could find and made her way to Napoleon's table, her heart beating faster with every step. What was it about him that stirred such agitation within her? Was it his aura of power? When she arrived, Napoleon gazed intently into her eyes. She felt an intense inner conflict as their eyes met–should she drop his gaze or not?

"Venison stew, our best dish," she murmured.

Napoleon didn't take his eyes off her.

"What was that scowling woman saying to you in the kitchen doorway?"

Anne chuckled, happy for the excuse to prolong their conversation.

"That's just my mother. She's suspicious of any man who talks to me."

"She's not wrong, you know. A beautiful girl like you needs someone to watch over her."

She'd been through this before. It was a tale as old as time; the concerned looks, the patronizing smiles, the not-so-subtle attempts to insinuate themselves into her life under the guise of being her protector. Yet, somehow, this time felt different. Anne was pulled, questioning what this particular man wanted from her. Was he after her beauty? Her youth? Or perhaps it was the thrill of playing the hero, of having a damsel in distress to rescue and claim as his own?

"I'm not helpless. I can take care of myself," Anne retorted, tossing her long dark hair.

"I'm sure you can," he said lightly, lifting a spoonful of stew to his lips and tasting it. "Good stew."

Anne let out a nervous giggle, her cheeks flushing as she attempted to hide her embarrassment.

Violet glanced from the kitchen doorway, tapping her foot impatiently. She could hear Anne's laughter from the other side of the room, making her uneasy.

"Anne! Anne!" she hissed quietly.

But Anne was in another world, having forgotten her waitressing duties. Napoleon's adventurous lifestyle fed her curiosity about the world beyond the safe walls of the tavern.

As the night dragged on, Anne sought any excuse to talk more with Napoleon, while Violet, smelling danger, struggled to keep her only daughter away from a man famous for bringing destruction wherever he went.

The late hour came, and Anne busied herself with cleaning tables while the tavern's guests began seeking places to rest. Violet approached Napoleon's table and handed him a key to his room.

"If you'd kindly follow me, I'll show you to your room," she offered, forcing a polite smile.

Napoleon nodded his agreement and rose to follow her. Anne moved gracefully towards a nearby table, attempting to conceal her real aim of getting closer to him, making her presence known—or so it appeared to him. Napoleon leaned in, his breath warm against her ear.

"Meet me in my room tonight," he whispered. His words sent a shiver down her spine.

Without a word, Anne turned and walked away, her steps deliberate and measured. She sensed Napoleon's gaze on her, intense and uncertain. Her departure left a charged silence in the air, thick with unspoken questions. As she disappeared around a corner, Napoleon stood rooted to the spot, his mind a storm of doubt and hope. Had he misinterpreted the signals? The lingering glances, subtle touches, and charged conversations—were they mere illusions? Or did Anne feel the same way?

"Are you coming?" Violet's voice pulled him from his thoughts.

Meanwhile, Anne's mind was equally tumultuous as she sought refuge in the kitchen's solitude. She paced the space, attempting to distract herself from the words that echoed in her head—*meet me in my room tonight.* Her attraction to Napoleon was undeniable—his charisma, his power, his... eyes. The thought of a secret meeting sent waves of anticipation through her. Yet, a cautious voice in her mind—one that sounded a lot like her mother's— warned her. "This is dangerous," it whispered. "You're playing with fire."

Anne plunged her hands into the cold water and began washing the mugs. Time seemed to stretch as she grappled with her decision, as she did her best to tidy the kitchen while her mother was gone. She dreaded the moment when she would have to go to sleep, and the night would end.

"Anne," came Violet's voice from down the hall.

"Yes, Mama?" Anne answered uncertainly as her mother appeared in the doorway.

"I'm going to bed. Hurry up and go to sleep; tomorrow is a long day."

Her mother gave her a pointed look, and Anne sighed deeply, biting her lip.

"Straight to bed," Violet said in a stern voice. Then she paused, and sighed heavily. "You're a good girl. I trust you, it's them I don't trust."

Anne nodded, feeling a mix of conflicting emotions surge within her. Her mother touched her cheek and wished her sweet dreams.

"Yes, Mama," Anne murmured, kissing her on the forehead and picking up her broom.

Anne's heart raced. A half hour had passed since her mother went up to bed and she finished sweeping, and in all that time she'd stood frozen with uncertainty by the hearth. What was the right thing to do? She heard her mother's words echo in her head—*I trust you*—and she knew she should sleep. Still, the draw was irresistible. How Napoleon looked at her made her feel like the only one in a crowded room. The sparks that flew with every stolen glance and *accidental* touch were mesmerizing. But was it genuine? Anne shut her eyes, trying to navigate the chaos of her feelings. Was this sensation profound enough, true enough, to risk... everything? For what? A fleeting desire? "It's just attraction," she insisted to herself. "Nothing more than a simple infatuation."

Yet, as she spoke, doubt crept in. Could it be more? A silly thought crossed her mind, and Anne nearly laughed at its absurdity. Love? With Napoleon? The notion was absurd. "Don't be a fool," she chided herself, shaking her head at her naivety. Yet the idea, once conceived, refused to vanish completely. It lingered at the edges of her mind, a perilous prospect that excited and frightened her.

Napoleon's invitation echoed persistently in her mind. Anne glanced at the clock. Time was running out. She could go to him to explore this alluring connection, regardless of the risks. Or she could go to her room, safe, left only with thoughts of what might have been.

All of a sudden, she remembered her mother climbing the stairs with Napoleon–without the usual jug of water. What if he became thirsty in the night? A steely resolve settled over Anne. This was no longer about her conflicted feelings or the electric tension that seemed to crackle between her and Napoleon. No, this was about duty; the reputation of her mother's inn depended on her. "The perfect excuse," she murmured, a small smile playing at the corners of her lips - one she could justify without a hint of impropriety.

Napoleon paced the confines of his room, his usual composure shattered by a storm of conflicting emotions. The flickering candlelight cast dancing shadows on the walls, mirroring the tumultuous thoughts in his mind.

"Why did she turn away?" he muttered, gripping his disheveled hair. "Not even a word... a nod. Nothing."

The memory of Anne's silent departure replayed in his mind, each iteration fueling his growing frustration. He, Napoleon Bonaparte, the rising star of the French military, reduced to this state of uncertainty by a mere glance - or lack thereof.

"Could I have been played?" The thought struck him like a physical blow. His fists clenched at his sides as anger bubbled up within him. "Was she only toying with me?"

He strode to the window, staring into the darkness without seeing. "How could I be so stupid?" he berated himself. "I'm Napoleon, for God's sake. The golden boy of France's army. I know better than to let my guard down." A bitter laugh escaped his lips. "And for what? A nobody girl?"

Yet even as the harsh words left his mouth, he felt a pang of regret. The image of Anne's face floated before him - her sparkling eyes, her radiant smile, the melodious sound of her voice. The anger drained from him, replaced by a calm that soothed and unsettled him.

"No," he whispered, shaking his head. *c'est impossible!*

But as the minutes ticked by and his room remained empty, doubt crept back in. Napoleon's gaze darted to the door for what felt like the hundredth time. The inn was silent now, everyone surely asleep. Everyone except him, alone with his thoughts, waiting like an eager *boy* who had just been fooled.

C'est impossible! he said again, but the word sounded hollow even to his own ears. Caught between action and hesitation, Napoleon realized that for all his military genius, he was utterly unprepared for this particular battle of hearts.

A new thought struck him, igniting a spark of hope. Maybe... he mused, his eyes widening. "Maybe she thinks I'm sleeping?"

The idea took root, growing stronger with each passing second. Of course! Anne was considerate and... mindful. She wouldn't want to disturb him if she thought he had retired for the night. A slow smile spread across Napoleon's face, his confidence returning. He moved to the door, his hand hovering over the handle. Should he open it? Leave it slightly ajar as an invitation. As he listened intently for any sound in the hallway, he found himself more exhilarated than he had ever been on any battlefield.

"What am I doing? This is crazy." Anne thought to herself warily as she walked to Napoleon's room. Each step felt like an eternity. Finally, she reached his door, which was closed. The hallway was heavy with silence. Anne's heart raced as she approached Napoleon's door. As she neared her destination, a sudden wave of rationality washed over her.

"I'll just leave the water by his door," she thought, attempting to quell the tumult of emotions within her. It was the sensible thing to do, the safe choice. Just as she bent down to place the jug on the floor, the door swung open. Anne found herself on her knees before Napoleon, struck mute with a potent cocktail of embarrassment and unexpected desire.

"I...we forgot to bring you water," she blurted out.

Napoleon's face was stern and impassive, a mask that betrayed nothing of his inner thoughts. Suddenly, Anne was gripped by fear. Had she misinterpreted his invitation? What if she'd woken him?

"Well," Napoleon said, his voice carefully controlled as he fought to conceal his excitement at Anne's presence, "bring it in."

Anne debated her conflicting emotions. His authoritative tone both irked and thrilled her. She couldn't deny the excitement that his commanding presence ignited within her. Taking a deep breath, Anne made her choice. She followed her heart into his room, even as her mind screamed caution. The door closed behind them with a soft click that seemed to echo in the silence.

The room was shrouded in darkness, save for the flickering light of a single candle by Napoleon's bedside. Despite having cleaned this room countless times, Anne stumbled, feeling as if she were entering uncharted territory. She placed the jug on the bedside table, acutely aware of Napoleon's gaze upon her. As she turned to face him, Anne noticed his eyes were fully alert, burning with an intensity that frightened and exhilarated her.

"I apologize for disturbing you."

"I was hoping to be disturbed."

Anne dragged her hand along the windowsill.

"You are quite the topic of gossip around here," she said.

"Is that so?" His eyebrow arched with interest, an amused smile tugging at the corners of his mouth. "And what do the villagers say?"

A thrill passed through Anne. Never in her life had she flirted with a stranger; nor had she bothered about any thick-skulled village boys. Yet somehow, in his presence, all of the anxiety she felt when she kneeled at his door with the jug melted away and she knew just how to act.

"That you are a man of great ambition," she began, twisting her hair with her finger, "and that your heart is as guarded as a palace."

"Then it seems I must correct such rumors," Napoleon said, striding towards her and capturing her hand gently in his. "For you have breached my heart's defenses without a single weapon."

Anne's musical laugh rang out in the silence. Napoleon remained solemn.

"Anne, do you believe in destiny?"

"Destiny?" she echoed. The word hung between them, charged with possibility.

"Because I do, now more than ever." His fingers brushed against her cheek.

"Then let fate take its course," she whispered, emboldened by the fire in his eyes.

Napoleon's arms encircled her, and she felt as if she were the spoils of a victorious campaign. Their lips met with a fierce desire. Anne's panting breath danced rhythmically upon Napoleon's senses as she gradually eased back from the fervor of their kiss. The candle's soft glow cast undulating shadows across the room. An owl hooted in the woods behind the inn, and a night breeze teased the curtain hovering over the barely open window.

Entangling her fingers in his hair, Anne pulled Napoleon to her as if she could somehow merge their souls. He interpreted that as consent, allowing his hands to wander along the curve of her back, tracing the contours of her body with a reverence that left her breathless. The world around them faded into obscurity, and the beating of their shared heartbeat was the loudest sound they knew. Nothing else existed but the two of them, bound by yearning. In the dim light, the imposing figure of Napoleon seemed to melt away into something else, transforming from indomitable legend into an eager, desirous young man who gazed into Anne's eyes with an unspoken plea for understanding.

"Anne," he whispered, his voice barely a whisper. "In the heat of battle, I am unyielding, relentless. But with you..." His words trailed off as he searched her face, seeking solace in her warm brown eyes.

"Go on," she urged gently, intrigued by the flicker of uncertainty.

He took a deep breath, his fingers trembling slightly as they brushed a stray lock of hair from her forehead. "With you, I am just ... a man. A man moved by the same passions and fears as any other."

Anne's heart swelled at the admission. She felt her own vulnerability mirrored in his confession. "That is the man I wish to know," she said softly, her hand resting over his, steadying it.

They fell onto the bed, Napoleon's trembling fingers unlacing Annie's chemise. As they held each other, the warmth of their connection starkly contrasted with the chill of the night air creeping in from the window. In that embrace, Napoleon found not just refuge but a rare glimpse of peace–a treasure he would carry with him into the uncertain dawn.

"I must leave with daybreak," he whispered, "but I make you this promise, Anne: wherever the tides of fate may carry me, I will return for you."

He leaned in, his lips brushing hers with a kiss that sealed his vow. "And I surrender to you, Anne. To the thought of you, to the memory of you–to the promise of what awaits us when I return."

"Then I shall hold you to that promise," she murmured.

***

The following day, Anne, having crept down to her solitary bed behind the kitchen, was awoken by her mother's knock on the door.

"Time to get up; we have a lot to do," Violet said gruffly. "*Mon dieu*, you look terrible, did you even sleep?"

Anne sighed and plodded out of bed. She soon realized she had over-slept–breakfast was in full swing. The small tavern was a riot of half-dressed soldiers stuffing themselves with bread and tartines. Orders had come through for Napoleon to lead the artillery at Toulon. As she cleared empty plates and baskets, Anne looked around frantically for her lover, finally spotting him consulting his watch near the door. They locked eyes and shared a brief smile. Then Napoleon raised his arm and commanded his men to prepare for their departure.

Avoiding Violet's searching gaze, Anne slipped out the back door and ran to the stables where Napoleon's horse stood saddled and waiting, stamping its feet in the early morning chill. When he came at last, he didn't seem surprised to see her. His eyes found Anne immediately, a flicker of something - relief? desire? - passing across his face before it settled into a mask of calm authority.

Anne's breath caught in her throat as he drew near, her heart pounding a rapid tattoo against her ribs. Without a word, Napoleon's hands found her waist, pulling her close with a gentleness contrasting sharply with his commanding presence. His eyes, dark and intense, searched hers for a moment, seeking permission or perhaps reassurance. Then, with exquisite slowness, he leaned in and pressed his lips to hers.

The kiss was soft at first, almost tentative, but it quickly deepened. Anne poured everything she had into that kiss - her fears, her hopes, her dreams - savoring every sensation as if it might be her last. Her mind raced with conflicting emotions - elation, fear, desire, uncertainty - but she pushed them all aside, focusing solely on the feel of Napoleon's lips against hers, his strong arms around her.

As the kiss finally began to slow, Anne was reluctant to let go, to return to reality and face the consequences of their actions. She held on for a few seconds longer, committing every detail to memory - the warmth of his breath, the taste of his lips, the solid strength of his body against hers.

"I need to go, Anne; this is my chance to prove myself and become someone," he said with determination.

Anne nodded, although her heart was screaming in protest. She wanted him to stay, but what was the use? He was a soldier with a brilliant career ahead of him—she knew this was something she couldn't change. Just then, Napoleon pulled a strange silver pendant out of his pocket, split it in two, and placed one in Anne's hands.

"This the most valuable thing I possess," he said as he looked into her deep brown eyes and wiped away a tear. "Now you know I will come back for you. Keep it safe until my return."

Napoleon's eyes, dark and intense, locked onto hers. He seemed to understand her silent plea, his body leaning almost imperceptibly towards her. Anne longed to throw herself into his arms, but the sharp sound of boots on gravel shattered the fragile moment. A man's voice called out, urgent and insistent, "*Capitaine*! We must depart immediately!"

"I'll be there momentarily," he barked, his voice carrying the unmistakable tone of authority.

Napoleon turned back to Anne, his eyes softening for just a moment. He opened his mouth as if to speak, but no words came. Then, with a sharp nod, he strode past her towards his waiting horse. Anne followed, her steps leaden, watching as he mounted the magnificent steed with practiced ease. She wrapped her arms around herself as if to hold onto the lingering warmth of the moment they had almost shared.

With one last glance back at her, Napoleon reluctantly spurred his horse. For a fleeting second, she saw a flicker of regret in his eyes, a silent acknowledgment of what might have been. A single tear ran down her cheek as she watched him ride away towards Toulon.

It was the last time she ever saw him.

2

As the days blurred together and news of Napoleon's victories spread across the land, Anne's dream of seeing her lover again gradually faded. A heavy sensation tugged at her heart whenever she pulled the pendant from its secret hiding place under the floorboards and held it in her hands. The elegant craftsmanship glistened in the light, holding captive her fleeting memories. She ran her finger over the intricate design, entranced by its beauty, mesmerized by its perfect symmetry. Turning the pendant over, she traced the broken tail of an 'N' engraved on the back. With a gentle caress of her finger, she slowly traced the edges of the pendant. Little did she know that hidden within her was another token of her vanished lover, blossoming into something new.

"Excuse me, *mademoiselle*. May I have a moment of your time in private?" came a stranger's voice.

"What for, sir?" Anne replied. She cocked her head. "You seem familiar. Have you been here before?"

The stranger watched her take a closer look at his face, trying to jog her memory.

"Yes, *mademoiselle*. Several months ago. We came with ... my battalion," he replied, keeping his voice low.

"Is this about Napoleon?" Her tone wavered between excitement and concern.

"Please, *mademoiselle*, not here," he said firmly, glancing around the room and catching a few gazes straying their way. "It's crucial that I speak with you now, far from prying eyes."

Anne needed no more prompting. She led him to a secluded corner near the kitchen. It was then that his gaze settled on her swollen stomach. A child in this dangerous time would weaken Napoleon and endanger Anne's life. The stranger's duty to his general and the sudden pang of worry he felt for Anne were at odds. Yet, understanding the depth of Napoleon's attachment to her, he couldn't carry out his orders without ensuring the girl's safety first.

As they made their way to the kitchen, a pair of eyes bored into them. Anne's mother stood at the stove, demanding to know what was happening. The stranger took a moment to gather his thoughts.

"My name is Jean-Philippe Dubois. I bring a letter from Napoleon," he said at last. "And I have been tasked with retrieving the gift he left to Anne before his departure."

"A letter?" Anne interrupted.

"But ... I noticed that Anne is with child. Is it ... his child?"

Violet's breathing become shallow. Anne hesitated for a few seconds before nodding her head. It was a moment of truth for Jean-Philippe, in which he proved to himself that he was a man of honor.

"This changes everything. I need to get both of you to safety. News of this could threaten not only your lives but the future of Napoleon and France itself. Enemies lurk in every corner of this kingdom."

"Leave? Why?" Anne protested. "Couldn't he protect me best if I was with him? What about my mother's tavern?"

"Don't be naive," Violet interjected. "I told you to stay away from him, and now look what's happened. This man is right. What did you say your name was?"

"Jean–Philippe, Madame," he repeated. "I don't know how long we have; it's not safe here anymore. Let me take you to a secure location, and then I will inform Napoleon about the situation. He will know what to do. But we must leave tonight."

Anne struggled to compose herself, but Violet's face expressed bitter resolve.

"I will send word to my husband's brother that he must take charge until everything is under control. Anne, please go gather your belongings. Stay calm and collected; we do not want to attract attention."

"I promise to protect both of you, for the sake of the love *mon général* carries for you, *mesdames*," Jean-Philippe said reassuringly.

Despite his words, a chill ran down his spine.

***

The night was cold and silent; frost had formed on the tips of the grass, creating delicate patterns that sparkled faintly in the dim moonlight; they left without alerting anyone. Jean-Philippe was filled with a thousand worries and fears about their unknown fate; he only knew that they had to go as far away as possible. Suddenly, he heard horses in the distance, and his heart sank. Who could it be at this late hour? They quickly steered their own horses off the path and hurried along, trying to outpace what seemed like certain danger.

"Quickly, head north and seek shelter! Stay out of sight and keep a low profile – you must not be detected!"

Violet nodded, her eyebrows knitted together with worry.

"Take this money and be cautious; don't trust anyone. I'll report everything to Napoleon. I'm sure we shall meet again, but for now, hurry! I'll distract them."

As the two women under his protection rode away, Jean-Philippe felt dread washing over him. Then he remembered – the pendant! In his haste to help them escape, he had forgotten his mission entirely. With no time to turn back, he quickly galloped off towards the sound of approaching horsemen, hoping to buy them enough time.

Five imposing figures soon encircled Jean-Philippe, brandishing torches and weapons. He attempted to feign surprise, but his heart was racing so intensely that it was difficult to keep his breathing steady.

"Where is the girl?" demanded a man in a dirty neckerchief. Jean-Philippe recognized him as one of the men who had been observing them in the tavern earlier, and his heart sank.

"What girl, *monsieur*?" he replied, trying to sound as composed and confused as possible.

"Don't be stupid. Tell me where the girl is, and maybe I'll give you a quick death," snarled his interlocutor.

"I'm here alone. There is no girl." His words came out more firmly than he'd expected, despite the terror that filled his body.

"We saw you talking to her in the tavern. It looked pretty important," another man drawled, his menacing eyes watching Jean-Philippe's every move.

"Oh, the girl at the tavern? Yes. Hmmm ... well, I was complaining about the bad food. My stew was stone cold. I travel quite a lot, and really, all one wants after a long day on horseback is a hot meal, am I right, boys?"

As he babbled, Jean-Philippe could hear the third man's horse snuffling and stamping behind him. The other men chuckled sinisterly, watching their leader circle closer. Jean-Philippe tugged the reigns of his own horse to meet the latter's gaze, and his mouth fell open in shock.

"You seem to know who I am," said the leader of the gang, a menacing man with a cleft chin.

A cold dread washed over Jean-Philippe. It was not this man he feared, so much as the man he worked for. He nodded slowly, trying to keep his emotions contained.

"Good," purred the leader. "And I know exactly who you are and why you're here. So, let's try this again. Be very careful with your answer this time. Where ... is ... the girl?"

Gathering all his courage, Jean-Philippe responded with a firm and steady voice.

"I don't know!" he cried out into the cold, still night.

As the sharp blade sliced into his flesh and he tumbled from his horse, Jean-Philippe was not without the satisfaction of pride, and faith that his sacrifice would prove worth it. His tormentor's words echoed through the encroaching darkness.

"Everyone wants to play the hero these days. Let's move. You two go north. We will ride south. *Find them.*"

As his attackers rode off and darkness enveloped him, Jean-Philippe couldn't help but wonder whether time would show his actions to be noble or simply foolish.

3

Ten years had passed since Gerard Moreau's wife died, leaving him alone to raise two sons. And yet, his life was full: where others saw obstacles, Gerard saw opportunities. His optimistic mindset was born not out of naivety, but rather forged through life's difficulties. Indeed, his weathered face, hidden beneath a slightly neglected beard, testified to a storied past, while his dark brown eyes twinkled knowingly among the books that populated his classroom. Gerard was a teacher, an especially dedicated one, valued by all who were privileged to study under him and come to him for guidance with their personal struggles. His passion and commitment to science, mathematics and adventure generated great admiration and respect in the town of Laval, where he'd lived and taught in the years since his wife's death. Few knew the precise details of his life before he came to settle down.

Richard, the eldest of Gerard's sons, stood discreetly by the open door and listened to his father teach with pride: he had inherited Gerard's passion for history and adventure. Gerard had promised to take Richard on a long journey one day to have an adventure of his own, but the prospect of this seemed increasingly distant as time went on. Two years had passed since becoming his father's teaching assistant, and they were both habituated to the easy rhythm of their work together. Richard was already in his early twenties, blessed with light brown hair and his father's striking dark eyes. He stood tall with an athletic figure, in all other aspects resembling his mother, which Gerard often pointed out by saying, "I can almost see her in you". It was a bittersweet compliment, considering that Richard's memory of his mother was fading fast.

Gerard's voice resonated through the classroom, his words carrying a weight that seemed to settle on the students' shoulders. As the golden late-morning light filtered through the windows, casting long shadows across the desks, he approached the culmination of his impassioned discourse.

"Throughout history," his eyes scanned the room, meeting the gaze of each student in turn, "we've seen individuals who've shaped the course of events and those who've merely observed from the sidelines." He paused, allowing the silence to build anticipation before continuing:

"Some indeed tell the stories, pass on knowledge, and preserve our collective memory. They are the custodians of our past, the storytellers who keep our history alive. Their role is crucial; without them, we'd lose our connection to what came before." He took a slow, deliberate breath, allowing his students the time to process.

"Then there are those who make the stories, the innovators and change-makers. They push boundaries, challenge norms, and forge new paths. They're the ones whose names echo through time, whose actions ripple across generations." He leaned against his desk, his voice softening.

"But here's the real question: Is it truly as simple as choosing between these two roles? Or is there perhaps a third option – those who learn from the stories of the past, critically analyze them, and use that knowledge to shape a better future?"

The students shifted in their seats, many sitting up straighter as they considered this new perspective.

"Your challenge," concluded Gerard.

A palpable tension filled the classroom as every dreamer in the room silently processed this question. No one spoke. Gerard broke the silence cheerfully. "That's all for today! See you on Monday. Have a good weekend."

The classroom was alive with mixed feelings; some students clapped and cheered, while others remained silent and unmoved. Richard made his way down the stairs to meet Gerard.

"Terrific lesson, Father," he exclaimed, patting his father on the back and helping him with a heavy stack of books. Gerard led the way out of the school, his strides filled with purpose and conviction. Richard struggled to keep up.

"History is a valuable teacher, no matter how unpopular its lessons may be," Gerard said confidently, waving to a passing gaggle of students. "My legacy is to ensure that others learn from the mistakes of our predecessors."

Richard nodded solemnly in agreement, though secretly he wondered which type of person he was: one who'd learn lessons from a book, or make history himself?

They reached the market square. Stall-keepers were beginning to pack up, though a few groups of tardy shoppers still milled about. Gerard was about to head for the road home, but stopped when he realized that Richard wasn't following him.

"Well, are you coming?" he called out to his son.

Richard had come to a standstill at the edge of a group of villagers, listening to a woman's tale from long ago. The story entranced Gerard, but part of him felt a sense of unease. The nostalgia drew him in, yet at the same time, he was repelled by it. He couldn't shake the feeling that things had changed, and there was no going back. It was amusing how some people were fascinated by old stories.

"Let's go find your brother." Gerard patted Richard on the back. As if startled from a reverie, Richard followed.

"Who knows why you two are so different," he said as they walked towards the central market, "you were brought up in the same way. You have the same mother, the same ..."

"Forget about it, Father," Richard interrupted. "Pierrick is a unique case, and we can't all be perfect in this family."

"Perfect? Me? That's ridiculous," Gerard scoffed.

"Well, I wasn't referring to you, Father," Richard responded, with the hint of a joke in his smile.

Gerard slung an arm around Richard's shoulders as they strolled further away from the emptying market, sharing a laugh.

"Good morning, Madame Fullette! How are you today?"
Madame Fullette was a petite, cheerful old lady who owned a quaint shop near the market. Her face was a roadmap of joy, etched with countless laugh lines that crinkled delightfully whenever she smiled – which was often. At the sprightly age of seventy-eight, she moved with a buoyancy that belied her years, her silver curls bouncing merrily as she bustled about her shop. Her store was filled with various goods, ranging from farm-fresh fruits and vegetables to practical household items. Her sharp wit and amiable nature made her a favorite among the locals, as she often helped customers with their grocery shopping. With her discerning eye for top-quality produce and friendly chatter, every trip to her store was enjoyable, leaving shoppers with packed bags and happy hearts.

"Good morning, Professor. You're here just in time," she said, rolling her eyes theatrically.

"In time for what?"

"To explain to your son what work is. He spends his days eating and sleeping!"

"Oh my, Madame Fullette!" Gerard apologized, going crimson.

"I've known Pierrick since he was a baby," Madame Fullette continued, "but Lord help me, I'm out of ideas. Even with the simplest tasks I give him, he finds an excuse to eat or sleep instead. Professor, he's convinced he deserves every single rest he takes. If only he were more like you, Richard."

Madame Fullette smiled slyly at Richard, and gently pinched his cheek, just like she did when he was a small boy. She turned her attention back to Gerard.

"As a father, all I can say is that you are his guardian angel. I only hope one day he will realize how lucky he is to have you."

Madame Fullette chuckled to let them know she wasn't really displeased. This was Richard's cue to go in search of his younger brother. He found Pierrick in a cozy spot in the back room atop a sack of potatoes, where he was snoring blissfully, his belly in the air and apple cores at his feet.

Spotting his one-year-younger brother in this amusing predicament, Richard couldn't resist the opportunity for a prank. He grabbed a bucket and filled it with cold water, then gleefully splashed it over Pierrick, who woke up with a start, sputtering and angry. Richard was doubled over with laughter, ready to dodge any retaliation that might come his way.

"You ugly goat, you'll regret this," Pierrick shouted, trying to grab Richard, who was still laughing at him.

"Oh, come on, it's just a little bit of water," Richard joked, stepping back quickly to avoid Pierrick's grasp.

"A little bit? You threw an entire bucket!" Pierrick retorted, shaking the water from his hair.

"Think of it as a refreshing wake-up call!" Richard mocked.

"What is that supposed to mean?"

"Well, I've been calling you for a while."

"Ah, so am I deaf now?"

"Your snoring muffled my voice."

"I don't snore!"

"You don't snore? Piglets would have much to learn from you!" Richard retorted. Pierrick lunged forward as his hand connected with Richard's cheek in a resounding slap.

"Fine, I guess we're even now," Richard chuckled, rubbing his stinging cheek.

"Not even close." Pierrick grinned, shaking his head. "You still owe me a dry set of clothes."

Madame Fullette and Gerard stepped into the room.

"What a delightful scene!" cried Madame Fullette in disbelief.

"Why are you soaked, Pierrick?" Gerard inquired.

"He just needed a little shower," Richard interjected hastily, waving a hand before his nose to indicate that Pierrick smelled bad.

Pierrick punched Richard on the arm in response. Madame Fullette's face grew stern.

"Have you finished yet?" she demanded with authority.

The boys apologized and bid her farewell.

"Goodbye, Madame," said Gerard, "and thank you once again for your .... forgiveness."

"Goodbye, Madame Fullette," Richard said.

"Goodbye, Professor, goodbye, boys. Pierrick, see you on Monday," she replied curtly as he tried to brush the dust from his wet clothing.

"Yes, Madame Fullette," mumbled Pierrick, shoving his brother on the shoulder.

"And try not to be late, do you hear me?" Madame Fullette added with a stern voice that seemed only to agitate Pierrick further.

Gerard handed Pierrick the bag with groceries as they left Madame Fullette's small store. The square had emptied but for the cheese monger, still lovingly packing away his remaining cheeses.

"Pierrick," he began, "when will you decide to take life seriously? You may not want to study, but you should at least take work seriously! Madame

Fullette has been very patient and understanding. Think about the example you'll set for your children when you have them."

Pierrick listened to his father's words reverberating like a physical blow. The truth in them stung, piercing the armor of his youthful indifference. He knew, deep down, that his father was right, but the weight of responsibility felt suffocating. At twenty, the world seemed full of endless possibilities, and the idea of narrowing his focus felt premature. His dark, close-cropped hair accentuated the sharp angles of his face, a face that bore an uncanny resemblance to his father's. But it was Pierrick's eyes that truly commanded attention - stormy grey orbs so deep they appeared almost black. Those eyes now flickered with a mix of defiance and uncertainty as he grappled with his father's expectations.

While Pierrick had inherited his father's striking features, their physiques couldn't have been more different. Where his father was tall and lean, honed by years of disciplined living, Pierrick's frame told a different story.

"I know you mean well, Father," Pierrick finally spoke, his voice a mix of frustration and resignation. "But I need time to figure things out... to explore. Isn't that what being young is all about?"

Gerard's brow furrowed as he contemplated his son's words, the initial surge of frustration giving way to a more nuanced understanding. He gazed at Pierrick, seeing not just the young man before him but echoes of his youth – the uncertainty, the desire for freedom, the resistance to predetermined paths.

"Perhaps," Gerard mused, his voice softening, "there's truth in what you say, son, and I'm not trying to force you into a mold. It's about helping you discover the best version of yourself." He paused, choosing his following words carefully.

"What if," he proposed, a new idea taking shape, "we look at this differently? What if I helped you explore options?"

He saw a flicker of interest in Pierrick's eyes, encouraging him to continue.

"I'm always in awe of your cooking, Pierrick," Gerard declared, beaming at his son. "You have such natural talent in that department. Why don't you pursue it instead of working in a grocer, which you clearly don't enjoy? Have you ever thought about opening your own restaurant and sharing your culinary skills with the world?"

Pierrick's heart swelled with pride at his father's words. "I've considered it, but the thought of serving a large crowd overwhelms me."

"Scared of hard work?" Richard taunted, jumping out of Pierrick's reach before he could respond.

'Ignore him,' intoned Gerard. 'Speaking of food, what are you going to cook for dinner? I'm sure it will be something special!"

Pierrick retorted: "For Richard, boiled cabbage and hard bread. For you, my dear father, boar stew with roast potatoes."

Their banter echoed through the marketplace, drawing smiles from passersby who could sense the underlying warmth and camaraderie between the trio. Gerard watched with amusements. It was not the life he'd imagined, but nor was it a bad life. Deep down, however, he feared that his sons were not content.

4

"Claaaaaire. Dinner's ready."

"Coming, Nana."

Claire carefully stepped down the old wooden stairs to the small room that served as kitchen and living area alike. Logs of wood crackled in the old but functional fireplace. Violet served up two steaming bowls of chicken soup she had cooked over the fire. The flames gave the humble house a golden, dreamy warmth. A faded rug covered most of the wooden floor, its once-vibrant patterns now muted by time and many footsteps. The focal point of the room was a well-worn rocking chair, its wooden frame polished smooth by years of use. Nearby was a sturdy table surrounded by four mis-matched chairs, and up the rickety staircase were two small, cozy bedrooms. Slanted ceilings followed the roofline, creating intimate nooks for reading or daydreaming. Despite its modest size, the house felt complete. Every item had its place, and every room held the promise of comfort. It was more than just dwelling; it was a home where memories were made, and love resided in every creaky floorboard and sun-faded curtain.

Willy, the old St. Bernard, lay on the hearth with his eyes half-closed, his tail twitching from side to side. He was content in the warmth of the flames, his nose alive to the smell of the soup.

"Do you need help?" Claire offered.

"Sit down, sweetheart," Violet said, smiling. "The soup's getting cold."

She cut two slices of freshly baked bread.

Violet felt a tinge of sadness in her heart as she watched Claire's eyes sparkle with excitement. She knew she was blessed to have such a spirited granddaughter, though she missed her own daughter, Anne, who'd died in childbirth. Claire had never known her mother, but they were so alike, and never so more than now that Claire had nearly reached the age Anne had been when .... Violet forced her mind to contemplate other things.

The soup was perfect, and Claire inhaled it hungrily.

"Nana," Claire asked slyly, "The butcher gave me free pork chops to take to you again. He's obviously in love with you, why don't you give him the time of day?"

"Nonsense," scoffed Violet. "Those chops were probably going bad."

Claire's eyes lingered on Violet's rich dark hair, shot through with enchanting filaments of silver.

"I'm serious, Nana. Why have you never married again? You're still beautiful."

"Hush," said Violet. "I'm over sixty, you know. I'm an old woman. I've done well alone practically all my life, what do I want from a man?"

"Tell me about your life," sighed Claire, sipping the last of her soup. "Tell me about your first husband. No, tell me about my mother."

It was a gamble: Claire knew her loving but strict grandmother didn't like talking about the past. The older she became, the more desperate Claire was to know where she'd come from, and yet her grandmother remained a closed book. "Let's leave the past where it belongs," she liked to say.

"Pass me your bowl," Violet said now. "You want more, I can tell."

Claire meekly passed the bowl and watched her grandmother refill it. As if sensing her disappointment and seeking to remedy it, Violet added casually, "I saw there's a fair three towns away tomorrow, in Laval. Would you like to go?"

Claire's eyes lit up with unbridled joy.

"Really, Nana? You'll let me go to a fair?"

Claire couldn't believe it; her grandmother usually avoided crowds, and rarely let Claire out of her sight. This meant Claire's amusements were few.

"What time will we leave? Where will we sleep? How long will it take to get there?"

Question after question poured from Claire's lips, each following so quickly on the heels of the last that Violet could barely keep up. The older woman's eyes crinkled with amusement.

"Slow down, my dear. One question at a time," Violet said with patience. "Let's finish our dinner. Émile has kindly offered to join us on our journey. He also has some errands to run, so we'll be setting off early in the morning."

Claire drank the last of her soup, a few drops spilling onto the table as her bowl clattered against its saucer. She apologized with a blush, jumping up for a rag to clean up her mess. Violet smiled as Claire rushed around the room at breakneck speed, banging pots and clattering plates. Everything was back in order in less than ten minutes, and Claire gave Violet a quick goodnight kiss before scurrying upstairs to prepare for the next day.

Violet's weathered face creased with a warm, affectionate smile as she watched her granddaughter bound up the creaky wooden stairs of their old farmhouse. The young woman's enthusiasm was palpable, her energy infectious, and for a moment, Violet felt a pang of nostalgia mixed with a hint of worry. At almost twenty-two years old, Claire was a young woman on the cusp of adulthood who had inherited more than just her mother's physical features. The same wild, untamed spirit that captivated and worried Violet in her daughter now shone brightly in her granddaughter. It was evident in the way Claire's eyes lit up when she discovered something new, her insatiable curiosity about the world beyond their small town, and her restless energy that seemed barely contained within the confines of their modest home.

Raising Claire on the outskirts of a sleepy rural town had been both a blessing and a challenge. The rolling hills, dense forests, and sprawling fields provided a picturesque backdrop for Claire's childhood, but also created a cocoon of isolation. The village population barely numbered twenty people, and most residents were either retirees or farmers, leaving few peers for a spirited young woman like Claire. Fewer people meant fewer connections, but it also meant fewer prying eyes, fewer uncomfortable questions, and, most important of all, less danger.

Violet sat back in her rocking chair with an aching heart. She knew she couldn't keep Claire sheltered forever, and yet she was terrified of losing her just as she'd lost everyone she'd ever loved: first her husband, then Anne.

Claire rummaged through her small wardrobe, pulling out clothes and tossing them over a chair. Amidst this whirlwind of activity, Willy shuffled up the stairs, finding a cozy spot on the bed to observe the chaos.

Claire and Willy shared a unique relationship that transcended the need for verbal communication. Their connection was built on a foundation of mutual understanding and companionship. Willy's responses to Claire's chatter were simple yet effective: a bark signaled agreement, while a snort or dozing off indicated disagreement. Nevertheless, Claire often liked to chatter to Willy out loud, often concluding their one-sided conversations with a heartfelt acknowledgment of Willy's listening skills, saying, "You're such a great listener, Willy – I don't know what I'd do without you."

"Willy," she cried out now, "tomorrow will be wonderful. A country fair! Dozens of stalls, people to talk to, new things to see, and Nana promised we'd buy fabric for a new dress."

Claire's monologue continued, although Willy struggled to stay awake. The cozy atmosphere and the gentle rhythm of Claire's voice made it difficult for him to keep his eyes open. After what felt like hours, Claire finally wrapped up her speech, stifling a yawn as she too settled on the bed to sleep.

"Goodnight, Willy," she murmured. There was no answer.

5

The rooster had not yet crowed, but Claire was already awake. She dressed quickly and hurried down the stairs, nearly stumbling. Violet was in the kitchen, packing a lunch. Claire eagerly grabbed a biscuit and glass of milk, observing her grandmother's actions with excitement.

"Why don't you take Willy to Madame Marie while I finish here?" Violet suggested.

Claire called out for Willy, who had just begun to stroll down the stairs, not in any rush whatsoever.

"Come on, boy, let's go see Madame Marie."

Willy followed reluctantly.

Claire stepped out the front door of their house, holding Willy's leash tightly as they walked towards the neighboring farm. The early spring morning embraced the land with a crisp, invigorating chill. As the first rays of sunlight pierced through the lingering mist, a gentle breeze whispered through the awakening world, carrying the promise of warmer days to come. Claire stopped for a moment, her eyes closed, face tilted towards the sky. She inhaled deeply, filling her lungs with the cool, fresh air that held hints of damp earth and budding flora. The sun's warmth caressed her skin, starkly contrasting the brisk air around her.

The farm was just beginning to stir. Chickens and ducks pecked the dirt for overlooked scraps. Marie emerged from the house with a basket full of food and began tossing morsels here and there. The chickens rushed toward her in a great flutter.

"Good morning, Madame Marie!" Claire greeted cheerily.

"Oh, morning, Claire," Marie replied warmly. "Good morning to you too, Willy. Are you ready to help?"

Willy wasn't up for helping. He was transfixed by a cat and mouse chasing each other nearby. He barked lazily at the cat, who paid him no attention.

Just then, Marie's husband Èmile pulled up in his dray. Monsieur Émile was a character straight out of a whimsical storybook, a man whose presence seemed to bring a touch of magic to the ordinary world. In his early sixties, he stood at a perfectly unremarkable height – not too short to be overlooked, not too tall to intimidate – but everything else about him was far from average. His face was a canvas of expression, dominated by bushy eyebrows that seemed to have a life of their own. They danced and wiggled with every emotion, often appearing to be in animated conversation with each other. Below them, twinkling eyes the color of a summer sky peeked out, forever crinkled at the corners from a lifetime of laughter. Émile's nose was a magnificent specimen, bulbous and red-veined, looking as though it had been borrowed from a circus clown. It was the kind of nose that begged to be honked, and indeed, Émile was known to produce a squeaky toy from his pocket to do just that when the mood struck him.

"Hop in, Claire!" Émile's jovial voice boomed, his bushy eyebrows dancing with excitement. "Let's go pick up your grandmother! We've got a date with adventure!"

Claire giggled as she clambered into the back of the cart.

He turned to his wife, Marie, who stood in the garden with a fond smile. Émile's eyes, twinkling like stars, met hers with a gaze that spoke volumes of a love nurtured over decades.

"Goodbye, my flower," he said, his voice softening to a tender rumble.

"Don't forget to water the roses with your tears of longing while I'm gone!"

With a flourish that nearly cost him his balance, Émile blew an exaggerated kiss. Marie, playing along with the whimsy that had defined their life together, reached out with graceful fingers. She plucked the invisible token of affection from the air with a delicate motion, her eyes never leaving Émile's. With a gentle touch, she pressed the imaginary kiss to her heart, right above the bright sunflower brooch that adorned her dress.

"Drive safely, you old goat," she called back, her voice warm with affection. "And try not to scandalize the girls too much!"

Émile winked.

She shook her head, chuckling softly. "That man," she murmured, her hand still resting over her heart.

In no time at all, they were off. Violet and Monsieur Émile chatted for most of the journey, their voices dulled by the rhythmic sound of the wheels rolling over uneven terrain. Claire was lost in dreams and paid no attention.

***

The town square was a chaotic blend of clashing sights, noises, and aromas. Farmhands scoured the market stalls for fabrics and other merchandise, acrobats performed dangerous stunts, and young girls shamelessly displayed their wares to earn a few extra coins. Stunned, Claire averted her eyes. Amidst the chaos, she caught sight of a young child attempting to snatch an apple – only to be met with a sharp slap from his mother. Claire couldn't help but giggle. She spotted more children singly happily around a schoolhouse, and a priest solemnly reading verses from Isaiah, luring passersby to seek refuge in his priory. Claire's head pivoted this way and that. Were those high society women examining exotic fabrics from Paris? Merchants trying to deceitfully pass off fake jewels as real? A fortune teller offering her services to the curious? Brigands taking advantage of the distractions to steal whatever they could from unsuspecting passersby? Soldiers were beguiled by lovely streetwalkers? Claire couldn't quite tell where the expectations set by her storybooks met with reality, but it all made for a chaotic yet fascinating atmosphere.

Émile slowly pulled the dray to a stop, allowing Claire and Violet to disembark.

"I'll see you at the end of the day. Be careful," Monsieur Émile cautioned.

"Thank you, Monsieur Émile," Claire responded as she hopped off the wagon. Violet and Monsieur Émile shared a few more words before saying their goodbyes.

"Fresh fish! Caught this morning!" a gruff voice bellowed from Claire's left.

"Exotic spices from the far east!" another vendor proclaimed, the aroma of cinnamon and cardamom wafting through the air.

"You stay close to me, Claire," Violet warned, her voice tinged with concern. "Fairs can be dangerous."

Claire nodded in agreement, still trying to take in everything around her. She noticed Violet's eyes scanning the crowd, ever vigilant. Suddenly, a stall selling brightly colored fabrics captured Claire's attention and she drifted over. After that, she became entranced by a fire-juggler. Without realizing it, she'd wandered away from Violet.

***

The Moreau family was also at the village fair. While Gerard conversed with a friend, Pierrick and Richard browsed through stalls, searching for anything that might interest them. Pierrick haggled with food merchants for the best prices, leaving Richard holding the bags of groceries.

"Come now, Madame," Pierrick cajoled a ruddy-faced woman selling plump tomatoes, "surely you can do better than that for a loyal customer?"

Richard was exasperated with the bustling crowd pressing in around him. He shouted for Pierrick to meet him at the end of the market. Out of the corner of his eye, he caught a glimpse of an unfamiliar girl in the middle of the bustling crowd. Her deep brown eyes shone with desperation. Despite his eagerness to escape the fray, Richard wanted to help her. Juggling the bags of groceries in his hands, he bellowed for Pierrick again. Pierrick gave a vague wave of his hand in response, as though asking Richard to wait just a moment longer.

Craning his neck to keep sight of the imperiled girl, Richard shouted something unintelligible and pushed through the crowd.

"Richard!" Pierrick yelled in bewilderment. "Where the hell are you going?"

Gerard appeared just in time to see his eldest son disappearing into a sea of people.

***

Claire was lost, turning in circles. All about, people squeezed past or bumped brusquely. The fair was nothing like the friendly place she'd imagined. She felt trapped by the crowd. Suddenly, a particularly forceful bump from behind sent Claire stumbling forward. In her panic to regain her footing, she inadvertently ripped the top button of her dress. The necklace she always wore, with its pendant made of the finest silver, swung into view.

Loitering by a spit upon which twirled a giant roasting boar, two brigands spotted the bright flash of metal. One was small with a pointy red goatee; the other was a towering giant with one green eye and one black. The one with mismatched eyes whispered something to a small, ragged child, who then ran towards Claire and tugged at her dress.

"Any coins, miss? Any spare coins so I can eat?"

Claire apologized wretchedly.

"All the money I have is with my grandmother. I've lost her somehow. Once I find her, I'll –'

The young boy grabbed her hand and pulled her down the alleyway.

"Come with me, lady! You can play with us. Please!"

Claire's eyes frantically darted around the busy market stalls, still searching for Violet. In her panic, she didn't realize she was being pulled away from the main square and towards a dark alley filled with puddles and dirty, squealing children. In a flash, the children scattered, and Claire found herself face to face with two menacing brigands blocking her only exit.

"We just want to talk," the giant smirked. His black eye fixed on her while his green eye wandered, sending a chill down her spine. Claire felt her heart racing and she prayed Violet had seen which way she went. The cheerful atmosphere of moments ago evaporated, replaced by a suffocating dread. A cold hand seized her shoulder. She tried to back away, but the grip on her shoulder was too tight. The man with the red goatee approached, and she felt her throat constrict as he yanked the pendant from her neck. Claire felt a surge of pain and fear as tears streamed down her face, leaving glistening trails on her pale cheeks. The world around her seemed to blur and spin; everything was happening so fast, and her young mind struggled to process the rapid shift from joy to terror. Her grandmother's words echoed - *fairs can be dangerous*.

The stranger clenched the silver pendant in his fist, feeling its weight and verifying its authenticity with his teeth. When he tasted the purity of the silver, he uttered a satisfied grunt and held it up to the light. With a smirk of satisfaction, he quickly tucked the pendant into his pocket.

The giant had not relinquished his grip. A putrid smell of alcohol and rot filled Claire's nose. The enormous brigand smiled, revealing yellow–stained teeth, and held a knife against her neck.

"You look as tasty as your jewel, lady. You don't mind if we have some fun, do you? We promise to make it quick," he growled.

The smaller man took up this line. "Stay still, and this will all be over quickly. But if you scream or give us trouble, it won't end well for you."

Claire quivered with fear. As her heart raced and her thoughts scrambled in search of safety, she blinked away tears and desperately looked for an opening between the two men. Summoning all her courage, she bit down hard on the giant's hand, eliciting a howl of pain. The man with the goatee brutally backhanded her, sending her crashing to the ground and adding a kick to the stomach. The shock of the pain took her breath away.

'Bitch!' raged the man with the goatee, forcing her down. "You're going to pay for that."

"Hold her down, Mardok," ordered the giant, his green eye rolling wildly. "This bitch is feisty."

Seizing hold of her boddice, he ripped it open, exposing her breasts. Claire cried out with fear and rage; one thought managed to break through the haze: something was very, very wrong. She tried to scream, to call for Violet, for anyone, but her assailant threw his arm over her mouth to muffle her cries and sneered mockingly.

Claire closed her eyes, her body shaking with sobs. She wished with all her might that she'd never come to the fair. All of a sudden, she felt her attacker's grip loosen as his piercing scream rent the air.

"Pigs! Let her go!"

The blur of a young man fell upon the brigands, raining merciless blows with a hard stick. The giant flinched and stumbled beneath the attack, unable to dodge or escape the onslaught. On his friend's cry, the man with the goatee released Claire and lunged forward, blade raised menacingly. The young man lashed out with the stick, but the darting brigand evaded it with a swift sidestep, his eyes blazing with hatred.

The giant lumbered to his feet and struck the young man on the back, seizing him when he stumbled. The man with the goatee stepped closer and snarled, raising his knife.

"This is not a good day to play the hero."

"Kill him, Mardok!" shrieked the giant. "Kill the bastard!"

Just as the brigand Mardok was about to lunge forward and stab the young man, Claire's instincts took over; she managed to reach the stick and swing it at the assailant.

"Behind you!" the giant yelled.

Mardok managed to duck in time and dodge the hit. He spun around and lunged at Claire, knife in hand. The young man swung his foot with all his might and connected with his attacker's heel. The painful impact made Mardok loosen his grip, allowing the young man to escape his vice–like grasp. Just then, the giant grabbed the young man's arm and violently yanked him away, sending two powerful punches crashing into his face. He tumbled to the ground near Claire.

"Are you alright, *mademoiselle*?" murmured Claire's defender, struggling to stay conscious.

Claire's heart thundered against her ribs; each frantic beat a desperate plea for survival. Her trembling hands clutched at her torn clothing, attempting to shield herself from the physical exposure. Her wide eyes darted frantically, trying to make sense of the chaos around her. The young man beside her was a mystery - a stranger who had materialized from nowhere to place himself between her and danger. His lips moved in what she assumed were words of reassurance or strategy. But the roaring in Claire's ears reduced everything to a muffled, underwater cacophony.

The brigands, momentarily thrown off by the young man's intervention, now regrouped with a predatory focus. Mardok, enraged, stepped forward, brandishing his blade.

Suddenly, out of the blue, a potato whizzed through the air and caught Mardok square in the jaw.

"Argh! What the f—"

Another potato hit him on the back, then the face, and he stumbled under a hail of potatoes.

"Ouch!" wailed the giant, his luck no better as he too was hit from all angles.

On the other side of the alley, Pierrick and Gerard were hurling potatoes from a bag with all their might. Pierrick's words were as incomprehensible as they were courageous. Taking advantage of the chaos, Richard got back to his feet and punched Mardok, making him lose his balance.

With adrenaline coursing through her veins sharpening her senses, Claire quickly joined in, momentarily forgetting her ripped dress and beating the giant with Richard's stick until, barreling through Pierrick and Gerard, he fled.

Realizing his imminent defeat, Mardok too tried to run. Pierrick grabbed a baguette and struck the fleeing figure's face. Gerard lunged forward ferociously; a clenched fist flew at lightning speed, crashing into the brigand's jaw and sending him spiraling to the ground like a ragdoll, his limp body crumpled in an unconscious heap. Gerard adjusted his jacket, a satisfied smirk on his face as he proclaimed, "That's how it's done."

Noticing Claire desperately trying to cover herself, Richard removed his jacket and draped it around her shoulders.

"Here, *mademoiselle*."

Claire clutched the jacket tightly around herself, her knuckles turning white from the force of her grip. The rough fabric against her skin was both a shield and a reminder of her vulnerability. Her hands trembled uncontrollably, betraying the fear that coursed through her veins despite her attempt at bravery. Claire's eyes darted around frantically, scanning her surroundings for any sign of continued threat. The adrenaline that had fueled her momentary courage was fading, leaving her feeling drained and vulnerable.

Gerard stepped closer and placed a reassuring hand on her shoulder.

"It's okay, *mademoiselle*. You are safe now."

"Claire! Thank heavens!"

Violet pushed past Gerard and Richard, her face alight with relief. Her joy soon turned to terror when she saw the state of her granddaughter. At the sight of her grandmother, the fragile composure Claire had been desperately clinging to shattered completely. With a choked sob, she broke into a run, her vision blurred by the tears that now flowed freely down her cheeks.

"Nana!" Claire cried out, her voice cracking with relief and lingering fear.

Violet's arms opened instinctively, enveloping Claire in a warm, familiar embrace as the girl crashed into her. The scent of lavender and home-baked cookies enveloped Claire, a comforting cocoon against the harsh reality of what she'd just experienced. Claire buried her face in her grandmother's soft cardigan, her small frame shaking with the force of her sobs. All the terror, the uncertainty, and the adrenaline of the past minutes poured out of her in a cathartic release. Violet's hand gently stroked Claire's hair, her touch a soothing balm to the girl's frayed nerves.

Gradually, Claire's sobs began to subside, replaced by hiccuping breaths as she struggled to regain control. She pulled back slightly, wiping at her tear-stained face with trembling hands.

"What happened to you? Who did this?" she demanded.

"I'm alright," Claire said bravely. "This kind gentleman saved me from ..." Her voice trailed off as she paled at the thought of the horrors she'd so narrowly escaped.

Violet surveyed the potato–strewn ground, Mardok sprawled unconscious. The thought of what could have happened to her granddaughter filled her with dread. She paled too, and embraced Claire. Meanwhile, Gerard held Richard's head, inspecting his bloodied face.

"I'm okay. I'm okay," insisted Richard, pridefully pull away. He felt suddenly shy around the young girl he'd so brashly saved mere moments ago. He stooped to help Pierrick, who was gathering up the few potatoes and vegetables he could salvage.

"Thank you all so much for helping my granddaughter. How can I ever repay you?" Violet asked with tears in her eyes.

Gerard stepped forward and bowed.

"It was our pleasure, Madame," he said with a polite flourish. "You should come with us. Let us help you, medicate you and fix the *mademoiselle's* dress. You cannot go about like this."

Violet considered the tattered dress and the blood and bruises on Claire's face as if anew.

"Thank you again," she said, with a touch of reverence.

"Gerard Moreau, Madame," interrupted Gerard. "This is my eldest son Richard, and my youngest, Pierrick."

"What fine and courageous gentlemen. Thank you all for your kindness. My name is Violet, and this is my granddaughter, Claire. Very nice meeting you all... even under these circumstances."

Claire looked up at the group, her face still tear–stained but with a trace of her customary sparkle returning.

Pierrick stood tall, his chest puffed out, nudging Richard in the ribs, relishing in the glory of his accomplishment.

"Maybe next time you make fun of me for loving food, you'll remember it was potatoes that saved your life," Pierrick said with a triumphant smirk.

"Thank you, Pierrick," Richard said as he pulled his brother in close for a hug.

Pierrick was taken aback – he hadn't expected such a heartfelt expression of gratitude. Richard winked at him, and Pierrick rolled his eyes in annoyance.

"Let's go. We don't want to be around when this fellow comes to," cautioned Gerard, disrupting the brotherly moment.

Pierrick and Richard finished salvaging the potatoes and the group wove through the bustling marketplace and down the long road. As they barreled through the dense crowd, Claire gasped.

"My pendant! It's all I have left from my mother! The one with the red beard stole it!"

"Go," commanded Richard, springing into action. "I'll meet you at the house."

Claire barely had time to express her gratitude before Richard had vanished. Rifling through the pockets of the still-crumpled figure in the alleyway, his fingers finally clamped around the stolen pendant, and he uttered a triumphant 'ha' before spinning on his heel and dashing away home.

6

Gerard flung the door wide open with an inviting gesture.

"Welcome, make yourselves at home," he said with a welcoming smile. "Pierrick, take our guests to my room and get what is needed to mend the young lady's dress."

"We are so very grateful; thank you, Monsieur Gerard!" exclaimed Violet.

"I will drop this off in the kitchen and be right back," Pierrick assured them as they stepped inside.

The Moreau family home was filled with fascinating trinkets, books, and paintings. Decorative glass bottles and figurines stood guard on shelves chock–full of old books and leather–bound journals. Oddly shaped abstract paintings covered every inch of wall space not taken up by mahogany bookcases. The embers still smoldering in the living room fireplace created a cozy atmosphere that made everyone feel welcome and at ease. The large table's surface bore the marks of countless meals shared, stories told, and laugher exchanged.

Pierrick deposited the packages in the kitchen and grabbed a small box before rushing back.

"This way, ladies," he instructed as he walked towards the second door down the hallway. "Make yourself comfortable. If you need anything else, whistle."

"Thank you, Pierrick," Violet replied.

He smiled as he closed the door behind them.

"Sit here, my darling Claire," Violet said. Her voice was stern but also full of love and concern. "Let's try to piece together what happened. What were you thinking? How many times have I told you to stay close to me?"

"I'm sorry, Nana. I didn't mean for this to happen."

Claire's lip trembled, and a sob escaped her throat.

Violet sighed heavily. "You were lucky this time, but it could have been so much worse," she said with relief and regret. "You must learn from this. Now take that dress off and let me see what I can do"

The gentle rustle of fabric and the women's soft murmurs continued until the dress was mended.

In the small but well-equipped kitchen, Pierrick moved with practiced ease, his hands deftly chopping vegetables for a hearty stew. His knife knocked rhythmically against the cutting board. He paused occasionally to stir a simmering pot, which released fragrant wisps of steam. Richard's breath hitched as he entered the house, directing his gaze immediately toward his father.

"I got it – but it's broken. Maybe you can fix it," he said, handing the trinket to his father. As Gerard took the pendant in his hand, all color drained from his face.

"This cannot be," he whispered. "I ... I know this pendant,"

Richard was confused. What could his father mean? Before he could ask, Gerard marched off to his study on an unknown mission. Desperate for clarification, Richard followed him.

Inside the study, Gerard was furiously shoving books and papers aside until he finally found an old journal.

"Yes, I knew it!"

Richard couldn't control his curiosity.

"What is that?" he begged.

"This, my son," Gerard replied with a ragged look in his eyes, "is how I met your mother."

Stunned by the sudden revelation, Richard couldn't help but wonder how his mother might have anything to do with a broken pendant worn by a girl none of the Moreaus had ever seen before this day. But before he could ask further questions, Gerard told him to help his brother with lunch, promising to explain everything later. Richard left, thinking about the mystery surrounding his parents and Claire's pendant. His thoughts were interrupted when his guests emerged from the bedroom and headed into the sitting room.

"Is everything alright?" Richard asked.

"Yes, thank you! We are so grateful for your help," effused Violet. "We should go now. If you could say goodbye to your father..."

"But to leave so soon? No, please, stay and have something to eat. Lunch is almost ready, and my father is trying to fix your pendant."

Claire's eyes widened in surprise. "You found it? Thank you!" she exclaimed.

"Yes, unfortunately the clasp was broken, and my father is trying his best to fix it."

"Can I at least help with lunch?" Violent insisted. "I can't just stand idly by. I'd be grateful if you could show me the way to the kitchen."

Richard pointed Violet towards the sound of Pierrick's chopping, though he warned her that his brother liked to work alone.

Meanwhile, Claire was strolling around the living room, taking in all of its wonders.

"What's this?" she asked, gesturing towards an antique brass telescope perched on a mahogany stand by the window.

Before Richard could answer, she had already moved on, captivated by a collection of vibrant seashells on a nearby shelf. "Oh, and these! Where did you find these?"

Richard chuckled warmly, amused by her unbridled enthusiasm.

"Those are from my father's travels in the Caribbean," he began, but Claire's attention had already shifted again. Her gaze fell upon a weathered map framed on the wall, its edges adorned with intricate illustrations of sea monsters and mythical creatures.

"Is this real?" she breathed, her voice filled with awe.

"Please, make yourself comfortable. You can sit by the fire and stay warm," Richard said kindly, gesturing towards a pair of plush armchairs. The flames crackled invitingly, casting a warm glow across the room.

"Is she being too nosy?" Violet interrupted, bringing in plates and cutlery for the table setting.

"Oh no, not at all," Richard smiled.

"Food is ready!" Pierrick announced, his voice carrying a hint of pride. "Enough chattering; it's time to eat."

The tantalizing aroma of a hearty stew wafted through the air, drawing the group's attention. The large, steaming pot took center stage, surrounded by colorful platters of roasted vegetables. The presentation was a feast for the eyes as much as it promised to be for the palate.

"Pierrick, this smells divine!" exclaimed Violet, inhaling deeply. "Is that a hint of rosemary I detect?"

Gerard joined them, and they all took seats around the table.

"Did you use that new herb blend you picked up at the farmer's market?" Gerard asked.

Pierrick nodded enthusiastically. "Indeed! I thought it would complement the root vegetables nicely. I hope everyone enjoys."

As they began to eat, appreciative murmurs and the clinking of cutlery against plates filled the room. The stew was rich and flavorful, the meat tender enough to fall apart at the touch of a fork. The roasted vegetables provided a delightful contrast in texture, their natural sweetness enhanced by the herb seasoning.

Claire closed her eyes as she savored a spoonful, the warmth of the soup spread through her body, bringing comfort and relief.

"It's nice to have some ladies here at this table," Gerard remarked. "It can get quite dull when there are only boys."

"Dull? I'm fun!" Pierrick interjected. They all laughed because Pierrick couldn't take the joke. Lunch passed pleasantly, the brothers joking and Claire enthralled by the group. She hadn't often been among boys her own age, and yet she felt completely comfortable, as if she was among family.

After lunch, they all gathered around the fireplace. Gerard started to tell stories from his past. Violet began cleaning up, but Gerard insisted that she sit down and join them.

"Oh, here. This is yours, young lady," he said, standing up swiftly and taking the pendant from his pocket. He slowly walked towards Claire and placed it delicately around her neck.

"Thank you so much; I can't thank you enough," she murmured gratefully.

"It's nothing. My pleasure."

Suddenly, Gerard hesitated, spinning towards Violet with a veneer of uncertainty creasing his face.

"If I may ask ... where did Claire get this pendant? From what I understand, it was her mother who gave it to her?"

Violet's expression darkened. Questions she had no wish to answer were forming on her host's lips. Her mind raced as she searched for an answer, her smile betraying the unease slowly creeping up inside her.

"Ahh ... well ... Claire's mother died in childbirth. I'm not too sure how she came across it. I think she perhaps found it lying on the ground somewhere."

Claire interjected innocently with the truth: "But Nana, you said my father gave it to her."

Violet, caught in her lies, froze guiltily. Gerard closed his eyes, taking a deep breath. Claire's words had confirmed his worst fears.

"Oh my, look at the time!" cried Violet. "We must go before Monsieur Èmile arrives, we can't make him wait. We need to get home before it's dark."

Some tension from the exchange lingered in the air, but Gerard could sense Violet's uneasiness and honored her reluctance to continue the discussion.

"Certainly, Madame. Is there anything else we can do before you leave?"

"No, thank you, you've done so much already. I cannot thank you all enough for coming to Claire's rescue; such bravery is a rare thing these days."

Claire didn't want to leave, but her pleading looks to Violet were useless.

"Come on, my dear; we have to go!"

Gerard grabbed his jacket; he and Richard had wordlessly decided to accompany the women as far as their meeting place with Monsieur Émile. Violet tried to talk them out of it, but they were determined to stay with the two women until they reached their destination.

***

As they walked down the street, Claire and Richard fell into conversation while Violet and Gerard shared a few brief words between awkward silences.

"So, you are a professor?"

"Yes, that is correct; I share the knowledge acquired during my long life."

"What topics do you teach?"

"Science and mathematics mainly."

"That sounds interesting."

"I should hope so, for my students' sake," Gerard jokingly remarked as she chuckled in embarrassment.

As they approached the crossroads that led out of town, Violet paused.

"I think this is the place," she said. Having fallen behind, Richard and Claire continued their conversation obliviously, while Gerard took this moment to confront Violet.

"Madame, I do not mean to invade your privacy again," he began cautiously, "but I can only assume this is a subject you are loath to discuss."

Violet's face shuttered with apprehension as the words sank in. She glanced around nervously.

"But there is something you need to know about that pendant. Call it fate or destiny, if you will, but I was part of a selected group of scientists that designed and created that pendant, and I don't think you know what it was intended for."

A chill ran down Violet's spine as she realized the gravity of Gerard's words. She recalled the long-ago night when she and Anne had fled their home, leaving practically everything behind. She felt dizzy with fear. Violet's unease was palpable and even caught the attention of Claire, who drew close, trying to overhear the conversation.

"Right now, there is no time," said Gerard. "This is not the place to explain more, but please listen to an old man – hide the pendant, do not wear it, and do not show it to anyone."

Violet nodded weakly in agreement.

"If you require a safe place to stay or more information regarding the pendant, do not hesitate to seek me out – my door is always open."

The tension broke suddenly as Monsieur Émile pulled up in his dray.

"Hello, ladies," he greeted them with a warm smile. "How was your day? I see you've made some new acquaintances."

Claire quickly introduced everyone before exchanging goodbyes. With a few last warnings from Gerard and Richard to stay safe on the road, they climbed into the carriage with Émile and headed home.

Violet stayed quiet as Claire and Émile talked, Gerard's words echoing in her mind. What made the pendant so dangerous? A bitter taste filled her mouth as she pondered the apparent cruelty of fate. It seemed that life had an uncanny way of throwing obstacles in her path, testing her resilience at every turn.

"Nana. Are you alright?"

"What? Oh yes," Violet said, disorientated. "Sorry, I'm just a little tired, and ..." Violet trailed off at the sound of approaching hooves.

Six riders drew near the cart. Èmile pulled in the horses, stopping them abruptly and causing them to rear up in fear. As the dust cloud settled, Claire and Violet wiped the grit that clung to their faces and recognized none other than the brigand Mardok. All the events of a few hours previous came flooding back to Claire. Her enemy smirked at her.

"Is she the one?" the other man inquired.

"Yes. That's her. I remember that at least ..."

Before he could finish his sentence, the other man yanked a pistol from his jacket pocket. A loud bang echoed through the air, a bullet piercing Mardok's heart and sending him tumbling from his horse, gasping, "You ... fucking ... liar!" with his last breath.

Claire muffled a scream, covering her mouth with her hands. Èmile snapped at the reigns of the horses, commanding them to run, but a bullet found his stomach and he fell to the ground. In a flurry of motion, Violet jumped from the carriage and started running frantically back to town, Claire close behind her.

"Give me the pendant, Claire! It's safer with me," Violet demanded.

Claire's fingers trembled as she ripped the pendant from her neck, the delicate chain snapping with a sharp ping.

"Run!" Violet hissed.

They sprinted down the road, their long skirts billowing around their legs; each step was a battle against the restrictive fabric. Violet's dress caught on a jagged rock, yanking her backward with brutal force. She crashed to the ground, a cry of pain escaping her lips.

"Claire!" Violet gasped, struggling to free herself from the tangled cloth. "I'm stuck!"

Claire skidded to a halt, her heart pounding as she turned back to Violet. "Hold still," Claire gasped. She grasped the fabric of Violet's dress, working to disentangle it from the rock.

"Please hurry, Claire," Violet pleaded. "They're coming!"

Claire tried hard to keep her focus. With a ripping sound, the dress came free.

"Let's go!" Claire grabbed Violet's hand, and they both took off running.

The men on horseback charged forward as the ladies fled in terror. In a split second, they had seized Claire and thrown her onto a horse. Before Violet could react, she was knocked to the ground with a sickening thud and lay motionless. One of the attackers drew back his gun, ready to fire another shot – but man who'd shot Mardok ordered him to stop: "She's an old woman; leave her be."

The sound of hooves faded away until there was nothing but silence. Violet opened her eyes just in time to see them ride off into the horizon. Her heart sank as she screamed out:

"Noooooo! Claaaaaire!"

Gathering her strength, Violet raced towards Èmile, who was bleeding on the ground.

"Èmile! Oh no. My poor friend!" She quickly took off her scarf and pressed it against his wound. "We have to get you a doctor – now!"

Émile winced.

"No... it's too late for me. You must go ... it's not safe here."

Violet felt a tear rolling down her cheek as she grabbed Èmile's hand. "They took Claire – my Claire!"

"Who were they?" Èmile asked, dissolving into a fit of coughing.

Violet did her best to wipe the tears away and found courage inside of her. "Let's take one step at a time – first, we need to get you to the doctor, and then we will look for Claire. If they wanted her dead, they would have done it by now."

Gently, she pulled Èmile up from the ground and helped him walk towards the back of the carriage. Laying him down, she took the reins and drove towards town. The ride was bumpy but fast – Violet had no idea where to look for a doctor, but she knew that Gerard would know. When they finally arrived at the house, Violet jumped off the cart and knocked frantically on the door.

Richard opened the door.

"Madame Violet? Is everything alright?" His head whipped around, searching for Claire.

"We need your help. Èmile was shot in the stomach, and we need a doctor, please," she begged desperately.

Gerard rushed to the door, quickly assessing the situation. "Hurry, Richard, help me bring him inside. Fortunately, I'm a better surgeon than that old village sawbones. Pierre! Fetch my medical tools!"

"Where is Claire?" Richard demanded, helping the agonized Èmile off the carriage.

"She was taken," Violet stammered.

"Taken? By whom?! How? Where?" Richard's mind raced with questions as he imagined the worst.

Gerard scolded Richard sternly to focus and act fast as they lay Èmile down on the couch, then suggested a bottle of rum to soothe the pain. He told Violet to keep a towel near as he inspected the wound. Gerard instructed Richard to gently turn Èmile on his side so he could extract the bullet. Pierrick was told to hold a knife over the fire, ready if needed. As soon as the bullet was removed, blood began to flow, and Gerard poured rum on it before using the hot knife to cauterize one side of the wound, making Èmile scream out in anguish. Gerard repeated this technique on the other side of the wound, sealing it. Èmile passed out from the pain. Once finished cleaning up the blood, Gerard carefully wrapped Èmile's belly with gauze.

"Well, this is all I can do for now." He exhaled deeply as he stood up. "He needs to rest."

Violet asked worriedly, "Will he make it?"

Gerard nodded. "We got him just in time. Another hour and he would have lost too much blood."

She closed her eyes with relief, grateful to this family that had come to the rescue once again.

"Are you alright, Madame? What happened?" Pierrick asked, handing her a glass of water.

Violet finally recounted the entire story.

"Did you see which way they headed?" Gerard inquired, his forehead creased with concern.

"I saw hoofprints down the same road I took towards the city, but then they veered off," she replied anxiously. "I can't lose her; she's all I have left. First, my husband, then her mother, and now Claire. Maybe I'm cursed." Tears streamed down Violet's face as she spoke.

Gerard's expression softened, and he placed a comforting hand on the old woman's shoulder. "No, no, Madame – it is not your fault," Gerard reassured her. "The world is full of wicked people. It is not your fault."

Violet looked up at Gerard through her tears. "But what if I never see her again? What if they – "

"You mustn't think like that," Gerard interjected firmly.

"It's the pendant – that stupid pendant!" Violet sobbed.

Gerard nodded gravely. "I believe you're right. But how did they find out?"

"It must have been one of the thief who attacked Claire. He was there, and then one of the other men killed him in front of us." Violet remembered quickly.

Richard looked at Gerard and spoke up. "It would be best if you told her everything, Father. She deserves to know. We all do."

"Know what?" Violet questioned anxiously.

Gerard's breathing punctuated the heavy silence that had settled over the room. With a grunt, he pushed himself up from his leather armchair, his joints protesting the sudden movement. The old cabinet door opened with a soft whisper, revealing a collection of crystal decanters and bottles. Gerard's fingers trailed over the labels before settling on a bottle of rum, its amber liquid promising temporary solace. The clink of crystal against crystal rang out as Gerard carefully extracted four tumblers. He distributed the glasses silently, each recipient accepting with a nod of gratitude.

Violet settled into a worn leather armchair, her fingers drumming nervously on the armrest as she waited for Gerard to speak.

"Madame Violet," he began hesitantly, "maybe before I begin, could you explain how the pendant ended up in your family?"

Violet paused, inhaling deeply before gulping down the last of her rum. She recounted the day Napoleon had visited their tavern and shared the details leading up to Anne's tragic death, her voice trembling with emotion.

Pierrick was the first to break the silence. His voice wavered as he asked incredulously: "Wait ... are you saying that Claire is Napoleon's daughter? The ex–emperor himself?"

"Lower your voice, son," Gerard chided him.

Violet nodded in agreement. Gerard refilled his glass and asked, "Does she know?"

"No, she knows nothing about it; she only knows that her mother died giving birth to her and that her father was a nobody who never kept his promise," Violet said quietly. "Now it's your turn to tell me about this... *cursed pendant.*"

Gerard took a deep breath.

"Over two decades ago, I had recently moved to Paris for my scientific studies, surrounded by the culture and social life of the city. It was then that I met Napoleon – a young, ambitious officer with a unique charisma that drew everyone to him. We formed a deep bond over time, often gathering with our friends to share drinks and laughs.

"His ambition was unstoppable, like a raging wildfire that consumed everything. He surged forward with every mission as if he had been gifted with a divine power that propelled him to success and opened up new possibilities. His strength was unyielding. He had cultivated a powerful network of friends and allies that proved invaluable to his success.

"One night, Napoleon invited me to a secret meeting place, asking me to build an impenetrable safe. At first, I was skeptical that he asked me, a scientist, to build a safe, but he insisted. Napoleon believed scientists would bring a fresh perspective to the challenge of creating an impenetrable safe, potentially leading to groundbreaking solutions that traditional engineering might overlook. Everything seemed surreal as he impressed me with the secrecy and urgency of the request. The hefty price he promised tempted me greatly, yet I was concerned about accepting such a difficult task. My hesitation was palpable until Napoleon presented another scientist he had hired to team up with me. Her beauty overwhelmed me, but it was her intellect that overcame my doubts. Little did I know then that in accepting this challenge, I had embarked on a scientific odyssey and taken the first step on a journey of the heart. This is, of course, how I met my wife."

Gerard's eyes clouded; he was lost to the memory of those bittersweet days. Seconds passed in silence until Richard's sharp cough jolted him back to the present, forcing him to continue his story.

"We raced against the clock and worked tirelessly. The boys' mother was incredibly creative, always bringing fresh perspectives to any obstacle. Her intellectual brightness was irresistible, driving me to tackle every challenge that came our way with ingenious solutions. After months of relentless work, we created something incredible – a masterpiece of scientific engineering – an indestructible lock mechanism with a very distinct key. The key was designed as a pendant that could be split into two halves, adding an extra layer of protection. Only when these two pieces were locked together could they open the safe. The piece you possess is fundamental to unlocking the safe. Without it, the safe is impenetrable."

Violet gasped, as understanding dawned. Gerard continued.

"Napoleon's sense of amazement and satisfaction was almost tangible when we unveiled the completed safe. After a generous payment, we were sworn to secrecy by Napoleon, who warned us that our lives depended on this oath. When I dared to ask what the safe was intended for, he sternly warned us that the less we knew, the safer we'd be. That was the last time we saw him; we married soon after and moved to Laval."

The room was still until Violet shattered the silence with her most burning question.

"Then why on earth did he give Anne a piece of the key; and who is after the pendant?"

Gerard, taking in Violet shrewdly, coughed and rubbed his chin.

"From what you said," he mused, "I can only assume that he was intending to come back for it. So long as no one knew that he had left the half pendant with Anne, the security of the safe would not be compromised."

Richard cut in. "Then who was the man who shot the brigand Mardok? Somehow, news of the missing pendant got out."

Gerard's brow furrowed, his mind racing to unravel the complexities of the delicate situation before him.

"As Napoleon's power grew across Europe, he wove an intricate web of relationships – friends and enemies alike, especially in wealthy and influential families. But one thing is certain: whoever is after Claire's half of the pendant must want what's inside that safe."

Struggling to maintain her composure, Violet asked, "So why did they take Claire if they were after the pendant?"

"They must also know who Claire is. Maybe they're trying to use her as some sort of leverage; after all, Napoleon still poses a big threat. Otherwise, I can't understand it," Gerard replied with a heavy heart. "I don't have all the answers, but... I do know someone who might know more."

"You do? Who is it?" Richard asked, surprised.

Gerard opened his mouth to respond, but Violet interrupted, her voice shaking.

"Claire doesn't have the pendant! When they attacked us, I took it for safekeeping. I assumed she would be safer without it."

Violet's fingers quivered as she pulled the pendant from her pocket, the significance of its presence causing as a hushed reverence filled the room.

Her hands shook involuntarily as she lifted it before her, the glinting metal reflecting light across the conflicting emotions on her face. How could such a small piece of metal make powerful men fight tooth and nail? What secrets did it protect?

Gerard's face became very solemn.

"Then we must assume they will come looking for it soon. We should leave first thing in the morning."

Gerard kindly offered Violet his bedroom for the night, but she couldn't shake off her concern for Èmile. Their friendship began twenty years ago, on the day she came to the quaint village of Briacé with little Claire. She wanted to be close to him and keep an eye on him, so the boys set up a makeshift bed for her on the floor before going sleep themselves.

"I've already taken care of the fire; it should last through the night," Gerard said, his kind words filling Violet with gratitude.

"Thank you all for your generosity and kindness. I am truly at a loss for words."

"It is our pleasure, Madame. Please try to rest well tonight."

Violet lay still in the quiet living area; her mind drowned with worry as she listened to the comforting crackle of the fire. Beside her, Èmile appeared to be resting peacefully, but Violet couldn't let go of her concerns. Her thoughts were filled with the nightmarish possibilities Claire might be enduring. If only she had been more vigilant. What could she have done differently? She whispered a prayer, but even closing her eyes did not bring any relief.

8

Claire's heart pounded as the four men on horseback came to a halt and scanned their surroundings, looking for any signs of pursuit. Her mind raced with worries and questions as her muscles ached in protest from the jostling ride, and the sweat of the stranger holding her firmly in place had seeped into the back of her dress.

"We should rest for the night. It's a long way to Rouen," ordered the man who'd shot Monsieur Émile, circling round on his horse. Claire had overheard the others call him Louis.

"Where are you taking me?" Claire pleaded, trying to jerk away from her captor. Both Louis and the man holding her ignored her question, spurring their horses onward towards the nearest town. Soon they reached a seedy tavern on the outskirts, where they dismounted and tied up their horses.

"Do as you're told, and keep quiet," Claire's captor threatened.

She nodded mutely. Louis came closer and held out his hand. "The pendant," he demanded.

"I – I don't have it," stammered Claire, trying to conceal the fear in her voice.

But Louis wasn't buying it. "Lies won't save you. The pendant. Now!" he snapped.

"I swear, I don't have it! The thief you killed took it," she lied.

Louis leaned in even closer, his face mere inches from hers. The scent of tobacco and whiskey on his breath made her stomach churn. "Why was he chasing you, then?" he sneered.

Claire shut her eyes, trying to steady her breathing. Louis observed her with a cold, shrewd gaze. He idly scratched his stubbly beard, then took a small step away from her.

"We must find that pendant, Louis!" whispered Claire's captor anxiously. "He won't be happy if we return without it."

Roughly, he started searching for the pendant hidden in her clothes as she shrieked and tried to push him away.

"Enough!" Louis ordered, shoving the man back. "She doesn't have it!"

Louis cursed angrily as he tried to think of an alternative plan.

"We'll rest here for the night," he said at last. "First thing tomorrow, take all our men back to Laval and search for that... *stupid* pendant."

The tavern was full of smelly, shady, drunken men. Panic bubbled in Claire's veins as she was forced deeper into the inn, past tables full of carousers who leered at her hungrily. One of Claire's captors barked out a warning: "Anyone that talks to her or even looks at her meets death!" Claire had no choice but to stay by Louis's side as dinner and ale were ordered.

She tried to force down a few bites of the meal, but her appetite was much diminished. She was shaken, worried, and in pain. Was her grandmother alive?

Amid drunken shouts and laughter, Louis calmly surveyed the room. Fights erupted here and there due to the excessive amounts of alcohol consumed by the patrons. Sitting next to Claire, Louis watched his men chug ale at a neighboring table and exchange crude jokes. His face bore the marks of a man who had seen too much and aged prematurely by the rigors of his line of work. Those pale grey eyes, once perhaps bright with youthful idealism, now resembled storm-tossed seas – turbulent, yet eerily still on the surface.

They were windows to a soul burdened by the weight of unspeakable memories, each blink holding a secret that gnawed his conscience. His demeanor hinted at a man trapped in a perpetual battle with his inner demons, grappling with struggles invisible and incomprehensible to others. Yet, it was the impenetrable mask he wore that truly unnerved those around him.

Claire took a deep breath and summoned her courage to speak up.

"What do you want from me, sir?" she asked boldly.

Louis was unfazed by her question, sipping his ale and munching on cheese.

"I have no idea who you are, what you want, or where you're taking me," Claire persisted.

A piece of cheese stuck in Louis' teeth, causing him to smack his mouth with his tongue. He paid no attention to Claire's questions.

"I demand an answer!" she cried.

"Do you, now?" he replied flatly.

Claire begged him to believe she wasn't involved in whatever he thought she was involved in, but Louis only gave her an irritated look, muttering something about being quiet and eating her meal. Claire tried to obey, but the food tasted like sawdust in her mouth. Glancing around, she noticed a solitary man drinking alone, taking no notice of all the roughhousing around him. He seemed less dangerous that the others – but was that deceptive, was he actually the most dangerous of all? Claire felt powerless; she could not gauge these people's true intentions. In less than twenty–four hours, her life had been turned upside down. Just then, Louis banged his fist on the table and stood.

"Listen up!" he shouted out loud to the tavern. "I need four men to ride with me to Rouen Castle. You will be paid handsomely, but only once this girl is delivered – alive and unharmed."

There was a noticeable pause at the name of 'Rouen Castle'. Three men rose, unsteady on their feet, but most stayed put, seemingly debating whether it was worth the risk.

"I need one more! Don't make me ask again!"

Out of the corner of her eye, Claire saw the solitary man stand and approach Louis.

"I'll come with you if the pay is good," he said, in a thick accent Claire couldn't place, having never left her village before.

"And who are you?" inquired Louis in a suspicious tone.

"You can call me Vincenzo," he replied confidently.

Louis assessed him sternly, seeming to find him adequate. The man before him exuded mature confidence and a youthful physique, with broad shoulders, a narrow waist, and muscles evident beneath his tailored clothing. His dark, thick hair, flecked with silver, added a distinguished yet vibrant air, complementing his intense espresso-colored eyes that surveyed the room with practiced precision. His Mediterranean heritage shone through in his olive skin and strong facial features, with high cheekbones and a rugged yet softened handsomeness. Vincenzo's meticulously trimmed beard and superior quality attire, understated but refined, reflected his life as a soldier for hire who values elegance.

"An Italian, eh? Alright then. We ride at dawn. Your only job is to protect the girl at all costs, and see that she doesn't escape."

He then addressed the table of his own men, destined to return to Laval on the morrow.

"Jean!" he snapped at the man who'd kept Claire pinned to his horse after her kidnapping. "Bring the girl to her room, tie her up, and stand guard at the door. Nobody comes in or out."

With that, Claire was unceremoniously hoisted upstairs by her captor Jean, who was clearly upset about being pulled away from the festivities. He shoved Claire into the room, chained her waist to the bedpost, and glared menacingly.

"Stay put," he grumbled as he backed away, threatening her with severe consequences if she dared to try anything suspicious.

"What if I need to pee?" she demanded.

"There's a bucket beside your bed. Now shut your mouth." He slammed the door and locked it from the outside.

Claire's heart raced as she frantically pulled at the chain binding her to the bed, fruitlessly hoping to free herself. Suddenly, she heard Louis's voice ringing through the corridor, ordering Jean to open the door. She quickly turned onto her side and pressed her eyes closed, feigning sleep and hoping her shallow breath wouldn't give her away. Louis scouted the room suspiciously. When he eventually backed out of the room, Claire released a long–held breath. Finally giving in to exhaustion, she drifted off into a fitful sleep, tormented by the long day's events.

***

Claire was jolted awake by the sound of keys turning in a lock and a door banging open. Her chain jingled and she was disoriented for a moment, struggling to determine how long she'd been asleep. Across the room, she saw Louis giving orders to four men who looked dressed to depart; she assumed they were heading out to search for the pendant that caused such tremendous disruption. A wave of fear washed over her as she contemplated what this meant for her grandmother – had she found refuge somewhere, or returned to Gerard and his sons to seek help? What about poor Monsieur Émile?

Louis gestured to Claire to come to sit at a table opposite the bed, where she could see a loaf of bread and two small pots of butter and jam.

"Eat," he said calmly, "we are leaving soon."

"I'm not hungry."

Louis gave her a cold stare.

"It doesn't matter what you want. I must ensure your safe delivery, so eat and keep quiet."

Swallowing nervously, Claire tore off a piece of warm bread. She could feel Louis's dark, icy eyes watching her. The tension in the air remained palpable, a silent reminder of his power over her. A quiet knock sounded at the door, and Vincenzo slipped in.

"We are ready to depart, *signore*," he said to Louis. To Claire, he added politely, "This way, *signorina*."

As they exited the tavern, she heard the clop of horses' hooves against the cobblestones and bristled at the indignity of being silenced and ordered around like some puppet.

"Where are we going?" she pleaded. "What's at Rouen Castle?"

Yet again, Louis answered her with steely silence.

Vincenzo helped Claire onto her horse. With an electric buzz of adventure, the riders spurred their horses into a wild gallop and soon disappeared in a sinister cloud of dust.

9

Five travelers huddled in a sturdy cart journeying through thick forest. Beams of sunlight filtered through dense branches, creating a dotted pattern on the forest floor that danced with each gentle breeze. As they pressed on, the forest began to thin, allowing the merciless sun to beat down upon them. Spring was ending, and the days were getting hotter.

Violet found solace in the trees' presence, their sturdy trunks a testament to endurance and resilience. They gave her courage. Sensing worry in her silence, her new friend Gerard attempted to occupy her with interesting trivia and stories about the tiny towns they passed along the way. The trek was more challenging than expected, and the cart provided little comfort. They took turns riding and resting while Èmile recovered in the back to regain his strength. Pierrick repeatedly whined about the heat and scarce food, providing Richard with ample opportunity to tease him.

Just as the sun began to set on the horizon, they spotted the imposing silhouette of a château emerging from the fog. As they arrived at the majestic gates, their anticipation and excitement rose. Gerard immediately asked to meet with the baron of the house, and the guards led the travelers into a grand hall. The interior was surprisingly cool, a welcome relief from the sweltering heat of their journey. Flames flickering in a massive fireplace lit up the cavernous space, casting long shadows on every surface. The crackling logs provided just enough warmth to maintain an ideal temperature in the chilly space.

"Who is this friend of yours, again?" Richard asked his father, his voice low and guarded.

"He's one of my oldest friends."

"Can we trust him?" Violet asked, her eyes narrowed. "He could very well be the one after Claire."

Gerard shook his head.

"He'd never do anything so despicable – not even for a priceless pendant. I trust him, or we wouldn't be here now."

It was clear that Richard was not convinced. Pierrick piped up: "I hope they bring some food. It's been hours since we ate."

Richard shot him an annoyed look, but his stomach rumbled in agreement.

"Urgent matters or not, we still have to eat," Pierrick muttered defensively.

The group fell silent once again, each lost in their own thoughts. It felt like an eternity passed before they were met with a stern greeting from the baron himself.

"Gerard, my friend!" the baron exclaimed warmly as he opened his arms for a hug. Gerard was taken aback when he saw Charles Dupont, the man who had been one of his closest friends back in Paris. His old friend's appearance had changed drastically; his once-dark hair had surrendered to the march of time, now a shock of silver that caught the light. Deep furrows had etched themselves around his grey eyes. Despite the weariness that clung to them, there was still a spark of the old humor Gerard remembered so fondly. The most distinctive feature of his friend's appearance remained those peculiar ears – larger than most, they protruded slightly, giving him an almost elfish quality. In his youth, they had been a source of gentle teasing, but now they seemed to suit him perfectly, enhancing rather than detracting from his unique charm. Yet, for all the physical changes, the essence of the man remained unchanged. His smile, when it broke across his face, was as warm and genuine as ever, lighting up the room and instantly putting those around him at ease.

"What brings you to my house? How long are you staying? And who are your friends?" Charles continued, his eyes scanning the group with curiosity. Gerard's unexpected arrival had caught him off guard.

"These are my sons, Pierrick and Richard," Gerard announced with pride, gesturing towards the two young men standing beside him.

Charles's eyes widened in surprise, a smile spreading across his face. "Oh my, how time flies. Two grown men now. It is an honor to meet you both," he exclaimed, stepping forward to shake their hands.

"And these are our friends Violet and Émile," Gerard continued, introducing the rest of their party. Violet gave a polite curtsy while Émile offered a respectful nod, wincing as he clutched the bandage at his side. Charles greeted them warmly, but his keen eyes didn't miss the underlying tension in Gerard's demeanor.

"I'm afraid this is not a social visit, my friend," Gerard said quietly, his voice barely above a whisper. He leaned in close to Charles, lowering his voice even further. "Is there a more private place we can talk?"

Charles nodded curtly and issued quick, precise instructions to his household staff. "Please attend to the needs of our guests. Ensure they are comfortable and have refreshments."

His voice was calm but carried an unmistakable note of authority. Once the servants were tending to the other travelers, Charles led Gerard down a long hallway lined with lavish decorations. Their footsteps echoed softly on the polished floor as they approached a heavy wooden door at the end of the corridor.

Inside Charles's private study were shelves overflowing with books, maps, and curious artifacts from his travels. As Gerard entered, Charles followed and closed the door firmly behind them. Gerard was invited to sit in this sanctuary of adventure and knowledge while Charles poured two glasses of aged brandy. As they sipped the smooth liquor, memories flooded back.

"It's been far too many years, my friend," the baron sighed, his voice tinged with remorse. "I was very sorry when Emma passed away. I wish I could have been there for you."

Gerard nodded in acknowledgment and quietly murmured, "She was one of a kind. The best of us."

To distract himself from becoming too emotional, he quickly introduced a topic more pertinent to his visit.

"When was the last time you saw ... him?"

Charles paused.

"Who? Napoleon? Hmmm ... I briefly saw him last year before his abdication when I was in Paris for business. And you?"

"Since before we got married ... I haven't set foot in Paris since then," Gerard said sadly, looking down into his glass.

"He wasn't acting like his usual self," Charles continued. "He seemed to be suspicious of almost everyone."

"Hmmm, perhaps the weight of responsibility was getting to him," Gerard replied thoughtfully.

After a moment of silence, they both lifted their glasses in a toast to their long-standing friendship.

"You seem worried, Gerard," Charles probed gently. "What can I do for you?"

Gerard shook his head apprehensively. "I don't know where to start. I'm afraid that revealing too much could put your life at risk."

The baron laughed at this suggestion. "My life? Ha! My friend, I'm lucky I lasted this long. Shoot, and do not worry about me – I am all ears."

Gerard hesitated for a brief moment. He cleared his throat and spoke softly.

"You know about Napoleon's obsession with science and how he occasionally called upon my services for some of his side projects ... but you don't know the circumstances under which I met Emma."

"Napoleon introduced you two. Right?"

"Yes, but it wasn't a social gathering. We were hired to build an indestructible safe ... but we never knew what he wanted to protect."

"Did you ask?"

"Whenever I attempted to ask, he would hesitate and change the subject without giving me an answer."

"Knowing Napoleon, I'm not surprised," Charles continued, sipping his drink.

"Recent events have ... resurfaced that part of my past, almost as if the safe is haunting me." Gerard murmured.

"What events?" Charles asked cautiously, sensing unease in his friend's voice.

"Well, we crafted a unique key to unlock the safe ... and recently, it reappeared. Along with some surprising news." He took a deep breath. "What if I told you that Napoleon has an illegitimate daughter?"

Charles' eyes widened in disbelief.

"So, it's true?" he murmured under his breath, understanding pervading him like a fog. "This explains a lot."

"You don't seem surprised by this story!" Gerard remarked suspiciously. "What do you know?"

"Finish your story first," Charles urged.

Gerard provided information about the safe and explained that Napoleon's illegitimate daughter, Claire, had been kidnapped the day before. The woman Charles met earlier was her grandmother, who was desperately looking for her granddaughter. The, key, he said, took the form of a pendant necklace.

"What about Claire's mother?"

"Died in childbirth."

"Hmm."

"Whoever took Claire knows about the safe – and who she is!" Gerard continued.

Charles was still connecting the dots. "I've heard rumors of men looking for a pendant of some kind – most often whispered in seedy taverns between brawlers and shady characters. I never paid much attention – what surprised me was their relentless search for it. There were even rumors of Napoleon having a secret daughter, but you know how unreliable gossip can be. But, if what you're saying is accurate, who could be capable of orchestrating such an audacious feat?"

"I don't know, but something doesn't feel right." Gerard responded.

Charles remained silent, letting the information sink in and contemplating a possible solution. "I know someone who can help us make sense of this. He is highly connected and may also be able to help your endangered friend."

"Who?" Gerard demanded.

"Mortimer du Udille, the Marquis de Rouge; surely you know him."

Gerard felt his heart quicken. He knew of the Marquis, of course – strange stories and warnings about this mysterious man abounded.

"I think I met him once," Gerard said with hesitation. "Can he be trusted? What if he's involved in all of this?"

Charles smiled and released a reassuring guffaw.

"Mortimer? You don't actually believe the rumors, do you? His reputation is just a clever cover-up, spread to intimidate his enemies. Don't worry, my friend. I have maintained a good relationship with him over the years, and I'm sure he can help. It's also the perfect opportunity to catch up with him. It's been quite some time since we last saw each other."

Gerard paused to weigh their options carefully. He let out a deep sigh, resigned to the fact that there was no other way for them to uncover the truth.

"Then I shall accompany you!"

"Oh, no no, my friend," Charles replied firmly, patting Gerard's shoulder. "It is best if I go alone – we're not young men anymore, and you need to rest after your tiring journey, and relate our plan to your friends."

Gerard sighed heavily and reluctantly agreed, knowing Charles was too noble-minded to take no for an answer.

"I'll leave first thing tomorrow with a couple of my men," Charles said firmly as they approached the door. "I should be back in two or three days."

Charles rested his hand on Gerard's shoulder as they entered the grand hall. The rest the group sat huddled together, gobbling a sumptuous dinner in tense silence, when Charles and Gerard finally joined them. Violet and Richard immediately abandoned their seats and rushed over, while an unfazed Pierrick continued to eat without so much as a glance in his father's direction.

"Are you finished with your dinner? Allow me to show you to your rooms," Charles proposed.

Gerard clasped his hands in gratitude. His dear friend strode boldly down the hall, issuing orders left and right to any servant that crossed his path. Gerard smiled, watching fondly as Charles' adventurous and optimistic spirit was reignited for what lay ahead. That night, he closed his eyes and slept peacefully.

10

The first light of the morning shone off Rouen Castle, its walls towering menacingly over the surrounding forest. Every tower was staffed by watchful eyes, scrutinizing the horizon for any possible threat. This stronghold was legendary for its impenetrable defenses – nothing could breach its walls. Meanwhile, tantalizing scents from the kitchens within could make any soldier's stomach rumble with hunger. The air around the castle was filled with tension and despair as peasants gathered outside the gates to pay their taxes. With fear in their eyes, they knew what would happen if they did not yield what they owed.

Mortimer lay in bed naked, three ladies running their hands expertly over his body. One worked her way up to his face, but he turned away, refusing her touch. Despite the skilled ministrations of these three women, Mortimer remained unmoved and emotionless, oblivious to their caresses. He was lost in a whirlwind of thoughts.

Suddenly, an abrupt knock at the door jolted Mortimer from his thoughts, and a soldier entered with urgent news.

"Sorry, to bother you, sir," he began hesitantly. "There is news about ... you know."

"About what?" Mortimer snapped irritably.

The soldier gestured meaningfully towards an imaginary pendant hanging from an invisible chain around his neck.

"Speak clearly; I can't understand you," Mortimer ordered.

"It seems that Louis found the pendant," came the soldier's reply.

With a wave of his arm, Mortimer dismissed the ladies hastily, throwing them their clothes as they scrambled for the exit. Donning a robe, he poured wine into a silver cup and gestured for the soldier to enter and shut the door behind him.

"Speak!"

"As I said," the soldier continued, "Louis found another pendant."

"Where?"

"Near Laval. In a young girl's possession."

"A girl?"

"Louis believes it is the girl you are looking for. The age matches. It could be her," came the reply.

The words had barely left the man's lips before Mortimer was trembling, savoring the moment he had anticipated for over two decades.

"Quickly, send ten men to accompany Louis on his return journey. Bring the girl here unharmed. Keep this matter quiet. No one can know. No one."

With that, the soldier bowed and closed the door behind him, ready to execute all orders without hesitation.

For Charles, it was as if the two-day expedition would never end. But finally, he reached the main gates of Rouen Castle and a sense of relief washed over him. "I'm too old for all this traveling," he muttered. The guards recognized the noble insignia on the shields of Charles's men and granted them entry.

"Welcome, Baron. I will inform the Marquis of your arrival," a servant announced with a bow.

The main hall was a mess, remnants of Mortimer's last party still strewn about. Embers glowed in the fireplace and a curious dog sniffed for left-over food scraps. Servants scurried about, tidying up the tables as quickly as they could. Charles made his way towards the fireplace, hoping its heat would ease his fatigue. His men sat at the table, chatting loudly and sniffing the wine dregs, laughing loud enough to wake up anyone who may still be asleep nearby.

Mortimer burst into the room like a whirlwind of color and sound. His voice, a rich baritone that seemed too big for his diminutive frame, filled every corner of the space, demanding attention and admiration in equal measure. Perched atop his head was a blond wig that defied gravity and good taste. It was a masterpiece of excess, each perfectly coiffed curl gleaming under the chandelier's light. The wig bobbed and swayed with his animated movements, a living entity that somehow managed to complement rather than overwhelm his flamboyant personality.

Mortimer's attire was a symphony of sartorial splendor. His suit, cut from fabric that shimmered with an almost opalescent sheen, fit his compact frame like a second skin. Every detail, from the intricately embroidered waistcoat to the diamond-studded cravat pin, spoke of a man who viewed dressing as performance art.

Despite barely standing five feet tall, Mortimer seemed to tower over everyone in the room. The heels, cleverly disguised by flared trouser legs, were masterpieces of illusion, giving him a boost without the obvious tell of platform soles. He moved with the grace of a dancer and the confidence of a king, each step purposeful and somehow both delicate and commanding. His face was a canvas of expression, eyebrows arching dramatically, eyes twinkling with mischief and intelligence. When he smiled – often – it was with his entire being, lips parting to reveal perfectly white teeth in a grin that was equally charming and slightly unnerving in its intensity.

Mortimer's hands, adorned with rings on nearly every finger, fluttered through the air as he spoke, punctuating his words with gestures that were part conductor, part magician. Each movement seemed choreographed for maximum impact, drawing the eye and emphasizing the theatricality of his presence. Though not the friendliest host to all, he was always welcoming to Charles.

"I couldn't resist stopping by to see how my dear friend is faring!" Charles declared with a playful grin, wrapping Mortimer in a warm embrace.

"It's good to see you too," Mortimer said, gesturing at a servant to bring out the finest wine for their reunion.

"Are you staying here or just passing through?" inquired Mortimer.

"We'll see ... I have something important to discuss with you – somewhere quieter than this."

Charles followed Mortimer to a different room, where the latter closed the door behind them. He then spilled the full story, not leaving any details out. Mortimer listened intently, trying to mask his inner turmoil. He alone knew the secret of his own culpability – a secret with the potential to break their friendship apart. Should he act surprised or tell the truth? Would Charles take his side?

Charles leaned forward, his eyes shining with hope and admiration, concluding, "I thought of you immediately. You always seem to possess a wealth of knowledge on the most obscure subjects."

Mortimer looked at his friend, astounded by his trustworthiness and naïveté.

"I'm not surprised you got mixed up in this," Mortimer replied carefully. "Did you talk about this to anyone else?"

Charles shook his head.

"Not at all." He paused for a moment before continuing with more conviction. "I wouldn't trust anyone other than you with this information ..."

"You did well, my friend," Mortimer interjected, not allowing Charles to finish his statement. "And since you seek my help, I will be completely frank. Put this girl and her pendant out of your mind and move on."

Charles couldn't believe what he was hearing. "You want me to forget about it? Do you understand the significance of this information if it's true?"

"I have my reasons for secrecy, Charles. You know I worked closely with Napoleon on confidential operations," Mortimer replied sternly, steepling his fingers.

Charles frowned.

"What kind of operations?"

"The kind that could get you killed," Mortimer retorted. His eyebrows, meticulously groomed to geometric perfection, remained as still as carved stone, defying the natural expressions of human emotion.

"One of those operations involved finding this pendant."

"And ...?" Charles pressed, his suspicion growing.

"We never were able to find it. But I did learn that the pendant held sentimental value to Napoleon, though he had no idea he had a daughter," Mortimer explained, feeling his friend's skeptical gaze.

"But you did know?" Charles prodded.

"I had my suspicions. But as you know, people talk, and not everything can be taken seriously." Mortimer scratched his perfectly shaved chin, affecting casualness. He'd always been a skilled liar, though it pained him to use his gifts on Charles.

"All I can say is that every time we got close to finding the pendant, my men were ambushed and killed. The trail would go cold, and I was left with wasted resources and dead soldiers."

"Do you have any leads on who might be behind these ambushes?" Charles asked, growing more concerned by the minute.

"If I did, I would have taken drastic measures by now," Mortimer hissed through clenched teeth. "But I'm sure there's something shady about that secret society."

"What secret society?" Charles inquired.

"It was a covert and bizarre organization, collaborating with Napoleon on one of his scientific ventures. You're familiar with his passion for science."

He paused for a moment, undetectably gauging Charles's gullibility.

"Wait, weren't they working *with* Napoleon? What changed?" his friend demanded.

Mortimer gravely shook his head. "I'm not so sure anymore. They were the only ones that knew about these missions." He paused grimly. "Perhaps they decided it was too risky and cut all ties with Napoleon. Or maybe something else happened – I wouldn't put anything past them. Whatever it is they're trying to hide must be powerful."

Charles fell back in his chair as if hit by a gust of wind. He blanched at the implications of Mortimer's words. What had he gotten himself into? Mortimer met Charles' gaze with unwavering intensity.

"My dear friend Charles, I understand your desire to help those in need. It is a noble trait. However, you cannot fix every problem that comes your way. In this particular case, trust me when I say that getting involved will only make things worse. You did the right thing by bringing this issue to my attention. Rest assured, I will do everything in my power to assist. But please, let me handle it."

Charles remained silent, mulling over Mortimer's words. Mortimer felt a surge of determination, knowing he would do whatever it took to keep his mission safe.

"This pendant operation is deeply personal to me. In its pursuit, I have made countless sacrifices and lost many of my men. You don't need to get involved in this dangerous game, and there is no reason for you to put your life on the line."

Charles hesitated at Mortimer's words; he wanted to take action, but he knew it was beyond his capabilities. He found himself nodding.

"You may be right. This problem is likely beyond me; you should handle it."

"Then it is settled," Mortimer said, scratching his ear.

"Are you sure that you don't need any help? I could write to Napoleon, and he may have some insights that could –"

"No!" snapped Mortimer. Then he gathered himself, adding calmly, "It would be best if you didn't, spies are everywhere. Let's get your friends to safety first. The last thing I want is to put more people at risk. They must come here, where I can protect them."

Struck by the sincerity and care in Mortimer's voice, Charles acquiesced.

"You are right. I'll let you handle this. What do you want me to do?"

The men spoke for several more minutes. Charles agreed to take a short rest while Mortimer assembled a company of his best men, who would ride to Charles's home and escort his friends back to Rouen Castle and Mortimer's protection.

After Charles departed for his rest, Mortimer paced restlessly around his study, torn between conflicting emotions. He considered himself a true patriot who always put his country first no matter the sacrifice, but now he questioned whether his political aspirations were more important than a valued friendship. Though ambition and loyalty warred within him, Mortimer couldn't deny the pull towards power and success. He knew it was time to take action; whatever the outcome, he couldn't let anyone stand in the way.

Charles dozed off on a comfortable couch in a small parlor, enjoying soothing sounds coming in from an open window: birds chirping, and a gentle breeze that brushed against his face. He was so exhausted that at first, he didn't hear the gentle but persistent voice calling out to him.

"Baron?" the voice persisted.

When he finally jolted awake in a daze, he saw a timid figure standing before him. Though his body begged for rest, Charles knew there was no time to lose. As he approached the entrance, Mortimer intercepted him with concern. "Are you sure you don't want to rest some more?"

"Not at all," Charles replied. "I feel quite refreshed, thank you so much for your help. I won't forget."

Mortimer smiled before turning towards his men and giving them one last warning glance. With a final wave goodbye, Charles climbed atop his horse and ordered his men, accompanied by Mortimer's entourage, to venture out of the fortress gates.

11

Louis stood atop the hill, surveying his vast surroundings. The marquis's land spread out before him in every direction. Beyond the forest rose the towers of Rouen Castle, filling Louis with anticipation and relief; he knew he was bringing success to his master. The matter at hand was severe, yet he couldn't help but look around for any sign of his men returning with the pendant. He wanted to wait for it, but Mortimer was already expecting him and knew how important the girl was to him – delaying arrival could bring about negative consequences Louis wasn't prepared for.

Meanwhile, Claire tried to steady her breathing. Her heart was racing from the long hours of riding. She wasn't used to riding long distances, much less traveling so far away from her home. She had often dreamed of traveling and meeting new people, but this was not how she thought it would be. She rode with Vincenzo, who'd been assigned to protect her and seemed determined to receive full compensation by fulfilling his duty. With her, he was gentlemanly but distant. He monitored the other men almost as closely as he monitored her. So long as the journey lasted, she knew she was safe from the dangers the brigand Mardok had threatened her with. And yet, that journey had nearly reached its end.

An order from Louis pierced the air, and the entourage began galloping towards Rouen Castle. The others closed ranks around Claire. Her heart

raced as they neared the mighty castle gates – people fled their approach
as their horses thundered down the road without regard for anyone or anything in their path. Finally, they arrived at the castle entrance, where everything was huge and grand, more intimidating than anything Claire had ever
seen. She rode through the castle courtyard fearfully.

The courtyard was bustling with activity, and the guards were on high
alert. Everywhere Claire looked, she saw soldiers, far too many to count. It
felt like she suddenly became the center of attention as every eye fixed on
her. Vincenzo helped her off her horse. He, too, was taking careful notice of
their surroundings. This was his first time entering the castle, and he kept
a watchful eye for anything unexpected.

Louis gave orders, and most soldiers dispersed to their posts. He walked
over to Claire, commanding her to follow him, and handing some coins
to Vincenzo.

"Take these and be on your way," he said dismissively. Claire glanced
at Vincenzo, secretly hoping he would stay with her. She didn't completely
trust him, but compared to the other men, he'd treated her with respect.
Despite her reservations, she felt safer with him by her side.

Vincenzo carefully examined the coins before responding with a sly
grin, "I wouldn't mind getting my hands dirty for the right price."

Louis scrutinized him. On the one hand, Vincenzo had proven himself
reliable, following orders without question, yet something about him still put
Louis on edge.

"Wait over there," Louis said gruffly. "I'll let you know later." He steered
Claire toward the main hall, pushing her along as they went.

Louis frightened Claire, as did the intrusive stares and noisy bustle all
around her. As they entered the castle hall, he ordered a female servant
to find Claire a room, followed by two soldiers to guard her. Louis stood
watching Claire depart with a sudden feeling of trepidation. He had been
Mortimer's faithful man for over two decades, entrusted with confidential

tasks and secrets that would make most people shudder. He was the one person who truly knew Mortimer's complex character, whose outward charm and diminutive stature belied a cunning and manipulative nature. Mortimer viewed the world as his personal chessboard and the people in it as pieces to be moved according to his grand design. He excelled at identifying others' weaknesses and desires, exploiting them with subtle precision to achieve his goals. Louis knew Mortimer would not take kindly to news of the pendant going missing – nor would he forgive anyone responsible for its loss. Would delivery of Napoleon's lost daughter be enough? Spinning on his heel, Louis went in search of wine in which to drown his anxieties.

Mortimer sat at the long table, eating his lunch surrounded by servants. As soon as he saw Louis, he invited him to join him.

"Louis. Come, sit, eat something. How was the trip? I hear you bring a pleasant surprise."

Louis obliged, servants bustling around as he sat, placing steaming roasts and fluffy soufflés all around him.

"It was," he said, filling a chalice with wine, "I found the girl."

"That wonderful news," drawled Mortimer. "Where is she?"

"I had her escorted to a room to freshen up. She is awaiting your orders."

Mortimer gestured to one of the servants.

"Bring her here," he commanded. Before Louis could take a breath of relief, Mortimer proceeded to the dreaded question. "And what about the pendant?"

Hesitating, Louis coughed and drank before carefully replying. "My men are looking for it, and we were ..."

Mortimer was staring intently into Louis' eyes.

"I was told the girl had the pendant," he said.

"That is what I was led to believe," Louis replied. He weighed his fondness for his own head against Mortimer's known disdain for excuses. "But ... it was my fault. I should have been more cautious. I have men looking for it, and we have a good lead. There was an old lady with the girl, apparently they were assisted by some local villagers."

"The old lady is her grandmother, and the villagers are a professor and his two sons," Mortimer cut in, wiping his mouth with a pristine white napkin.

Louis was stunned. How did Mortimer know this?

"Oh, don't look so surprised, Louis. You know I've got eyes and ears everywhere."

Mortimer revealed the previous night's conversation with Charles as Louis felt the tension drain out of him.

"If everything plays out as it should, this two-decade hunt will end soon. And let's hope they do find the pendant ... or else you will have to go back and find it."

Mortimer's sharp gaze pierced through Louis, who dropped his eyes and turned his attention to the buffet before him: he was famished, after all.

"What should we do with the girl?" Louis asked, shoveling food onto his plate.

"Oh, I think she may be the key to defeating Napoleon for good."

"Isn't he defeated already?" Louis sneered as he leaned forward. "He's in exile with no power and –"

Mortimer cut off Louis' words with a sharp growl.

"As long as he is alive, he poses a threat." His voice low and intense, Mortimer added, "We cannot afford to underestimate him."

"Do you think he's aware of her existence?" Louis asked between enormous bites of roast duck.

"No, and this could play in our favor if we're smart enough. We've successfully eliminated any links that could lead back to us. I must keep up the appearance of loyalty until the end. We are so close to ..." Mortimer paused, realizing he was about to reveal too much.

"Did anyone from The Serpent Watch spot you?" he asked instead.

"No, we were strategic about our stops and traveled lightly," Louis replied with confidence.

"Double the guards on the walls – just in case."

Just then, one of the guards forced Claire into the dining room and the two men fell silent. Louis shoved his chair back and commanded his men to approach. Claire felt her feet sink into thick carpet, her legs shaking with each step as the guard pushed her along. She had been scrubbed clean and given a new dress and shoes, but she could not wash away the fear that engulfed her. As she scanned the room for any sign of comfort, her eyes locked onto Mortimer's.

Mortimer chastised the guard for his rough treatment.

"We are in the presence of a beautiful lady," he purred with a warm smile, standing up and extending his hands in a welcoming gesture. Louis nodded to the guard to leave, hoping to avoid further complications.

"I apologize for my men's behavior," said Mortimer to Claire. "they can be quite uncivilized at times."

Claire froze, unable to move from her spot in front of Mortimer. The short man before her appeared friendly and charismatic, but his demeanor exuded power. She knew she was at his mercy, and a tingling sense of dread crawled down her back.

"You must be famished," Mortimer continued, his voice faintly mocking as he gestured at Claire to take a seat. "I bet my men were not as welcoming as I am."

Claire slowly recovered the use of her limbs. The smell of meat made her mouth water, and she soon realized there was no use in resisting. Grudgingly, she accepted the stranger's invitation and took a seat. No sooner had she sunk her teeth into a turkey thigh did a rapacious hunger strike her. She ate recklessly and noisily, apologizing between bites, trying to maintain some semblance of manners. The taste of the warm food was comforting and reminded her of Violet's cooking. But soon the harsh reality set back in, and dread once again suffused her. Glancing around the room, she saw that the servants had left, leaving her alone with Mortimer and Louis.

"It's alright; if I wanted to hurt you, you'd know by now," Mortimer reassured Claire with a smile. "So, tell me ... where are you from?"

"From Briacé," Claire managed to choke out while still chewing.

Mortimer's brows furrowed. "I've never heard of it," he said, turning towards Louis, who shook his head.

"It's a tiny village of farmers," Claire whispered, feeling vulnerable and exposed.

"Ah. So, you are a farm girl?"

The man's voice cut through the silence. She continued eating, trying to ignore Mortimer's questions and suppress her emotions. With every passing second, she felt her fear escalating.

"Is your father a farmer too?"

Claire stopped chewing. Apprehension for her grandmother's safety only added to her distress.

"I never met my father," she finally whispered, her eyes cast down.

"Sorry to hear that. And what about your mother?"

Claire could no longer contain herself. With unbridled vehemence, she took courage and revealed her true self:

"May I ask what this is about? Why am I here, and why all these questions? I don't know who my father is, and my mother is dead. I am a simple girl who lives on a farm. I had the most dreadful week; this has been an unending nightmare ever since your men captured me! I haven't done anything wrong; I just want to go home." Claire let out a sob as tears streamed from her eyes.

Mortimer smiled – his flair for the dramatic at play – savoring every moment of Claire's anguish. He stood slowly and walked towards her, draping a cloth over her shaking shoulders. His touch made her skin crawl with revulsion.

"It's quite alright, my child. I did not mean to unsettle you ... You have to excuse my men; they can be somewhat brusque because they are simple soldiers who don't know any better. But you are safe here."

"Please, sir, I want to go home," Claire begged, her lip quivering. "Why am I here?"

"I will explain everything. Louis, no more questions – can't you see how scared the girl is? Try to enjoy your lunch. We can talk after you are rested."

Louis, who hadn't spoken a word, was taken aback; nevertheless, he was familiar with his master's games, so he played along. Lunch concluded without further emotional outbursts, and then Claire was led to an enormous bedroom.

A female servant showed her around before hurrying away, shutting the door behind her as a guard took first watch outside. It was the largest room Claire had ever encountered; the bed was at least five times bigger than her tiny bed back home. There was also a magnificent writing desk with an immense mirror above it, an enameled basin filled with water, and soft towels laid nearby. Was this what being a princess felt like? All this extravagance, and yet she was confined within these four walls, all alone in a new world.

Her gaze fell upon an arched window offering breathtaking views of rolling hillsides – farmers working their land and horses galloping freely. The sight reminded Claire of home, freedom, and her beloved grandmother. She tumbled onto the bed, releasing a deep sigh as the weariness from her travels finally lulled her into a dreamless slumber.

12

Claire jolted awake. She had dreamed of Violet and her dog, Willie. She could feel the sun fading through the window, signaling another day drawing to a close; how long had she been here?

She got up from the bed slowly, her feet dragging across the floor as if they were made of lead, and stumbled towards the basin of water. Splashing cold water against her face, she shivered and shook the remnants of sleep from her eyes. With one final glance towards the fading sunlight, Claire fixed her dress and hair and opened the door. Two guards stood to attention, their eyes boring into her.

She spoke firmly: "I'm ready to see the Marquis."

One of the guards nodded curtly and left in silence. The other, still standing sentry at the door, glanced downwards with a knowing look.

"Please wait inside!" he said, but Claire refused to be treated like a powerless prisoner; she demanded to be taken to where she wanted to go. Without saying a word, he pushed her inside and firmly shut the door.

She slumped onto her bed in frustration as her mind raced with all the potential outcomes of this meeting with the Marquis. And what would happen next? Time seemed to stand still as she lay waiting on the bed, her frustration growing by the minute. She stared aimlessly at the ceiling, wishing she had something – a book, a game, anything – to distract herself with. All she could do was wait.

Suddenly, she heard an ominous stomping of feet and voices coming closer and closer until, finally, her door swung open. Louis appeared and invited Claire to follow him. She sprung up immediately and followed. They walked through a long corridor until they reached the same room where they had eaten lunch earlier. Mortimer was standing there with two massive black bull-mastiffs sprawled at his feet. As soon as she entered, their menacing heads snapped up, muscles rippling under impressive fur coats. She thought of gentle Willy. Just as abruptly, the dogs laid back down again, sensing that she posed no danger.

Mortimer invited Claire to sit. All servants and guards hastily vacated the room.

"I trust your rest was good?"

Claire smiled politely and said that the bed was very comfortable. One of the dogs got up curiously and made its way over to her, sniffing around before flopping down beside her and pressing itself into her legs for attention. Claire couldn't help but giggle softly under her breath as she ran her hand through the dog's fur. Mortimer's lips barely curved into a smile, almost as if he were envious of the friendliness his dog showed her. His eyes were dark and unreadable, his presence intimidating despite his attempts at hospitality.

Claire reluctantly pulled away from the dog, feeling the weight of Mortimer's stare upon her. Uneasy yet determined at the same time, she bravely took it upon herself to break the awkward silence.

"Why am I here, and what do you want of me?"

Mortimer weighed each word carefully before speaking. He reasoned that manipulating the girl's emotions and playing mind games with her would result in a better outcome than simply enforcing his authority.

"You are here for protection," he began.

"Protection from what?"

"From who you are. From what you are."

"Who I am? I'm no one. How could a farm girl pose a threat to anyone? I was robbed and taken prisoner against my will," Claire replied in confusion.

"You are my guest, not my prisoner."

"I don't feel like a guest. I have been brought here without my consent, and I am being constantly watched."

"I apologize for that, but it is necessary to keep you safe."

"So does this mean I can leave whenever I want?" Claire asked hopefully.

Mortimer seemed to be enjoying the conversation immensely.

"Let's just say it would be best if you remained here for now."

"So I *am* a prisoner, just not behind bars."

"Oh, that could be arranged if you prefer." Mortimer's words were devoid of pleasantry, and Claire felt her rebellion stifled by his response. She chose her words carefully.

"That's not what I meant. I apologize. I thank you for your hospitality, Marquis."

"Good. I'm glad we cleared this up."

"Please, who is after me, and why?"

Mortimer fixed her with a stern gaze. "Let's just say some very powerful people want to take advantage of your father and use you to do so. You should stay here until I can ... guarantee your safety."

"My father?" Claire was filled with a mix of confusion and curiosity.

"You really don't know who your father is?"

"He's a nobody," she spat fiercely. "A lying, heartless man who left my mother pregnant with nothing but a broken promise to cling to."

"Ha, ha, ha. Is that what you were told?" Mortimer said, with a hint of sarcasm in his voice. "And what about the pendant?"

Claire felt her defenses rising as she answered him. "I don't have it – I already told your man that."

"Right. Then who gave you the pendant?"

"My mother. It's the only memento I have of her."

"You don't know anything about its origin?"

"What's to know? It's just a worthless pendant – except for its sentimental value. I don't understand why all you people are so obsessed with it."

A tense silence followed until Mortimer spoke again. "Have you ever considered, my dear Claire, that the items we inherit might carry more than just sentimental value? That perhaps, they bear secrets waiting to be unlocked?"

Claire glanced at him, her brow furrowing slightly.

"Secrets?" she echoed, curiosity coloring her tone.

"However," Mortimer continued, "unveiling such secrets often requires ... assistance."

"Assistance?" Her voice quivered slightly.

"Of course," he assured her. "One needs resources, protection – someone to navigate the treacherous waters that flood such endeavors. I, for one, am offering my services to ensure your safety and success."

Claire looked up at him, her eyes reflecting the turmoil of her thoughts. Trust wrestled with doubt, the allure of adventure clashing with the instinct to guard herself against deceit.

"Protection?" She pondered the word, its implications stretching out like the shadows around her.

"Think of me as your ... guardian angel in this quest," Mortimer proposed, the silkiness of his voice wrapping around her like a cloak. "Together, we can uncover the truth, and who knows what wonders might await us?"

Claire kept her eyes on Mortimer as he began at last to reveal what she longed and feared to know.

"That pendant belonged to your father, and I've searched for it for many years. When your parents met, they fell in love instantly. Your father gave your mother the pendant as a guarantee of his return, but when he came back, she was gone, nowhere to be found."

Mortimer stared into Claire's confused eyes, the intensity rising as he continued.

"Your father and I tried finding her for years without success; he was consumed by his desire to do so. Every time we got close, our men were ambushed and killed."

"Killed?" Claire murmured, both stunned and skeptical. "By whom?"

Mortimer shook his head and replied solemnly, "We don't know."

Claire stared at him incredulously before replying, "This makes no sense!"

Mortimer chuckled, hiding his irritation.

"I know this must come as a surprise, but I assure you that everything I am saying is the absolute truth."

"What reason do I have to trust you? Perhaps it's you who wants the pendant." Claire countered.

"Careful, mademoiselle," he sneered, his veneer of civility shattering. "I have been most accommodating thus far, but my patience has its limits."

"I apologize, Marquis, I didn't mean to –"

"I am one of your father's most loyal allies," Mortimer interrupted.

Claire scoffed. "An ally? What is he, a king?"

"He was the emperor of France, Napoleon Bonaparte."

Claire rolled her eyes in disbelief. "Oh please, that's just not ... You're having fun at my expense."

"Why don't you ask your grandmother? She may be able to tell you more."

Claire froze as she looked into Mortimer's sly eyes.

"Do you know my grandmother?!"

"I do. I do," he lied. "The loving and ingenious Violet."

Claire furrowed her brow in confusion, "She never mentioned anything about you."

"Well, it seems there are many things she failed to mention. As for me, I'm more than happy to answer any questions you have. This is an opportunity to change your life and live like royalty. All I ask for in return is your help."

"My help? For what?" Claire asked, trying to make sense of Mortimer's cryptic words.

"Let's just say your father needs a little ... motivation. And you can provide that."

"Motivation for what? My so-called *father* doesn't even know I exist. How could I possibly motivate him?" Claire was becoming increasingly perplexed.

"Oh, but you can. You see, all you need to do is write Napoleon a letter and tell him who you are. I'll even assist you in writing it." Mortimer's tone was sinister, and Claire couldn't shake off the feeling that there was more to his plan.

"I don't mean to be rude, but this feels more like a..."

"Be careful how you finish that sentence," Mortimer interrupted.

Claire stopped to think again, but there was no other way to say what she needed to say. "It seems you're using me to get something from my ... from Napoleon."

The air around them seemed electrified. Mortimer stayed still in his seat, his gaze never leaving hers. Claire's questioning appeared to back Mortimer into a corner, his patience wearing thin. Suddenly, he exploded with frustration.

"You're much smarter than I gave you credit for. You're also stubborn and quite annoying," he added, sneering.

Claire felt a chill run through her body as she saw darkness fill Mortimer's eyes. Slowly, he approached her chair, standing only inches away. He glared down at her.

"I wanted us to work together ... but you had to go and ruin everything, didn't you?"

"I ... I don't understand. What do you mean?"

"SHUT UP!"

His words hit Claire like a physical blow, and her heart sank even lower. Mortimer stood and started pacing back and forth, his gaze full of cold intensity each time he looked at Claire. He could easily end her life, but there was a nagging feeling that she still had a role to play.

"Let's play a little game. I'll ask a question, and you give me an honest answer. Sound good?" he resumed, composing himself.

Claire was utterly horrified; she'd never felt such fear in all her life. She was shaking uncontrollably, tears streaming down her face. Mortimer couldn't help but feel a sense of delight.

The first question was straightforward: "Where is the pendant?"

"I don't have it," Claire sobbed, hiding her face in her hands.

"Get a grip! We're just having a conversation. Would you rather I extract your answers through torture? Because that could be arranged."

He gave her a cold, threatening look.

"I don't have ..."

"I KNOW you DON'T have it. I asked you WHERE is it?"

The words rolled off Mortimer's tongue with disgust, and Claire squeezed her eyes shut, trying to devise a convincing fib to protect her beloved grandmother from harm.

"I... I ..." Her voice cracked beneath the weight of Mortimer's gaze, and he slowly leaned forward, parroting her words in mocking tones.

"WHERE!" he shouted, making the dogs bark, and Claire jump from her chair. With no way out, she blurted out the truth.

"My grandmother has it!"

Claire stayed frozen in her chair, wishing she could shrink into a tiny ball and escape this nightmare. How had everything turned upside down so quickly? Mortimer's fake kindness was a perfect disguise for his true malicious intentions. Claire had never felt such intense trepidation as when Mortimer rang a bell, calling two guards to his side.

"Take her to the tower," he ordered coldly. "No one is allowed to speak to her. No one! Bring Louis here immediately!"

The soldiers grabbed Claire roughly and dragged her away.

13

As the two soldiers marched through the courtyard towards an isolated tower, Claire felt invisible eyes stabbing her like sharp thorns. She heard Louis ordering his men to increase the guard on the castle walls. Suddenly, Claire spotted a familiar flash – it was Vincenzo, apparently one of her new guards. As he scanned the perimeter, his gaze met the silent plea Claire's eyes as she was dragged towards the tower. What did he think of all this, she wondered. Was he friend of or foe?

"Welcome to your new residence ... *mademoiselle*," one of the guards sneered, slamming the heavy iron door shut with a resounding clang that seemed to reverberate through Claire's very bones. Louis took a moment to look around and ensure everything was in place before heading back to the castle to meet Mortimer.

"You asked for me?" Louis inquired, approaching his superior. "I couldn't help but notice that you sent the girl to the tower."

"I am considering altering our plans for her," Mortimer replied, spinning a globe distractedly.

"Do we still need her? She doesn't have the pendant," Louis inquired.

"She's Napoleon's daughter, surely we'll find a use for her. Let's keep her here for now. Keep her locked up in the tower, and don't let anyone speak

to her. We'll see if isolation breaks her strong-willed nature," Mortimer declared. "Did you double the watch?"

Louis nodded.

"Good."

Mortimer walked to his study, the sound of his boots pounding on the
hardwood echoing through the hallways. Shoving open the door, he sat
at his desk and contemplated his next move. Time was of the essence. He
grabbed a quill and hastily scribbled an urgent message.

My dearest Napoleon,

*I hope this letter finds you well despite the challenging circumstances of
your exile. As your steadfast supporter and friend, I feel compelled to
reach out to you in this time of great upheaval for our beloved France.
Throughout your meteoric rise to power, I have been your unwavering ally,
working tirelessly behind the scenes to ensure your success and the glory of
our nation. You may recall the promise you made to me long ago – a promise of a place by your side when the time was right. I held that promise
with unwavering faith, believing in your vision and our shared destiny.
However, as the years passed and your influence grew, I found myself still
waiting in the wings, my potential unrealized. More troubling still was
the realization that you harbored a power of immense significance that you
chose to keep hidden from me. This secret, this lack of trust, cut deep into
the very foundation of our relationship.*

*Now, as you face the harsh reality of exile, I find myself in a position to
salvage what remains of our great nation's future. The specter of royal
tyranny looms once more, threatening to undo all that we have fought so
hard to achieve. In this critical moment, I extend my hand to you once
again, offering my services and unwavering dedication to the cause. If you*

are unable or unwilling to wield the power you have kept hidden for so long, I pray you to consider entrusting it to me. With it, I could continue our work, ensuring that France remains on the path to greatness you so brilliantly laid out.

Before I conclude, there is a matter of great importance that I must bring to your attention. The pendant – the one that has been the subject of much speculation and intrigue – has come into my possession. More significantly, I have also located your daughter. It may come as a surprise to you, but you do have a daughter from your brief liaison with the tavern girl Anne. Rest assured, she is safe and well and currently under my protection.

I eagerly await your response, my dear Napoleon. Together, we can still shape the destiny of France, even from afar.

Yours faithfully –

Mortimer signed the letter with a bold **M**, then hastily folded it and sealed it with hot wax, his family seal pressed deep into the envelope. With a sharp wave of his arm, he summoned his loyal messenger and bellowed orders for secret routes and safe delivery to Napoleon no later than two days. The messenger bowed and raced off into the night without further questions.

As the sun set and the day dipped into darkness, the heat of the day gave way to cooler temperatures. The sentinels standing guard in the castle courtyard lit fires to keep warm. Claire could find no relief in the tower cell as she lay on a cold, hay-covered floor. The small, tattered blanket provided little warmth or comfort against the chill. The dungeon was shrouded in shadows, the only light filtering through a small barred window near the ceiling. She could make out the vague shapes of previous prisoners' desperate engravings on the walls, a testament to their own struggles against the darkness that now sought to claim her. The guards posted outside the cell huddled together, bundled in thick coats, as they sipped their ale and chuck-led maliciously at Claire's shivering form in the corner.

"Do you need someone to warm you, eh?" one of them called out.

A second guard laughed.

"How about we come closer and take a nice little nap together?"

Claire shrank into the corner, desperately trying to pretend like she wasn't there.

"Hey, I'm talking to you!"

"We aren't supposed to talk to her, remember?" the other guard warned.

A wicked gleam entered the eyes of the first guard.

"Right, no talking. But no one said we couldn't have a little fun."

Now both guards were grinning knowingly at each other.

"You keep her still and quiet, then we switch. Let's make it fast."

Claire understood the guards' intentions all too well, but there was no-where for her to escape. She was locked away in a tall tower with barred windows. The two soldiers slowly unlocked her cell and approached her, smooth words dripping from their tongues.

"You're not supposed to be in here!" she shouted at them defiantly.

"Listen to her. We're not supposed to be in here!" they cackled cruelly as they moved closer.

"If you touch me, I'll tell Louis," Claire threatened.

One of the guards acted scared for a moment, before the other lunged forward and clamped a hand down hard over her mouth, pinning her arms with his free hand. The other man's eyes widened in glee as he pulled down his trousers. With a mighty surge of adrenaline, Claire managed to muster enough force to kick the man square in the face and send him crashing to the ground.

"Ooooh, you bitch!" he shouted.

Like a rabid dog, he bit her leg, making Claire scream in pain. Just as he was about to have his way with her, a voice interrupted the scene.

"What the fuck are you doing?"

Vincenzo stood there, holding a plate of food for the prisoner.

"Mind your own business, new boy," spat the guard holding Claire's arms. "Leave the food and go."

For a moment, Vincenzo just stood there. Then –

"Why? You want to keep all the fun for yourselves?" he replied with a wicked grin.

The men exchanged glances before hooting and hollering for Vincenzo to join them in their unholy act. Claire's eyes filled with tears – she felt strangely betrayed by Vincenzo, who was coming closer and closer, until suddenly he lunged forward and cast a knife straight into the throat of her pants-less attacker. Blood spewed over Claire's face like a macabre shower and she watched him collapse dead at her feet. The other man released Claire in panic but was too slow to prevent Vincenzo froming throwing another knife into his chest – killing him in moments.

Claire screamed as Vincenzo turned to her, but he quickly soothed her with comforting words: "Are you okay? Did they hurt you?"

"I'm fine – fine," she insisted, although she was trembling still.

Meanwhile, the commotion had caught the attention of other guards nearby, who rushed over to investigate.

"What's going on here?!" one yelled as he burst through the door.

Seeing their compatriots lifeless on the floor inside the cell and Vincenzo trying to help Claire, they stormed in. The guards yanked Vincenzo up and punched him twice before tossing him into another cell.

"Trying to free the girl, you traitor? Call Louis."

When Louis arrived at the tower, he immediately demanded an explanation.

"Is this true? Did you kill my men?"

"I did," came Vincenzo's calm reply.

"And what was your plan after rescuing the girl? To fly away?"

One guard jeered and the others laughed.

"I only followed orders to bring food to the prisoner when I found your goons assaulting her. They threatened me when I tried to stop them and I defended myself; it's as simple as that. Wasn't it clear we weren't allowed to talk to her? Let alone rape her."

Louis exhaled heavily and grudgingly ordered Vincenzo's release.

"I'm starting to feel like I'm surrounded by idiots. My patience for this stupidity is wearing thin." His cold gaze landed on Vincenzo. "You will stay here tonight and guard her. The rest of you, return to your posts! If I hear so much as a peep out of place, I will end you myself."

Vincenzo was left alone with another man to watch over Claire. Louis stepped out of the tower with one last warning: "No talking ... or fucking the girl. And stay alert!"

Both nodded before Louis angrily stormed off, muttering, "What a pair of idiots."

Quavering in the corner, Claire's emotions were a mix of fear and coldness as she studied her new keepers. She locked eyes with Vincenzo, silently thanking him for shielding her from her attackers. Vincenzo snatched a tattered blanket from the neighboring cell and hurled it toward Claire; with a barely perceptible nod to avoid arousing suspicion from his comrade, Vincenzo returned to his post, a silent promise to do what he could, however small it might be.

As the night wore on, the castle grounds settled into an eerie silence, the only sounds coming from the flickering embers of dying fires and the distant hooting of owls. Most guards slumbered in their posts though some patrolled the grounds. Claire clung to a prayer she'd learned from her grandmother, repeating it like a mantra. Exhaustion overcame her, and she drifted into a fitful sleep, wondering if the next day would bring salvation or torment.

14

Violet woke early to bid farewell to Èmile, who had decided to risk returning home; he feared worrying his wife more that he cared for his own health. "Please give my regards to Marie, and thank you for everything, Èmile," Violet said fervently, pressing her forehead to his hands. "May you continue to recover quickly."

"I will say a prayer for Claire. Stay safe, my friend," Èmile replied.

As Violet watched the cart transporting Èmile disappear into the distance, she wandered into the garden, desperate for a distraction from her worries about Claire. Everywhere she looked, servants were bustling around, taking care of every need. She wished she had the courage to take off on her own and search for her granddaughter without delay, but Gerard's wisdom and patience kept her enthusiasm in check. Despite the beauty of the flowers that surrounded her, Violet felt nothing but conflict as she tried to reconcile her desire to keep hope alive with the fear that no news meant something terrible had happened.

Violet's attention was drawn to a man pushing a cart of fresh fruits and vegetables into the courtyard. He reminded her of home and Èmile. The man's penetrating gaze bore into her; his eyes, sharp and unwavering, seemed to pierce through her very being as if searching for hidden secrets. A thick, unkempt beard adorned his face, peppered with streaks of grey that hinted at a life filled with hardship and experience. The beard merged seamlessly into his long, unruly hair that cascaded past his shoulders, moving slightly in the breeze. It was clear from a single glance that this man was no simple farmer. His posture exuded an alertness, his muscles taut beneath his worn clothing, his hands, calloused and scarred, told tales of wielding weapons rather than plowshares. No, this man was unmistakably a soldier, or perhaps more accurately, a seasoned warrior.

She quickened her step and broke away from his stare as she hurried towards the château entrance. Casting one last look over her shoulder, she saw the man still staring in her direction.

"Everything okay?" Gerard asked when Violet entered. She jumped from shock, lost in thought.

"Oh heavens!" she said with a nervous laugh. "Someone was staring at me ...."

"Should I get the guards' attention?"

"No, no, it's nothing. I'm probably just paranoid. I'm alright now." Before Gerard could ask anything else, she changed the subject. "Have you heard any news from Charles?"

"Not yet, but I'm hopeful something will come today."

"I hope so; I can't stand waiting here doing nothing. It's been almost three days, and Claire ..." Violet began to tear up, and Gerard comfortingly put an arm around her shoulders while they walked together toward the living room.

"Everything is going to be alright, Violet. Charles will bring good news," he reassured her, although deep down, he was concerned too.

The long table in the dining room, stacked with fresh fruit and baked goods, emitted an enticing smell. Pierrick was the first to indulge, entranced by a breakfast he didn't have to prepare. Life seemed almost perfect at that moment, and he could have stayed there forever. Richard, Gerard and Violet soon joined him. Pierrick, his mouth full of food, managed a muffled exclamation of "Morning!"

"Good morning to you," Richard said sarcastically. "Nice to see you waking up at a decent time."

Pierrick ignored his brother's provocation. Violet sat motionless and silent, lost in her thoughts.

"Madame, there is a man that would like to speak with you," a servant announced from the corner of the room.

"With me?" Violet replied in surprise, her eyes widening in confusion.

"Yes, he is outside, and he said it is important. Should I tell him to come back later?"

"No, it's ok. I'll come."

Gerard stood up and followed Violet towards the entrance. The man who had been fixated on Violet earlier stood there waiting anxiously, twirling his beard between his fingers.

"How can we help you, sir?" Gerard interrupted as they neared the door.

The man quickly composed himself, looking at Violet intently.

"It's really you, Madame?" His dark eyes locked onto hers.

Violet was unable to place him anywhere in her memories, but something about him felt strangely familiar.

"Madame, it's Jean-Philippe. It has been many, many years. I'm afraid it's my fault you fled your tavern that long ago night ... You may not recognize me now with my beard."

Jean-Philippe ran his hand over his now-bearded face, hoping to prompt Violet's memory. Violet gasped in recognition, memories from the distant past flooding back.

"Please, come inside," she murmured nervously, leading Jean–Philippe into the dining room, followed by a confused Gerard.

Inside the dining room, Violet offered Jean–Philippe something to drink, which he politely refused.

"I'm glad you're safe; I've been looking for you and Anne for many years," Jean–Philippe declared sorrowfully. Violet's heart felt heavy, remembering the circumstances under which they had met and all that had followed. Wasting no time, she introduced Jean–Philippe to the others as the man that had saved her and Anne many years ago. Then, addressing Jean-Philippe, she swiftly recounted what the years had brought: Anne's death, the birth of Claire, their quiet, idyllic years on the farm, and the pivotal theft of the pendant. Her words spilled out rapidly, her voice rising and falling in volume as she tried to cram a lifetime into mere moments. When Violet was overcome with emotion, Gerard picked up the narrative. He was careful not to give away too much information on Charles' whereabouts and his meeting with Mortimer, as he still wasn't sure how much he could trust this stranger.

Jean–Philippe remained still and silent throughout the breathless account, taking in every word. He understood how much this woman had been through, and yet she had found the strength to move mountains to save her last living family member. As the story came to a close, Jean–Philippe took a deep breath.

"I can't fathom all you've endured, Madame. On the day we were separated, I had an awful confrontation with the man who was pursuing Anne. After they failed to obtain any information from me, they stuck a sword into my side and left me to die. Miraculously, I somehow made it out alive, thanks to the help of a farmer. I recuperated and regained my strength over time. I swore never to rest until I found you and Anne again. However, I never could ascertain whether the Marquis du Udille's men had reached you or...."

At the mention of the Marquis, the tension in the room skyrocketed. Everyone swapped uneasy glances.

"Did I say something wrong?" Jean–Philippe asked with trepidation.

"Are you referring to Mortimer?" Gerard asked for clarification.

"Yes, Mortimer du Udille," Jean-Philippe confirmed, puzzled by the sudden change in atmosphere. "He's been searching for the pendant for years."

It was Gerard who finally spoke.

"Two days ago, my friend Charles went to ask Mortimer for help in search of Claire. I'm sure Charles has given him all the details – now I'm worried for his life."

Jean–Philippe sprang into action, the urgency in his voice palpable.

"If you trust this man Charles and he is not in Mortimer's pockets, then he is indeed in grave danger, as are all of you. I don't think you realize how much. Mortimer has a deceptive nature; he may seem kind and helpful at first, but that's only because he wants something from you. Things may have already taken a turn for the worse."

Gerard interjected, "We can't just leave, we must wait for Charles to return!"

Jean-Philippe was pale.

"That would be folly. There is no guarantee your friend will return – or that he'll return alone. You may wish to risk your own life, but would you risk the lives of your son's? Or the life of this brave woman?"

The expression on Gerard's face suddenly changed as he grasped the magnitude of the situation. Just then, they heard the sound of horns and clattering hooves: Charles was back – with reinforcements.

"Good news, my friends," Charles declared cheerfully as he walked through the door. "But first, I need a drink."

Gerard grabbed his arm, urgently demanding his attention. "I need to speak with you, Charles. It's important!"

"What is it, Gerard?" Charles didn't break stride as he made his way toward the parlor. A servant came forward to offer him a basin of water to wash his hands. Weary from the long journey, he accepted without hesitation. As Charles dried his hands on a proffered linen, Gerard ushered him into a quiet corner where he quickly updated him on Jean–Philippe's recent revelation.

"Are you certain about this?" Charles furrowed his brow in confusion.

"These days, I'm uncertain about everything. However, I don't think we can trust Mortimer, nor his men," Gerard replied.

Charles remembered the oddly serious conversation he had with Mortimer a few days before, and the feelings of doubt he had repressed. He passed a trembling hand over his face.

"My God," he whispered. "What have I done?"

Gerard laughed loudly as if Charles had just told a hilarious joke and whispered through his teeth, "Pretend nothing is wrong. We must not raise suspicion. The men who travelled with you are watching us closely."

Adopting poker faces, both men turned toward Charles's study.

"Please see that our guests have everything they need, food, water ..." Charles beseeched his manservant, before leading Gerard away. Seeing this, Jean–Philippe trailed behind them, leaving Violet, Pierrick and Richard in the parlor with the ragtag company of Mortimer's men.

With a heavy sigh, Charles sank into the oversized couch's plush cushions, exhausted from his long journey. He shut his eyes and took a deep breath, trying to relax. Gerard poured him a glass of aged cognac.

"Just what I needed," Charles said gratefully. His eyes landed on Jean–Philippe. "Who is this gentleman?"

"A pleasure to meet you, sir; my name is Jean–Philippe."

"Right! And it's you who believes my old friend Mortimer isn't to be trusted?" Charles continued, getting straight to the point.

"I served under Napoleon, sir. I've known Mortimer for years, just like you. While on a secret mission for Napoleon, I was ambushed by one of Mortimer's men and left for dead. Trust me, Mortimer is not the man you believe him to be. I learned that the hard way."

"What do you know about what I believe or not?" Charles demanded, his voice gruffer than he intended.

"That you are simply a poor judge of character is the best-case scenario for us," Jean-Philippe replied shortly.

Charles stiffened.

"I am a man of honor," he said. "Though I don't suppose there's any way I can prove that to you."

The heavy silence that descended seemed to know no bounds, and with every passing second, suspicions mounted. As much as Charles resented the stranger's implications, his own thoughts raced frantically, unable to find any proof that would absolve Mortimer in the eyes of all.

"When I spoke to Mortimer," he began, taking a restorative sip of cognac, "he knew about the pendant, and Claire. He was very eager to take over, demanding that I step back. He claimed this was for my own protection, but deep down I suspected he had another motive. Still, I trusted him. He has always been extremely devoted to our nation's interests, so I assumed his actions were motivated by a desire to protect France."

Theories flew swift and wild about what motivated Mortimer to plot against Napoleon, but every answer only seemed to spawn more questions.

"What are we going to do now?" Charles asked warily.

Dread settled into the group. Gerard suggested that until they could devise a plan, they should delay their departure by having one of them pretend to fall ill. With no other options left, the three men decided to risk it. Gerard volunteered to be the faker, apologizing to Charles for dragging him into this mess.

"No, my friend," said Charles, his expression darkening, "It is not your fault. I need to know who my friends are, and I need to know how involved Mortimer is in all of this. If your accounts are true, he will pay."

Watching Charles's face, Jean-Philippe said, "Maybe because I have no choice but to trust you, I choose to believe you're an honest man."

At this, Gerard poured cognac for himself and Jean-Philippe, and the three men clinked glasses in a somber toast.

Back in the parlor, Mortimer's army commander, Captain Gaul, sauntered in with an air of forced casualness. His sharp and calculating eyes darted around the space, taking in every detail before settling on Violet and the boys. There were only two men in Mortimer's employ that he trusted: Louis and Gaul, each bound to him through distinct yet equally potent ties. Louis, the first of Mortimer's trusted confidants, was a paragon of loyalty. His devotion was not born of fear or coercion but rather a genuine belief in Mortimer's cause.

In stark contrast stood Gaul, whose penchant for cruelty extended far beyond the bounds of normal human behavior. This twisted inclination made him an invaluable asset to Mortimer, who often leveraged Gaul's proclivities to maintain a facade of clean hands. Gaul became the instrument through which Mortimer could enact his most brutal schemes, allowing him to distance himself from the grim realities of his machinations. Gaul's appearance was a study in contradiction. He cultivated the image of a refined gentleman, his hair meticulously styled with a perfect part on the far left side of his head. His green-grey eyes, which might have been striking in another face, seemed to hold secrets of unspeakable deeds. Despite his efforts to embody sophistication, an undeniable aura of menace clung to him like a second skin.

A smile that didn't quite reach his eyes spread across his face as he approached and extended a hand towards Violet. Something was off about the gesture, a hint of insincerity that caused her to drop his hand quickly and fiddle with a loose thread in her skirt.

Gaul turned his attention to the boys. "Pleasure to meet you, lads. Are you enjoying your stay?" he asked.

The boys exchanged uneasy glances, picking up on the tension radiating from Violet. Pierrick nodded while Richard mumbled a noncommittal, "It's alright."

Undeterred by their lukewarm responses, Gaul pressed on, peppering them with questions about their journey and plans. With each inquiry, his eyes seemed to gleam with an ever-increasing intensity, as if he were cataloging each piece of information for some unknown purpose. As the conversation progressed, Violet felt a growing sense of unease. Gaul's words were pleasant enough, but something sinister ran beneath the surface. His laughter came a beat too late, his smiles never seemed genuine. It was as if he were playing a role, and not particularly well. When Gerard, Charles and Jean-Philippe returned from the study, their return was eagerly welcomed. Jean-Philippe's eyes lingered upon Gaul's face a moment too long.

"I don't feel very well," Gerard said, clutching his stomach. "I think I'd better lie down for the rest of the day."

The statement was met with a wave of intense emotion from the others. Gaul bristled at this news and reminded Charles of the timeframe they had agreed upon with Mortimer. Charles forced a disingenuous smile, assuring him that a small rest would do the trick. The entire group migrated upstairs, as no one wished to remain alone with Gaul. In the hallway outside his room, Gerard explained in a whisper that his illness was a sham, and he related the dire situation they were in.

"Mortimer's men mustn't suspect anything, so some of you had better go back and act normal until we figure out a plan. I don't want anyone getting into any more danger than we're already in."

Violet piped up, worried: "Did he say anything about Claire?"

"No," Gerard replied, "but we think we know who is behind this. I am almost positive that Mortimer has Claire, or at least he knows where she is."

As the brothers headed for the stairs, Pierrick's eyes lit up with a devious plan.

"What if we kidnapped that strange man, Gaul, and forced him to tell us where Claire is?"

"Kidnapping? Really? That's your brilliant idea? Are you crazy? We don't know the first thing about kidnapping someone!"

But rather than being discouraged, Pierrick seemed emboldened by Richard's words.

"Think about it. We could get Charles to help and do it while he sleeps. It's not a bad idea. I'm going to tell Charles," he declared, determinedly spinning on his heel.

"Pierrick, wait! Think about this for a minute," Richard pleaded as his brother strode off, but Pierrick was already gone. Reluctantly, Richard headed to the parlour alone and tried to act natural.

"How is your father?" Gaul asked.

"He's doing well," Pierrick replied, not thinking of the consequences of his words. "I mean, he will be, he just needs rest. I think tomorrow he should be better."

Gaul eyed him suspiciously, but just then Richard and Charles entered. The latter came over and offered Gaul a glass of cognac. Richard grabbed Pierrick by the arm and steered him out of the room before he elaborated further upon the 'plan' in that too-loud whisper of his.

"What is wrong with you? We need to keep up appearances and you're marching me out of the room, like that's not suspicious!" hissed Pierrick.

Richard opened his mouth to issue a fiery rebuttal. Noticing the two brothers, Jean–Philippe's hurried over to pull them farther away from any prying ears.

"What's up with you two?" he asked, looping an arm around both of their shoulders as they began to walk away.

"Nothing, just reminding my brother to THINK before he says or does something stupid," Richard snapped.

"Think? Really? JP, you seem like a man of action, what are your thoughts?" Pierrick retorted.

"*JP?* Really, Pierrick?" At this point, Richard was furious with anything Pierrick suggested.

"JP! I like it!" said JP mischievously, adding fuel to Richard's fire.

"How about we kidnap Gaul while he sleeps and force him to tell us where Claire is?" said Pierrick in a rush.

"Enough!" exploded Richard. "We can't just go around kidnapping dangerous lunatics!"

"Wait," JP said cautiously. "Maybe that's not a bad idea."

Pierrick swelled with pride.

"You see?"

"What? Are you actually giving him credit for his stupid idea?" Richard cried out in disbelief.

JP didn't back down. "Stupid or not, it may be our only option right now. Gaul is a very dangerous man – I've met him before. In order for this to work, it needs to be done quietly without arousing any suspicions. Let's not tell your father – I don't think he would approve of you two getting involved."

It took much debate to convince Richard, but he finally agreed on one condition:

"We go to Charles first. If he says no, it's off the table, agreed? Both of you?"

Both JP and Pierrick agreed and they all three shook hands. They resolved to find the right moment to talk with Charles away from Gaul's watchful eyes.

Richard was shocked when Charles unexpectedly endorsed their stratagem and gave them details on how to proceed.

"We can't leave anything to chance, and this may be our only shot; I'm trusting you to keep this between us," Charles warned.

Pierrick couldn't contain his enthusiasm. "So, what's next? What are we doing?"

"Jean-Philippe and I will take care of it," Charles said sternly.

"But this was my idea! I can help!" Pierrick insisted, fuming.

"I'm aware," Charles replied calmly, "but the risks are too high. Your father would never approve."

"Are you going to involve him?"

Charles glanced at JP.

"I think it's too risky. We need to keep up appearances that he's ill and resting."

"Then there's no need to tell him anything!"

Charles shook his head. "I'm not going to endanger you and lie to your father. I'll fill you in first thing in the morning. I give you my word."

Pierrick seethed with frustration, but no amount of insistence could sway Charles or JP.

15

As the day waned and the brilliant sunset cast its murky orange hues over the majestic château, the plan was set into motion. Most everyone was exhausted from the day's events and ready for a restful night, except those few involved in Charles' plan. The plan was straightforward: Gaul would be invited to Charles' study to discuss the journey to Rouen Castle, while Charles' trusted valet, Kofi, would assist Jean-Philippe in coercing Gaul. The interrogation would then take place in Charles' study.

Despite his excitement, Richard finally managed to fall asleep. His sleep was disrupted by Pierrick, who kept tossing and turning next to him in bed.

"Sleep," Richard muttered. "If you keep making all this noise, you will wake Father."

"It's not fair. It was my idea," Pierrick whined.

"Pierrick, drop it. We have no experience with this," Richard said.

"Where do you think they're keeping him?"

"Keeping who?"

"Gaul! Mortimer's man," Pierrick said, frustration evident in his voice.

"I don't know, and I don't care. Go to sleep," Richard said sharply.

Pierrick fell silent, though he couldn't tear his thoughts away from the plan and the fact that he hadn't been included. For the first time in his life, he craved the chance to be part of something bigger, to feel the thrill of adrenaline – and he wasn't scared. Why were older people so quick to dismiss him?

A quiet noise sounded outside the room, and Pierrick jumped from the bed.

"You hear that?" he whispered, but ran out of the bedroom before Richard could answer.

"Pierrick! Come back!" Richard hissed. Annoyed by his brother's obstinacy, he still followed out of a sense of obligation – who else would talk some sense into him? Taking extra caution to close the door as quietly as possible so as not to wake Gerard up, Richard hurried after his brother.

Pierrick felt elation rising within him as he quickened his pace. In the dark, he bumped into a small table and cursed under his breath. Richard rolled his eyes in exasperation. The brothers tip–toed through the hallway, their hearts pounding as they squinted in the dimness.

Even with the faint moonlight filtering in through the windows, it was difficult to see. Suddenly, Richard and Pierrick spotted two shadowy figures moving outside and froze fearfully.

"Something isn't right," Richard whispered.

"Let's check it out," Pierrick said, taking a step forward.

In the dim light of a candelabra, JP and Charles huddled tensely in the latter's study.

"What if he doesn't tell us anything? We can't just let him go," said JP.

"We don't have many options left," Charles sighed. "Where is Kofi? He should be here by now."

At that moment, there was a crash. Richard and Pierrick tumbled through the door, looking sheepish.

"What are you two doing here?" cried Charles. "I thought I was clear enough!"

Pierrick smiled winningly while Richard opened his mouth to defend his innocence. He was cut short by a clatter from the end of the hall.

"Get up! Quickly, hide inside the cabinet!" Charles pushed the boys inside. "Not a peep, understand?"

With one final warning look, Charles closed the cabinet doors behind them.

JP stood watch over the door. Light appeared at the end of the hall, growing bigger and brighter as a group of soldiers came sprinting toward them. Something wasn't right – these weren't Charles' men, they were Mortimer's men. Someone had betrayed them!

Hurriedly locking the study door, JP breathlessly informed Charles of their precarious situation.

"Kofi must've double–crossed us! That bastard!" cursed Charles.

"We don't have time for regrets – is there another way out of this room?" JP asked.

"Yes, there is secret exit behind the fireplace."

Charles ran towards the fireplace. Just then, Gaul's men started banging ferociously on the study door. Luckily, it was strong enough to hold back the intruders. JP remembered the two boys and shouted, "Outside now!" In hasty retreat from the cabinet, Pierrick knocked Richard over.

"Hey! Watch it!" Richard hissed.

"No time for this," JP replied, seizing a burning log from the fireplace as a torch and motioning for them to follow Charles.

The three rushed through the secret door. Charles instructed them to go down the stairs and turn right where the tunnel split. He promised that it would lead them into the forest outside the château.

"Good luck," he said, turning back around.

"Charles, what are you doing? You need to come with us!" JP pleaded, but Charles refused.

"They're after me. I'll delay them." He shut the door firmly in their faces before they could stop him.

"No! No, Charles!" They called out desperately, but the thick walls muffled their voices.

"They're going to kill him! We have to do something!" Richard pleaded,
but JP couldn't open the door no matter how hard he tried.

Charles stood before the ornate liquor cabinet, his trembling hand
reaching for the decanter of cognac. The familiar aroma of the aged spirit
wafted up, momentarily transporting him to happier times – evenings spent
in this very room, sharing drinks and laughter with Mortimer. How naive
he had been, how foolishly trusting. The weight of betrayal pressed down on
him, and Charles closed his eyes, allowing the memories to wash over him
as the loud banging on the door persisted.

As he took another sip of cognac, Charles felt a strange sense of calm
settling over him. The initial shock and denial had given way to grim ac-
ceptance. There was no escaping the web Mortimer had so carefully woven
around him. Years of manipulation and careful planning had led to this
moment, and Charles knew that fighting against it would be futile.

A rueful smile played at the corners of his mouth as he contemplated the
irony of his situation. He had always prided himself on being a good judge
of character, on his ability to see through pretense and falsehood. Yet here
he was, betrayed by the man he had considered his closest friend. Blindsided
by a complete deception.

Charles raised his glass in a silent, bitter toast to Mortimer's cunning, to
his own gullibility, and to the end of everything he had known and loved. As
the last sip of cognac passed his lips, the door to his study began to splinter
and he steeled himself for what was to come.

Gaul charged inside with his crew in tow, his eyes glinting with malicious intent.

"So, your little plan has failed, eh? I thought you were smarter than this."

Charles turned to Kofi, who cowered behind the armed soldiers. Kofi
quickly averted his eyes, not wanting to meet Charles' gaze.

"How much did he pay you?" Charles demanded.

Kofi refused to answer.

"Show me some respect!"

Gaul's eyes glittered with malicious delight, savoring every moment of Charles's distress.

"Oh, Charles," he purred, "you really should learn to value your men more... or someone else will." Gaul motioned to the man behind Kofi, who struck without hesitation. Charles watched Kofi's lifeless body crumple to the ground, a pool of crimson spreading rapidly beneath him.

"Happy now?" Gaul's gaze was fixed on Charles, who winced and lowered his head. "Mortimer didn't want you involved in this mess. But it seems things didn't go according to plan ... and we can't leave any evidence behind."

"What is his plan? Does he have the girl?" Charles demanded, imagining the worst.

"I suppose I can reveal his intentions now. After all, you won't be able to tell a soul," Gaul taunted. His men snickered behind him.

"Mortimer has the girl ... or had. I'm not sure if she is still alive," he mocked. "All he needs now is a particular pendant in the possession of one of your guests. As for the others, they just happened to be in the wrong place at the wrong time – but we're taking care of them."

Just then, a terrible scream from somewhere in the château shattered the stillness of the night. All color drained from Charles's face.

"Why are you doing this? These people are innocent. It's me you want, not them," Charles begged.

"No one is *truly* innocent – after all, they work for you," Gaul sneered.

Charles, who'd planned to turn himself over like a gentleman, without a fight, now sprang to his feet and grasped a decorative sword hanging on the wall. Gaul's sharp eyes followed laughingly; he was ready to defend against his quarry's futile attempts.

"You never give up, do you, old man?" he goaded.

Ignoring the mockery, Charles charged forward and swung his sword towards Gaul, only to have the strike effortlessly blocked and countered with a powerful blow that sent him stumbling back. Despite his valiant efforts, Charles struggled to keep up with the skilled swordsman and soon found himself on the floor with Gaul's blade pointed at his throat.

"Any last words?" Gaul drawled.

Charles's eyes narrowed in rage, and he opened his mouth to retort, but it was too late. With one swift thrust, Gaul's blade plunged into his throat. Twisting the blade with pleasure, he took sadistic delight in each shuddering gasp that escaped Charles' lips until one of the soldiers snapped him back to reality. "Gaul, he's dead."

Gaul withdrew his blade from Charles' neck and wiped it cleanly on his victim's robe before returning it to its sheath.

"Yes," he said curtly, "one must always be sure."

He barked orders for the old man and the old woman to be taken captive. Everyone else was to be slaughtered without mercy.

JP, Richard and Pierrick crept along a long, dark passageway illuminated only by the light of JP's torch. An oppressive silence hovered in the air, broken only by their labored breathing and the occasional floorboard creak. Charles' sacrifice hung heavy in their minds as they hurried through the darkness, desperate to find a way to rescue their father and Violet before Mortimer's men found them first. JP led the way. Suddenly, the path split into two directions.

"Charles said to turn right," JP whispered. The boys wordlessly complied, each lost in his own thoughts. Pierrick's were bleak: would his father be alright? He wished they had stayed home; life may have been dull there, but it was safe and comfortable.

"Pierrick, move!" Richard's voice shook him out of his reverie; he realized he had stopped walking.

"Shh, we're here," JP said.

They'd reached the end of the tunnel. A thick iron door separated them from freedom. They shoved it with their shoulders until at last it swung open with an ear–piercing screech. Fearful of alerting any soldiers nearby, JP hastily stilled the door and stamped the torch out with his boot. The three stood frozen for a few seconds, listening for any sign of danger but hearing only silence. Taking courage from the stillness, the three ventured outside, carefully surveying their surroundings. With mounting tension, they quickened their pace toward the château walls.

As they approached the main gate, both boys caught sight of their father captured and forced down the stairs along with Violet. Pierrick let out a cry. Richard grabbed Pierrick roughly, shaking sense into him.

"Stay down, or we're dead! And dead people can't help anyone," he hissed.

"They got Father!" Pierrick breathed, shaking.

"I know – I can see. Now shut up and think! We need a plan to save them," Richard continued between gritted teeth.

JP added, "Gaul wouldn't have spared them if he didn't think Mortimer would have a use for them. There are too many of them for us to fight head-on. We must be smart about this."

Pierrick reluctantly agreed and joined the group, huddling for cover behind a large boulder. The night was getting cooler, and the chill seeped into their bodies as they crouched on the ground. Many terrible screams rent the night. Richard moved closer to Pierrick, and they wrapped their arms around each other for warmth and comfort.

"What are we going do?" Pierrick asked, exhaling a shuddering breath.

"The most difficult thing to do; we wait," was the answer from JP.

After a few minutes had passed, JP and Richard raised their heads above the boulder. Corpses littered the grass around the château. The sheer brutality of the scene took their breath away. Amidst the disarray of the massacre, a soldier's voice called out to Gerard and Violet, ordering them to climb into a carriage. Their wrists were tightly bound together, and Gerard's face was bruised. As they watched, Gaul emerged from the château at the head of a small army of soldiers, an arrogant smirk on his face. It was clear he took great pleasure in ruthlessness.

JP snarled at the sight of this man who'd massacred so many innocent, defenseless people and showed no remorse. It was the same malicious look he remembered from the day he had been stabbed. The moment JP saw him in the château – those cruel eyes, that cleft chin – he'd known. Mortimer had a sinister gift for drawing the wickedest souls to him like moths to a flame.

A small eternity dragged by, each moment stretching out into agony. Mortimer's men had looted the château, and when they finally left, an unnatural silence fell. The night breeze itself seemed to come to a standstill, as if in horror at what had just taken place. JP, Pierrick and Richard crept warily back to the entrance of the château, hoping beyond hope to find survivors. Inside, the air was thick with the stench of death; the walls were painted in blood and tears. Their hopes quickly faded as they realized how much destruction had been wrought.

In Charles' study, JP found the baron's body bloodied on the floor. He spoke softly as he closed the man's eyes. "Though we did not know each other well or long, I will tell the story of your bravery till the end of my days. I promise you, your death will not be in vain."

After a respectful pause, Richard suggested they bury the dead. It was the least they could do.

The oppressive darkness cloaked their grim task, the rhythmic thud of shovels against earth a mournful percussion to their labor. Richard and Pierrick worked in silence, their muscles burning with exertion and their hearts heavy with an anguish that words could not express. The night air, thick with the scent of freshly turned soil and the metallic tang of blood, seemed to press down upon them, a suffocating reminder of the atrocity they were bearing witness to. The weight of each body seemed to increase with every grave as if the accumulated sorrow of seventeen snuffed-out lives was physically manifesting itself.

Richard's hands trembled as he laid a young woman to rest, her unseeing eyes staring accusingly at the star-studded sky above. He fought back the bile rising in his throat, his mind reeling at the senseless brutality that had brought them to this moment. Beside him, Pierrick's face was a mask of grim determination, but his eyes betrayed a profound sadness. The tall trees stood as silent sentinels, their branches reaching towards the heavens in a desperate plea for understanding, for meaning in this senseless act of violence.

The gentle morning breeze whispered through the leaves, carrying with it the sweet scent of dew-kissed grass. Richard, Pierrick, and JP stood in a ragged semicircle around the graves, their shoulders slumped with exhaustion and sorrow. The silence that had accompanied their labor now took on a different quality – contemplative, almost prayerful. Each was lost in their own thoughts, grappling with the enormity of what they had witnessed and participated in.

As the sun climbed higher, bathing the clearing in golden light, they all stood in quiet contemplation, hoping that some higher power would bring justice and guide these souls to a better place - perhaps even paradise.

16

Pierrick's eyes snapped open, his breath coming in short, ragged gasps. As reality slowly seeped back in, he became aware of the hard ground beneath him, so different from the soft bed he'd left behind. The musty scent of damp earth and decaying leaves filled his nostrils. He could feel the chill of the night air seeping through his thin blanket, causing a shiver to run down his spine.

Beside him, JP stirred, roused by Pierrick's sudden movement.

On JP's other side, Richard's rhythmic snoring continued unabated, a surprisingly comforting sound in the eerie quiet of the forest. Pierrick envied Richard's ability to sleep so soundly despite their circumstances. For the fourth night in a row, Pierrick found himself wide awake, unable to get a peaceful night's sleep. Questions swirled in his mind, each more unnerving than the last. What dangers lay ahead on their journey? Would they be able to rescue their father? The weight of these unanswered questions pressed down on him, making it hard to breathe.

JP reached out, placing a reassuring hand on Pierrick's arm. The simple gesture spoke volumes – a reminder that he wasn't alone and that they were in this together.

"Are you okay, Pierrick?" JP asked with concern.

"Yeah, just a bad dream." Pierrick rubbed his eyes sleepily as he stretched his stiff body.

"We should start moving," JP suggested. He shook Richard vigorously until he woke groggily from his deep slumber.

"What? Are we there already?" Richard mumbled in confusion.

"It's time to go," JP announced. Despite being exhausted by all that happened the night before, the brothers managed to prepare themselves quickly for the daunting journey ahead.

"We're going to need help if we want to stand any chance against Mortimer's men," JP said gravely.

"But where are we going to get help from?" Richard wondered aloud.

"Same way the rich do it – we pay for mercenaries."

"With what money?" Pierrick asked skeptically.

JP opened a bag of silver coins he had taken from Charles' office. The looters had somehow overlooked it. The two brothers were surprised, but seemed to approve of this unorthodox course.

"And I guess you know where to find such men?" Richard inquired.

"I do – but we have to move if we want to stand any chance of catching up with Gaul," JP replied. Spurred his horse forward into a gallop, he led them towards an uncertain fate.

The journey to Le Mans seemed to last an eternity. JP suggested it would be wise to avoid attention by conducting their business outside of town. They finally arrived at a small inn on the city's outskirts just as dusk fell.

The dank establishment was full of people from every walk of life, each with a different story etched upon his or her face. Some drank and laughed while others fought and argued. One unlucky fellow with a broken leg managed to play a lively tune on the piano. At the same time, his three drunken friends sang along, slurring words between gulps of ale and burps, barely able to string together enough words to finish the song.

"You want to find men *here*?" Richard asked, glancing about doubtfully.

JP nodded and moved toward the bar. "Sit, rest, and eat something."

Richard hesitantly took a seat, keeping an eye out for any patrons who seemed to study the three strangers a bit too closely. A plate of dark bread and cheese appeared on the table, looking rather more leftover rather than freshly prepared. Pierrick glanced at the plate with disgust, but hastily reformed his expression as soon as he noticed the waiter's scowl. Over at the bar, Richard noticed a quick exchange of words between JP and the innkeeper and some coins changing hands.

JP headed into a darkened corner of the room, beckoning a stranger over.

"Are you Remi?"

"Aye. And who might you be?"

JP ignored this.

"The innkeeper tells me you're the man I'm looking for," he said without further preamble. "I need ten men ready to fight, and I need them now."

The stranger fiddled with a pocketknife, his curiosity visibly roused.

"What for?"

"No questions," JP barked, throwing a small bag of coins onto the table. "Half now, half when it's done. I'll give details on the go."

"Not so fast. My men won't risk their lives for a mystery."

JP's eyes darted around the tavern.

"What do you know of the Marquis du Udille?" he asked.

The stranger's eyes grew dark and he spat on the ground.

"I know that his enemies are my friends."

JP smiled widely.

"Then consider me the very *best* of friends, my fine fellow."

Satisfied, the man moved nimbly through the tavern, assembling his company. JP strode back to where Richard and Pierrick were seated, snatching a piece of cheese off Pierrick's plate and taking a swig from his mug of ale. Displeased, Pierrick shot JP a dirty look but didn't say anything.

"Time to go!" called JP.

Outside the tavern, dim clouds threatened to swallow the night. The only source of light was the full moon, guiding them like a beacon forward into danger and darkness. A band of ten rough-looking men stood ready to join JP, Richard, and Pierrick on their harrowing quest. Observing the newcomers, Pierrick felt relieved yet nervous. His gaze fixated on a man with no eye and a deep scar that ran from his forehead to his chin. But the man's face wasn't the only part marred by scars; multitudinous tattoos covered his arms. As if sensing Pierrick's stare, the man's one good eye looked up and noticed his fascination. An awkward silence filled the air until ...

"One for each man I killed," he growled.

Unnerved by these cold words, Pierrick shrunk away. Laughter erupted from the rest of the group.

"Enough talking. Let's go!" commanded their leader, Remi. His imposing figure exuded an aura of quiet confidence and latent danger, a silent warning to any who might consider crossing him. Standing at an intimidating six-foot, his broad shoulders and thick arms were a testament to years of physical conditioning and hard-won survival. His face was a roadmap of a life lived on the edge. Deep-set eyes, as dark and impenetrable as obsidian, seemed to absorb light rather than reflect it. The grizzled hair atop his head was cropped close to his scalp - a practical choice for a man who couldn't afford the luxury of vanity. His jaw, usually clean-shaven due to patchy beard growth, was square and set with a perpetual tension as if he was constantly clenching his teeth against some unseen threat. A network of faint scars crisscrossed his face and neck, each one a story of violence and survival. The most prominent, a jagged line running from his left temple to the corner of his mouth, served as a constant reminder of his mortality.

Remi ordered all to mount their horses as they took off for Rouen.

After hours of riding deep into the night, JP pulled on the reins and stopped the horses. In the dim torchlight, he called for a meeting. His plan was simple – keep riding and catch up with Gaul and his men before sunrise. Some agreed with his idea, while others blanched at this first invocation of the Marquis du Udille. An argument broke out amidst heavy sighs and grumbles from those unsure about the risk.

Remi stood tall. "If any of you cowards think this mission is too dangerous, leave now! Otherwise, pull up your britches and let's get it done."

Richard and Pierrick looked around. After a moment, a man stepped forward to take his leave. "I'll, uh, pass on this one. If Mortimer knows about ..."

"Go," cried Remi, waving his hand in irritation. "Any other milksops?"

There was a short exchange of glances. No one else broke the line.

"Great. Let's continue," JP said calmly. "If we keep this pace, we should catch them before sunrise. The prisoners will be slowing them down. We must beat them to Rouen."

Remi's commanding voice echoed through the night: "One hour to rest, then we move!"

Richard and Pierrick couldn't help but admire the confidence with which Remi addressed his men. Despite the dangerous mission ahead, no one seemed fazed; it was just another day on the job. The two brothers could feel their adrenaline pumping as they prepared for what was coming. There hadn't been enough time to process what had happened, only to take action. They had to save their father and Violet!

17

Gerard lay awake in the back of the cart, his mind exhausted yet racing. Violet had wept herself to sleep beside him, her wrists bound by the cruel ropes that seemed to grow tighter and tighter as they traveled. Mortimer's goons stood guard around the dancing flames of a campfire, rotating shifts to stay alert. Gaul was soundly asleep, resting against a sturdy tree. Gerard couldn't believe someone who had caused so much harm could sleep so peacefully.

The hours dragged on endlessly. Gerard desperately wished for some peace or comfort. He reached into his pocket and pulled out his timepiece, only to find it was past four o'clock in the morning. His sons raced through his thoughts – had they escaped somehow? A glimmer of hope shimmered at the thought of Violet being reunited with Claire, but mostly the impending meeting with Mortimer filled him with dread. His thoughts were interrupted by the piercing cries of a male owl, a sound of deep longing that shook Gerard's soul.

The first rays of sunlight filtered through the dense leaves and roused the sleepers from their slumber. One of Gaul's raiders led Violet to a bush where she could relieve herself; Gerard declined. The group quickly resumed their journey, Gaul's demanding voice urging them to pick up the pace so they could reach Rouen by evening.

"Do you think Claire is alright?" Violet asked, unable keep her worries at bay.

"I'm sure she is," Gerard said reassuringly, although he too was filled with worry about what lay in store for them all. "She's too valuable to him."

Violet felt a chill run down her spine as she saw Gaul eyeing them both with a smirk.

"Don't worry," he snickered, "your cell will be more comfortable than the cart."

His crew laughed and Gaul spurred on his horse. Violet winced – each bump in the road sent a sharp pain coursing through her back. She started coughing.

"Are you okay?" Gerard asked.

"I'll be fine," Violet managed to gasp. "I must have caught a cold last night."

Gerard couldn't help but feel uneasy about Violet's health. She was an older woman, and the recent events had taken a toll on her both emotionally and physically.

Suddenly, an arrow flew from the shadows of the nearby trees, slicing through the warm air. The soldier riding next to the cart tumbled to the ground and his horse galloped away in terror. Deafening thumps of arrows and bullets barraged from the trees, and chaos rang out as everywhere bodies slumped against the sandy ground.

"Ambush!" shrieked a voice, promptly silenced by a bullet.

The riders towards the back of the group quickly dismounted from their horses and took defensive positions, while the driver of the cart dove into a bush. Gerard and Violet ducked as best they could. Gaul yelled commands amid the chaos, but it felt like the party was surrounded by a never–ending onslaught of artillery from all directions. One by one, their numbers dwindled. Realizing there was no stopping this deadly barrage of fire, Gaul spurred his horse and made a mad dash for safety. Even when a bullet hit his shoulder, he refused to slow down. Although he managed to escape, none of his men were as fortunate.

JP's veins pulsated with anger as he watched Gaul slip away into the distance. He knew he had to stop Gaul at any cost —the world would be safer without him. Springing to his feet and charging towards his horse with fierce determination, he was intercepted by Remi, who grabbed him by the shoulders and forced him to face reality.

"Don't be a fool," Remi hissed, his gaze intense. "We came here with a mission. Our job is done. He will get what he deserves soon enough."

JP glared at Gaul's departing figure, but he knew deep down that Remi was right. Reluctantly, he backed down, letting Gaul slip away into the horizon unscathed.

The clamor of battle had abruptly silenced the morning. Gerard and Violet remained huddled together, not daring to move or look up. Around them the air was thick with stirred dust and the whinny of terrified horses. Suddenly, the sweetest sound Gerard had heard in years filled his ears. "Dad? Dad? Are you okay?"

Gerard lifted his head in disbelief, his terror vanishing when he saw his two sons. Pierrick and Richard had come to rescue him. As tears of joy brimmed in his eyes, they worked quickly to cut the rope that bound his hands. JP observed the family reunion momentarily before stepping forward to take charge. This place was not safe. It was time to depart. Remi offered to lead them out of harm's way while his men quickly gathered any valuable items. JP urged everyone to hurry – they were close to Rouen Castle, and they needed to get far, far away.

Remi offered Violet some water before assisting her onto a horse. In a blink of an eye, they were racing away from the carnage that lay behind them. Despite the urgent pace, Violet cast one last glance over her shoulder. In her mind, she was raced in the opposite direction – toward Claire, still in captivity. With great effort, she forced herself to embrace the new hope that lay in the hands of this small yet unpredictable group of friends. She felt it in her bones – soon, she and Claire would be reunited.

18

Claire was shaken awake by the clanging of the prison cell door, followed by a muted thud. A guard threw her daily bread and cheese to the floor. She shivered at how he leered at her, one hand in his pocket, tongue picking away at something in his teeth.

Claire felt her body tense; the past few days had stripped her of strength and left her feeling empty and vulnerable. Her breath quickened as she looked up to see the man's eyes staring hungrily at her, his twisted thoughts visible on his face as clearly as if they were written there.

"What a waste," he muttered, before closing the door behind him. Vincenzo's eyes followed his every movement.

Claire took a moment to stretch her tense muscles before summoning the courage to walk over to the chamber pot in the corner. The guard's eyes followed her every move, eager to catch forbidden glimpses. Vincenzo motioned for him to turn around, and after some hesitation, he eventually acquiesced. Taking advantage of this chance, Claire immediately ran to the corner and lifted her dress to relieve herself as quickly as possible, wary that the guard might try to peek – which he did.

Vincenzo glared at the guard.

"What? Why do you even care? She's in jail," the guard complained.

"I'm just following orders. I don't want any trouble."

The guard made an annoyed noise through his nose before limping away, muttering something about food. Vincenzo nodded before settling back into his chair. In her cell, Claire hesitantly glanced at the moldy bread and cheese on the ground, her stomach growling. Despite how ravenous she was, she couldn't bring herself to touch it.

Left alone with Claire, Vincenzo took a piece of dried meat from his jacket. He also grabbed a half-empty bottle of ale and poured some into a cup.

"It's not much, but it's better than whatever they brought you," he said.

Claire accepted the gift, her emotions overwhelming her. In this dark place, Vincenzo's small acts of chivalry were her only glimmer of hope. She drank the ale before returning the cup to Vincenzo, then sat in the corner of her cell, hungrily chewing the jerky and praying that things would soon get better.

A sharp call cut through the morning air. Sentinels patrolling the perimeter of Rouen Castle had spotted a lone horseman bucking through the trees.

"Who goes there?" yelled one of the guards.

The rider was battered, bleeding, and holding onto his horse for dear life. The guards recognized him before he could answer and hastily opened the gate. He barely held on long enough to enter before collapsing onto the ground, groaning in agony from his wounds. The guards rushed to help him up with questioning glances. Before anyone could ask, Louis appeared.

"What the hell happened, Gaul?!"

Gaul managed to croak out the news:

"We were ambushed three hours from here ..." His shoulders trembled as pain wracked his body with each syllable.

Anger flashed across Louis's face.

"Ambushed?! By whom? And where are the rest of my men?"

"The old man's sons got help and attacked us. All our men are dead."

Louis cursed under his breath, knowing Mortimer would not take kindly to this news.

"Get yourself patched up by the doctor," he ordered gruffly. "When you report to Mortimer, you better have a positive spin on that story."

Mortimer was sitting at his breakfast table in the main hall when Louis cautiously entered. Immediately sensing something amiss, Mortimer bellowed between mouthfuls of food: "Don't just stand there! Spit it out!" Taking a deep breath, Louis answered quietly.

"It's Gaul – he's back."

"That's good news, isn't it?" Mortimer said, his tone flat. "Why are you standing there like your old cat died?"

"He ... he's alone," Louis said hesitantly. "Barely alive."

Mortimer settled into his chair and took a sip of tea, silently waiting for Louis to continue. When the silence became too much, Mortimer prompted him, an edge in his voice:

"Go on."

"They were ambushed this morning, not far from here. It appears that the two sons of the professor somehow managed to escape and get help. That's all I know so far ..." He trailed off with a hint of optimism in his voice, adding, "... but Gaul should be able to provide more details ... sir."

The air between them grew chilly. Mortimer broke the silence first, a note of anger seeping into his voice.

"Where is Gaul now?"

"He's with the doctor."

Mortimer pushed himself away from the table, snatching a piece of toast as he headed out the door.

"Let's go check on the patient, shall we?" he declared, gesturing for Louis to lead the way. The two made their way toward the doctor's quarters in heavy silence.

"Leave us," Mortimer ordered, his voice a low growl that sent shivers down the doctor's spine.

"I'm almost done," the doctor replied nervously, rushing to finish stitching the wound.

Mortimer didn't answer. Instead, his piercing gaze swiveled to Gaul. Sensing the threat, Louis stepped forward and grabbed the needle from the doctor's hands. He glared at the trembling physician, who quickly scuttled out of the room without another word.

Mortimer's voice echoed menacingly in the deathly quiet room. Gaul knew that every word spoken brought him closer to unspeakable torments. His desperate explanations hung in the air like a cloying fog; Kofi's revelation of Charles' betrayal was at its center.

"Charles, why did you have to be so stubborn?" Mortimer sighed under his breath.

His jaw clenched as he recalled their last conversation. If only Charles had listened and been willing to compromise. That stubborn integrity, once a trait Mortimer had admired, now forced his hand, pushing him to take actions he had hoped to avoid.

Gaul tried to convince Mortimer that his men had done their job and taken the professor and old lady as agreed, with nobody else would left alive.

"But you did leave someone alive, didn't you?" Mortimer questioned with an icy edge.

"They were so young and inexperienced," Gaul stammered. "I didn't want to waste any more time."

"And you believe this other man whom you mentioned was with them?" Louis asked.

"Yes ... um ... Jean–Philippe something," he stuttered, trying to remember the name.

"Did he escape as well?" Louis added chillingly.

Gaul gulped, unable to form an answer.

"I see." Mortimer stepped closer to Gaul, who flinched. "You tried; you did what you could. Right?"

Gaul found a spark of hope and managed to murmur, "I did. And I will fix this if ..."

"Oh, I know. I know," Mortimer purred before stepping even closer. "You are fortunate to have the information you have, and that you've seen the boys' faces and this Jean–Philippe guy. Although the mess you made can't go unpunished."

He uncovered Gaul's bloody wound.

Gaul gritted his teeth as Mortimer mercilessly crushed the wound, wrenching apart the coarse stitches. Hot blood poured onto the floor, and Gaul shrieked with agony.

"Consider this a warning. Fail me again, and you will not see the light of another day."

Gaul nodded, his mind reeled, grappling with the injustice of it all—one mistake. Gaul's hands, hidden from view, curled into tight fists. His nails dug crescents into his palms, the physical pain a welcome distraction from the emotional turmoil. He fought to keep his breathing steady.

Mortimer directed his gaze at Louis.

"Spread the word in all alehouses, whorehouses, thieves' dens – to everyone we know. I want to know where these *fils de pute* went. At this critical moment, we cannot leave any loose ends. Find them and bring them here!"

With that, Mortimer and Louis departed, leaving Gaul alone with his thoughts and his pain. A seething whirlwind of rage and vengeance coursed through his veins, fueled by the mere thought of the professor's sons, and that Jean-Philippe. He swore to exact retribution for the humiliation they'd forced him to endure.

The bustling courtyard was alive with anxiety following Gaul's arrival. Servants hurriedly prepared Mortimer's carriage: he was embarking on an important journey to Paris. Just as Mortimer was about to set off, another rider galloped into sight, shouting for the guards to open the gates.

"We found them!" he panted. "They're holed up in an old house about a half day's ride away."

"Get the men ready," Louis commanded, locking eyes with Mortimer.

Mortimer's eyes narrowed, his voice dropping to a dangerous whisper.

"Louis, the pendant is your primary objective. Secure it at all costs. Once you have it, bring the professor and the grandmother to me. Alive. I need them both." At this, his gaze hardened, brooking no argument. "As for the others ... I want no loose ends. Do you understand? No witnesses! I'll see you in three days."

Louis nodded. As soon as Mortimer swept through the gates, he directed his men to mount their horses and follow him.

Gaul limped out of his house, still suffering from his recent injury. He was met by commotion and chaos outside.

"What's happening?" he asked one of the soldiers rushing by.

"We found them, and we're going to get them," the soldier panted. Gaul looked around and saw Louis mounting his horse, ordering the men to move faster.

"I'm coming with you," Gaul shouted, straining to be heard over the noise. Louis turned around and saw the weak man standing there, barely able to stand up.

"Go back inside. You're no use to us like this."

With those words ringing in his ears, Gaul watched Louis ride off with twenty whooping men following close behind him.

19

JP and Remi stood in the shadows of an old abandoned house, discussing their next move. They had been lucky in their attack on Mortimer's men, but they knew they couldn't afford to test their luck again.

Remi instructed his men to prepare for departure.

"Where are you going?" he asked JP.

"I'm not sure yet, but eventually, our goal is to rescue the girl," JP responded.

Remi scoffed.

"Rescue the girl? You know she's already lost, right? And even if she is alive, it'll take an army to break into that fortress at Rouen."

Gerard stepped forward, determination evident on his face. "Then we shall raise an army!"

Remi clapped him on the shoulder. "I wish you good luck. We're out of here!"

"We'd better get moving, too," JP said. "It's not safe here."

The two brothers looked at each other nervously.

"Where are we going?" Richard asked.

Gerard gazed around the small group – JP, the boys, and Violet – and felt the weight of responsibility for what would happen next resting squarely on his shoulders. Summoning his confidence, he answered, "We'll go to Paris. I'll attempt to reach out to some old acquaintances."

Richard and Pierrick gave a cheer of excitement at this announcement while Violet looked worriedly at JP and asked, "Paris? What about Claire?"

JP sighed heavily and replied, "Violet ... there's no way we can save Claire without some real help – army-sized help. The castle of Rouen is nearly impenetrable – there's no chance of us rescuing her with just the five of us."

Gerard continued: "Rescuing Claire is our top priority, but we can't underestimate Mortimer any longer. Charles paid for that mistake with his life; dead people can't help anyone."

"I can't bear the thought of Claire being in that monster's clutches another day longer. She's the only thing I have left!" Violet sobbed.

Richard grabbed her hand. "You won't lose her. We'll get her back to safety, have faith."

She nodded and wiped away her tears. "Thank you," she said weakly.

JP rose to his feet as everyone scrambled to get ready for their departure. His voice was almost harsh in its urgency. "We've talked enough! We must leave now, it's no longer safe here."

When Remi bid goodbye to JP, he'd walked purposefully out the room and then slowed. He could hear the others discussing how best to rescue Claire. Memories he'd suppressed for years filled in his mind and his whole body tensed. Fists clenched at his side and fury surged through him.

"For fuck's sake, Remi, be a man!" he admonished himself.

He stalked towards his men with dark fire burning in his eyes.

"Listen up!" he bellowed, his voice carrying the authority of countless battles fought and won. The men snapped to attention, their eyes fixed on their leader with anticipation.

"Today, we have the opportunity to do something good, something honorable. It could be destiny's way of giving us the opportunity to right the wrongs done against those we love and care for. Not for some trinket or gilded prize, but to pay our dues in service of justice. Ignoring this opportunity would be foolish."

His voice rose again, filled with passion and conviction.

"I'm tired of mindlessly drowning my sorrows in ale and coin while pain and hatred swirl around me!"

A murmur of agreement rippled through the ranks. Remi paused, allowing his words to sink in.

"Now, our job here is done, and you are free to go ... BUT. Many of us have a personal score to settle with Mortimer and his lackeys. This is our opportunity to do something honorable, not just for ourselves but all the innocent people victimized by his tyranny. We can strike a blow at Rouen, weaken it, and make Mortimer pay for all the misery he has spread across this land!"

The energy surged as his men roared in agreement, ready to take on anything that came their way.

"You know why you are here. You battle your demons and prove your worth every single day. But if any of you aspire to have a lasting legacy beyond the alehouses and brothels of France, now is your chance."

A wry smile played across his lips as he added, "After all, it's not like you men have much else to do with your time!"

The men chuckled nervously at his words as his gaze swept across their faces, a wild glint lighting his eyes.

"Don't look so shocked, I haven't gone mad ... not yet."

He paused. Then, with a voice that carried the weight of destiny, he asked, "Now, what will it be?"

The men eyed each other warily, awaiting the first sign of who would break away or stay and fight. Remi was astonished when most of his men roared out a collective "Aye!" and eagerly followed without hesitation. The energy was electrifying as they all spurred their horses towards Gerard and the rest of the group.

JP was saddling his horse when he heard footsteps and whirled around.

"What are you doing here?" he asked in surprise.

"I also have unfinished business with that monster, you know," Remi retorted.

"But ... but we can't possibly afford your services!" JP exclaimed.

"Save it," Remi cut him off, raising a hand. A dangerous smile played at the corners of his mouth. "Revenge is worth so much more than money. Some debts can only be paid in blood."

"Yes!" Richard and Pierrick shouted with enthusiasm.

Taking a deep breath, Remi continued. "We should not waste our time going to Paris. I know a secret route that leads straight to the heart of Rouen Castle. But we must hurry; I'm sure Mortimer has already dispatched his minions after us. Follow me!" And with that shocking proclamation, everyone startled and adjusted their course, following Remi as he charged into the unknown.

The way plunged them deep into the forest. At last, a secluded wooden shed appeared. At once, Gerard asked, "What is this place?"

Remi's stoicism gave way to confidence. "What does it look like? It's a hideout. I built it, no one knows it's here. Let's pause to eat and plan our next move."

20

Violet and Pierrick laid a large cloth upon the ground and upended a sack of provisions. They had some apples, a half wheel of cheese, a slightly stale loaf of bread, and some jerky. Remi's men cracked open some ale, while Richard and Gerard searched for wood to start a fire. Before they could light it, however, Remi forbade fires. "We don't want anyone to spot us from far away."

Gerard whispered to JP, "A man of many secrets, this Remi. Are you sure we can trust him?"

JP replied gravely, "Trust is a big word. But he's had plenty of opportunities to betray us – and honestly, we have no choice but to trust him."

Everyone settled on the ground and shared the meager rations with camaraderie and hope. Then Gerard cut through the chatter with a pointed inquiry. "You mentioned you know a way into the castle? Where? How?" All eyes rested on Remi expectantly. He finished his drink before he spoke.

"Many years ago," Remi began, "during the time of Napoleon, I lived on the outskirts of Rouen. Mortimer had inherited his father's name and influence, and he quickly used that influence to seize control and manipulate everything in his favor. He was adept at keeping his acts secret from Napoleon, and soon he had absolute control over Rouen. Beneath his charming exterior, he is a skilled manipulator, exerting control and spreading fear throughout the land. No one would dare oppose him, knowing the severe consequences that would follow. Back then, I worked as a builder reinforcing the walls of Rouen Castle. Through countless hours of labor, I came to know not only the secrets of Mortimer's unseemly ambition, but every single nook and cranny of those mighty walls."

Remi paused for a moment and took a deep breath.

"I was married to a lovely woman who worked as a servant in the castle. Her name was also Claire." Violet's eyes widened at the mention of the name, which caused a stir in the room.

"Every day, she brought me lunch and we shared it by the trees, discussing our dreams for the future. Despite her humble roots, she was a brilliant woman."

Remi fell silent, and only spoke again with effort.

"But then, one day, she didn't come." Clenching his fists tightly, he went on, his eyes affixed to the ground. "I knew something was wrong. I questioned every guard, every servant, anyone who came out of the castle, trying to find clues to her whereabouts, yet no one seemed to know anything. In growing desperation, I searched for hours, anywhere she might have gone, hoping and praying for her safety. The next morning, when the castle servants went to the market for supplies, I followed them, and when we were out of view from the wall sentries, I asked them to tell me the truth. At first, they didn't want to answer; they ignored me. I knew they were scared. Finally, one girl stepped forward and told me everything."

Remi's face contorted in rage as he spat out the story. "Claire was doing her chores and crossed paths with Mortimer. He was drunk, and he tried ... to force her. When she screamed for help, he beat her to death."

Remi clenched his jaw.

"That monster ... he didn't just take a life. He took three. Claire's, mine, and ... our unborn child."

Tears fell from the hard man's eyes. Not a soul dared to speak.

"He had her corpse dumped in the river to make it appear as though she had drowned accidentally." Remi's voice broke. "All I wanted by then was to give my wife the dignity of a proper burial. And I did. But even after I'd laid her to rest, a blinding rage consumed me. I was ready to storm into the home of France's most powerful man and end his life with my bare hands."

Remi's gaze turned distant, reliving that fateful day. "As I approached those imposing gates, the guards saw right through me. My anger and fear were so palpable, so overwhelming that I ... I turned and ran like a coward."

His dark eyes, now brimming with shame, were cast downward. "I fled, finding refuge among mercenaries. I climbed their ranks and became their leader. As time passed, I let the memories of my wife fade, drowning them in blood and ale. I used to consider that a blessing."

The silence that followed was deafening. The weight of Remi's tragedy hung heavy in the air, a stark reminder of the depths of human cruelty and the devastating power of unchecked evil. Remi's men exchanged glances: they had never seen this side of their leader before. It was engendering in them a fresh respect.

"Life has a strange way of making us face our demons. You have brought back my memories of Claire and my hunger for justice."

JP patted Remi's shoulder and he handed him a bottle of whiskey. Raising his own flask, he said: "To all the Claires – may we bring them justice."

Everyone stood as one, united by the solemn toast, unyielding in their determination to face whatever lay ahead of them. No matter how high the price might be; they all knew that justice wouldn't come easily.

The plan was set in motion. Violet and Gerard would remain behind in the hidden cabin. Remi and JP had taken the reins of the rescue mission, with the boys joining the fray against Gerard's warnings, arguing that Claire would better trust her rescuers if she saw familiar faces.

"You boys promise me you'll come back alive. Promise me!" Gerard implored, his voice shaking as the group embraced one another one last time. Violet, eyes filled with tears, could only offer a silent prayer for the heroes' safe return – a plea that felt weak against the looming bleakness of the night.

21

The night was unbearably dark, with clouds blocking the moonlight. Seeing an arm's length ahead was nearly impossible. The forest before them stood like an impenetrable wall, its ancient trees reaching skyward with gnarled branches that seemed to claw at the fading light.

"We leave the horses here," Remi ordered. "And remember, no torches."

They dismounted silently, tying their mounts to nearby saplings. The horses nickered softly, sensing the tension in the air.

On foot, they followed Remi into the depths of the forest one by one, barely daring to breathe.

"Do you think Claire is still alive?" Pierrick whispered to Richard.

"Shhhh. Yes, she is alive. Now shut it."

Remi stopped abruptly, signaling they had arrived. The imposing castle walls towered over the men, and sentinels prowled below like vultures ready for the kill. The sheer size of the structure threatened to crush the men's resolve and shatter their trust in Remi. How could a mere handful of assailants hope to breach such an impenetrable fortress?

"See that tiny window below the small tower?" Remi whispered. "Directly beneath it is our way in."

He was met with dubious stares and incredulous interjections from the group.

"There's only water below," came one disgruntled voice. "How exactly is that our way in?"

"It is cleverly disguised," Remi began, his voice low. "There is an aperture you cannot see from here, built with rocks to look like a wall. But this part of the wall has been separated to let the water pass through – trust me, it leads directly under the walls of the tower!"

The men froze in disbelief; had Remi gone completely mad?

"Let's move! Crouch low and don't draw any attention!" Remi commanded.

JP and Richard were the first to heed his words, though Pierrick and the rest followed reluctantly. Just they reached the lake's edge, a sentinel suddenly appeared, a blazing torch lighting up their path. The men froze on the spot. Thankfully, the sentinel soon turned around. When the area was clear again, they slipped noiselessly into the water.

Suddenly, a man at the rear slipped on a rock, the noise echoing across the lake. JP's reflexes were lightning–fast: grabbing another rock, he hurled it far away in an attempt to disperse the sound of their presence. All of the men froze, submerging as much as possible beneath the surface of the water. The darkness surrounding them was so dense, they prayed that the sentinels couldn't see anything.

"What was that?" they heard a sentinel cry out.

"Must be an fox again," another replied.

Without another word, they all swam towards the entrance. Remi and JP arrived first, and Remi wasted no time locating where to begin work.

"Here!" he whispered. "Help me move these rocks!" Remi unsheathed his knife with a flick of his wrist and used its blade to ease the stones out of place. As expected, there was an unexpected gap between two of the larger rocks, allowing for the passage of water beneath them. Each man lent his strength one by one until eventually, a narrow tunnel opened up before them. They crawled in on their hands and knees.

Remi was the first to reach the other side, which terminated in an iron grid. Swiftly, he pushed it open with a creak loud to make everyone to freeze. No one dared to breathe. Remi's ears strained in the sudden silence, listening for any sign that they'd been discovered. Seconds stretched into an eternity as they waited, hoping, praying no one had heard. Miraculously, no guards came rushing. After a moment's pause, Remy thrust the grid fully open, his men snarling as they exited the small tunnel ready for action. Remy pointed towards a tower looming in the distance.

"Claire should be there," he said in a low voice.

The large courtyard between them and the tower teemed with sentinels patrolling every inch of the walls. Two soldiers, barely awake, slumped at the main gate. The group split in two directions and crept along the walls, closing in on their target. Richard and Pierrick were instructed to stay by the exit tunnel and keep watch; Remi's men were charged with executing the rescue plan.

At Remi's signal, they attacked; JP and Remi dispatched the guards at the main gate while the others raced upstairs, silencing any sentinel they met. JP and Remy barreled towards the tower door, only to find a guard securing it from within.

The guard at the tower door cursed audible.

"It's late," he grumbled. "Who the hell are you?"

"Let me in, brother," wheedled Remi. "I'm early, so what?"

As soon as they heard the door unlock, JP slammed against it with all his might. Together, he and Remi forced it open and killed the unfortunate guard. Their battle cries echoed off the walls and alerted the guards higher up inside the tower. Soon enough, a swarm of Remi's men joined them and quickly won the fight that ensued on the stairs leading up to Claire's prison cell. Panic struck fear into all those listening, and the dogs inside the castle began to howl with alarm. As soldiers emerged from their barracks, armed with swords clattering against their shields, they were met by silent arrows fired from high above.

Vincenzo and the other guard were jolted awake by the noise below. Claire too awoke abruptly. The hope that someone was coming to save her flickered through her. She huddled in the corner of her cell, trembling with anticipation for what was indeed about to come. The door burst open with a terrifying bang. Both Vincenzo and his fellow guard raised their weapons, but before the latter could strike, Vincenzo lunged forward and slit his throat.

"Vincenzo?" gasped Remi. "What the fuck are you doing here?"

"No time," Vincenzo said, grabbing the keys to the cell off the corpse and tossing them to JP. The lock clicked open, revealing Claire trembling and wide–eyed on the other side.

"Claire? I'm a friend of your grandmother's. We came to rescue you."

Claire's seized JP's hand. Though she was gripped with fear and mistrust, she had no choice but to go with these men.

"Who is this?" barked JP, gesturing at Vincenzo and they ran down the stairs. "Can we trust a man in Mortimer's employ?"

"Vincenzo? We can trust him." Remi confidently declared.

Breathlessly, Claire chimed in, recounting the moments of kindness Vincenzo had shown her throughout her captivity. As the group approached the bottom level of the tower, Remi seized Vincenzo's arm.

"Vincenzo," cried Remi, "I have further business here. Tell me, where is Mortimer?" His voice was heavy with years of pain and the promise of long-awaited vengeance. Vincenzo hesitated, as if the words themselves were painful to utter.

"He left this morning for Paris," he finally said. "I'm sorry, Remi, but he's not here."

The news hit Remi like a physical blow. For a moment, he stood frozen, his dream of revenge slipping through his fingers like sand. Then reality came crashing back, and Remi's eyes snapped into focus. They were still in grave danger.

"We need to move. Now!" Remi's voice cutting through the tension. "To the tunnel grate! Go!"

They spilled out into the moonlight, where Richard and Pierrick rushed toward them.

"Claire! You're alive!" Richard could barely contain his emotion.

"Richard! Is it really you? How did you ...?"

Pierrick appeared over his brother's shoulder, beaming with joy.

"No time for chatter. Let's go!" cried JP as they charged through grate.

They'd nearly reached it when a loud shot rang out, and JP crumpled to the ground. Remi wheeled around and spotted JP dragging himself away from the barrage while Pierrick raced to help him up, just in time to avoid being hit by another round. Pierrick pulled JP behind a barrel and tried to staunch the wound while Remi surveyed the area. In the smoky light of a fallen sentinel's torch appeared a wounded Gaul, barely able to stand straight, feverishly reloading his gun. Hatred burning brightly in his eyes, which glittered in the firelight.

"That bastard," Remi growled. He reached for his gun and charged headlong toward Gaul, who was still reloading.

Spotting Remi, Gaul tried to limp back. But it was too late: Remi had already pulled the trigger, and Gaul fell to the ground, blood pumping from a fresh wound. Remi was aiming for a final shot straight to Gaul's head when the sound of galloping horses and soldiers echoed through the night. Louis and his men had returned.

22

Full of adrenaline, Remi raced back to his friends. Grabbing JP with one hand and Pierrick with the other, he propelled them toward the secret tunnel. Claire was already halfway through when JP slammed the metal grate shut behind them, locking Remi and himself out.

"What are you doing?" Vincenzo demanded.

"We have to buy you time," Remi insisted. "Follow the boys, they know the way back."

"We can't leave you here!" Richard pleaded frantically.

"Don't be a fool," JP replied, his eyes flashing with urgency. "We came here to save Claire – now go! We will be right behind you."

"Don't argue with dead men," said Vincenzo grimly. "Go!"

As the main gates burst open and Louis and his men charged through, Remi and JP sprang into action. Bullets flew from their guns with deadly accuracy. The thud of bodies collapsing to the ground filled the air.

"Form a perimeter! Don't let them escape!" Louis's voice cut through the chaos, steely and determined. "I want them alive!"

Soon his men had surrounded Remi and JP, forcing them to surrender their weapons.

The acrid stench of gunpowder mingled with the metallic odor of blood. Louis surveyed the aftermath. Fallen combatants lay strewn across the courtyard, their lifeless forms a testament to the brutality of the assault.

One of Louis's men approached at a sprint, his face ashen. "Sir, the girl ... she's gone."

"*Merde!*" Louis's roar reverberated off the ancient walls. "What the fuck just happened? How did a worthless gang of mercenaries manage to infiltrate the castle?"

He whirled on Remi, who stood with his steel-gray eyes fixed on Louis. "You! You will tell me who you are and who sent you? SPEAK!"

Louis slammed his fist into Remi's face. Blood spurted from Remi's lip, but he only laughed smugly in response, delighted to antagonize Louis. He looked up at Louis with an expression of triumphant smugness. He could well imagine Mortimer's reaction when he heard about what had occurred.

"Lock him up," Louis barked at his men. "I'll deal with him later."

Louis turned towards JP, who was clutching his bleeding wound and struggling to stand. His eyes were blank, having failed to recognize JP from their deadly encounter twenty years back. As Louis surveyed the bodies of his men strewn across the ground, rage consumed him.

"Kill him," he commanded.

The soldier standing behind JP drew his weapon and aimed it at JP's head, ready to pull the trigger.

"Wait!" came a quivering plea behind them. "WAIT."

Gaul staggered forward, clutching the bleeding wound near his liver where Remi's bullet had exited his body. Louis and his troops watched in disbelief.

"Why? Who is this man to you?" queried Louis, as one of his men rushed over to assist Gaul.

"He knows ... he knows every ..." Gaul gasped before collapsing to the ground, unconscious.

Remi and JP exchanged quick glances, then seized their opportunity. Thrusting his head backward, Remi smashed the nose of the soldier holding him with enough force to make him double over in pain. A second soldier was caught off–guard as Remi charged forward like a rampaging bull and slammed into him with bone–crunching force. With lightning reflexes, JP seized a dagger from the ground and plunged it deep into Louis' heart.

"Remember me?" JP snarled.

Incredulous confusion contorted Louis' features. As his vision clouded, he recognized the man who delivered the fatal blow. It had been two decades since he, Louis, had him killed him for daring to protect Anne. How was it possible that he was still alive? Louis gasped out his final words: "You ... should ... be ... dead."

As Louis's body crumpled to the floor, Remi and JP dashed for the tunnel. Having grabbed the gun from Louis' corpse, JP fired shots at anyone who dared to pursue them. Remi wrenched open the grate leading into the tunnel. With precious seconds ticking away, they slammed it shut behind them and jammed it with a blade. The sounds of pursuing soldiers echoed in their ears as they raced farther down the treacherous tunnel. Adrenaline coursing through their veins, they sprinted faster than ever toward the dark waters, which promised them their only chance at salvation.

"Head to the opposite bank!" shouted Remi as they plunged into the lake. "They'll expect us to go to the woods!"

The strategy worked. As they swam away from the fortress, they could hear Mortimer's men shouting out commands at the tunnel's exit and barreling toward the woods. After what felt like an eternity, they crawled out of the ice–cold waters and staggered away. The heat of the day had burnt off and the evening chill was all the colder because they couldn't dry off. Just when it seemed like they would never find shelter, they stumbled upon a small barn. Soaked and shivering, they crept inside in search of warmth.

The cows mooed gently and the air smelled comfortingly of dung and hay. Just as they'd settled down for the night, a dog rushed in, barking wildly. Hardly another moment passed before the farmer stormed in, wielding an old sword and a torch. Remi and JP stood up, arms raised.

"We mean no harm," Remi said hastily, "we just needed shelter."

The farmer stepped closer, holding his sword tight as he inspected them for signs of danger.

"If you could provide a horse or two, we can pay," Remi added, his voice barely audible above the wind.

The farmer's eyes lingered on Remi's small bag of coins. After a long pause, he agreed to help them, providing his only horse and two warm blankets.

"She may not look like much," he grunted gruffly, "but she'll get you where you need to go."

Remi took the reins, feeling a brief pang of guilt for taking the farmer's only horse. At least the money they were giving him was enough to buy three horses.

"We were never here and you never saw us," Remi said, mounting the horse and giving JP a hand up. "For your own safety."

With that, they galloped off into the night.

23

FEB. 25, 1815

Napoleon sat on the porch of his villa, basking in the last timid rays of sunlight. His eyes burned with a fierce nostalgia. The sounds of laborers toiling all around him were drowned out by the deafening roar of the memories that consumed him. Memories of Paris, where he reigned supreme and wielded immense power. But also memories of tragedy – the sudden death of his beloved wife, the betrayal of his closest friends, and ultimately, his downfall. Despite it all, Napoleon couldn't shake the feeling that his story was not yet over. He often contemplated suicide, but believed that destiny still had plans for him.

A messenger appeared, interrupting his reverie.

"What is it?" Napoleon snapped without opening his eyes.

"An urgent message for you, sir," the messenger replied nervously. Napoleon's interest was piqued when the messenger mentioned Mortimer's seal.

"Fortunately, not all of my friends have deserted me."

Napoleon motioned for the letter and dismissed the messenger. As he read it, a range of emotions coursed through his body. Memories of Anne rushed back into his mind, filling him with a renewed sense of hope. Years ago, this hope had driven him to search for her tirelessly, but as time went on, it seemed to fade away. The letter provided no information about Anne's whereabouts or well-being. Was she still alive? And a daughter? The pendant was found? Was this a cruel joke? Mortimer wasn't one to joke about serious matters; he had always been a trusted friend. But how did he even know about his secret? He spoke of its power, so he knew its potential. Questions burned in Napoleon's mind. This unearthly power had been his most closely guarded secret, and yet here was Mortimer, displaying full knowledge of it.

A deafening ringing reverberated in Napoleon's ears as he struggled to make sense of the implications of this revelation. At last, his eyes snapped open, and he gasped for air as if emerging from a deep-sea dive. The world around him fell into an eerie silence, amplifying the deafening scream of his thoughts. He could feel the weight of the past months bearing down on him, crushing his spirit and filling him with despair. Suicidal thoughts once again threatened to consume him, but he clung to one phrase like a lifeline: "I am Napoleon." These words transformed into a mantra that echoed through his mind and spilled out of his mouth in a guttural roar.

"I AM NAPOLEON!" he shrieked, crushing the letter in his fist.

The peaceful sounds of gardeners and servants tending to the expansive grounds of Villa di San Martino abruptly stopped as everyone's attention shifted in the direction of the shriek. Napoleon could feel the stares burning into him. Several soldiers rushed towards him, weapons ready to defend against any threat. Thinking quickly, Napoleon gave orders for his trusted commanders to assemble at once, before darting back into his study. It was his sanctuary, where he could strategize and plan without any distractions or judgment from others. His heart raced as he braced himself for the consequences of his outburst, knowing that his actions would have far–reaching consequences. In that moment, however, he was consumed by a fierce determination to protect the only thing he still possessed: his legacy.

Napoleon paced in front of the study window, ignoring the constant buzzing of whispers and murmurs that filled the room. One lesson he had learned from his past mistakes was the power of honesty – tempered with strategic omissions to protect his ultimate plans, of course.

"I have just received an ... interesting letter from the Marquis du Udille," he boomed, as every mouth fell silent and every eye locked onto his. "I can't reveal all the specifics at the moment, but it's time for us to reclaim France."

"Sir," interjected one of his generals, "there are whispers that the British are planning to send you away to St. Helena, fearing your supporters may incite rebellion against King Louis XVIII."

Napoleon's jaw tightened at this revelation. He had been patient long enough, waiting for the opportunity to strike back against those who had wronged him. It seemed the time had finally come.

"We've been steady long enough, we've been patient long enough, we've been silent long enough. The time for action is now, and we will no longer hold back."

A burst of enthusiasm and determination engulfed the room. Napoleon's loyal supporters had waited a long time for this moment to arrive.

"How many soldiers do we have at our disposal?"

"Just over a thousand, perhaps more," came the confident response.

Without hesitation, Napoleon gave his command. "Ready the troops. We leave at dawn!"

In a flurry of action, commands were issued, missives were dispatched, and hurried preparations were made. As Napoleon's spirit reignited within him, his doubts dissipated, and his strength surged. He could feel the fire in his body growing hotter each second, fueling his unwavering ambition. Soon enough, his enemies would face his unrelenting wrath. The wait was over. Napoleon was ready to reclaim his throne by any means necessary.

24

The ride to safety was filled with an electric tension of hope and anxiety. Claire felt like the night would never end. She kept turning around to ensure that Richard and Pierrick were still behind her. As she felt the breeze rush through her hair, Claire smiled in joy and relief, for freedom was a feeling like no other.

One of the men ahead threw his arm up to signal the company to stop. Instinctively, Vincenzo leapt off his horse and crouched low, slowly inching forward. With a sense of dread rising, he asked, "What is it?"

"I heard horses," the man replied, barely above a whisper, "Could they be following us?"

The sound of hooves was now loud and unmistakable. It seemed they were coming from all sides with no way to escape. Vincenzo frantically instructed the men to take defensive positions and protect Claire and the boys, quickly pushing them into the group's center as the noise grew louder. Claire stifled a sob, and her eyes went heavenward as she prayed for salvation. The thought of being captured again after having just tasted freedom made her stomach churn.

Suddenly, they were surrounded on all sides by ten armed riders. Vincenzo bellowed for his men to raise their weapons and hold their ground. All eyes locked onto the lone man who dismounted his horse and broke through the circle, advancing confidently towards the cornered group. He greeted them calmly.

"We did not mean to startle you, but we needed to make sure you were not Mortimer's men."

Vincenzo's brows relaxed as he recognized the speaker's deep voice. A relieved chuckle escaped his lips.

"You old bastard! You gave us quite a fright!"

Vincenzo signaled for the men to lower their weapons. He eyed the man before him.

"You were expected earlier – what took you so long?" Vincenzo demanded.

"You went ghost on us, and tracking you down has been hard. Then I heard that you'd joined Mortimer's men to escort a certain girl – was it her?" came the reply.

Vincenzo nodded briefly, indicating the human wall around Claire. "It *is* indeed her."

The tension seemed to dissipate slightly as everyone heaved a sigh of relief.

"We need to get to safety. We left too much chaos back at Rouen, and I fear repercussions."

Richard, Pierrick, and Claire watched in confusion, none of them entirely sure what was happening. Within minutes, they were galloping off into the night with the stranger's company, no one daring to say a word, only grateful that they were still alive and well.

***

Violet sat on the small porch of the cabin in a creaky wooden chair, keeping watch through the endless night. She prayed for a miracle that would bring Claire back safely. The sound of her cough interrupted the stillness. Gerard stepped out of the hut and wrapped a blanket around her shoulders. A chill had settled over the land – the promise that morning was nearing.

"Thank you, Gerard."

Violet smiled at him. Birdsong echoed through the trees. Both listened, becoming aware of a new sound – riders were approaching, far more than had departed. Both she and Gerard stood frozen, uncertain if the riders were friends or foes.

Gerard breathed a sigh of relief when Richard and Pierrick rode into view, beaming. Gerard breathed a sigh of relief and looked up at the sky, grateful for his sons' safe return. Amidst the clouds of dust stirred up by so many horses, Violet eagerly searched for Claire, finally spotting her in the center of the group. She couldn't contain herself any longer and ran forward just as Richard helped Claire dismount. The reunion was more precious than either of them could have imagined. Tears streamed down their faces as they clung to each other for what seemed like an eternity, surrounded by joy and relief – this moment was worth it all.

But even amidst the celebration, Vincenzo knew they hadn't faced the worst yet. He looked on warily as Violet thanked each one of the men for bringing Claire back. His thoughts were interrupted when Claire approached him.

"I wanted to thank you for taking care of me and keeping me safe," she said with genuine gratitude.

"There's no need to thank me, *signorina*," Vincenzo replied, bowing his head gently.

"If you don't mind me asking ... who are you? I mean ... why did you ...?" Claire struggled to find the right words as she looked around.

Vincenzo could see her discomfort. He stood tall with a slight and confident smile. His intense, dark eyes met hers, and she couldn't help but blush and look away. "I know what you want to ask, and I promise you will get your answers. For now, I am glad you are safe," he assured her.

Claire lifted her gaze to meet his, feeling strangely at ease around him. "Thank you," she said softly before turning to rejoin Violet. Richard, observing this scene, felt a stab of uncertainty: how much could they really trust this mysterious man named Vincenzo?

At that moment, all heads snapped up: another rider was approaching. Although the small cabin was hidden deep within a dense forest, no one could shake the feeling of danger and vulnerability. Vincenzo squinted towards the horizon, his eyes narrowing as he spotted a horse boldly racing their way with two riders on its back. The closer they got, the more palpably relief emanating from Remi's men until, finally, Vincenzo burst out: "You lucky bastards!"

25

The next morning, a gentle breeze rustled through the leaves of the towering oaks and woke Claire, who couldn't help but be momentarily mesmerized by the beauty that surrounded her. A single leaf floated down and landed peacefully on the ground, bringing a sense of tranquility to her mind. She closed her eyes and took a deep breath, basking in the warmth of the sun's rays. With the temperature rising, she removed her blanket and fully embraced the day.

"Is everything alright?" Richard asked from a sleeping mat several paces away.

Claire's face lit up with a smile. "Yes, everything is fine. I was admiring the beauty around us. It's truly breathtaking." She gestured for Richard to look up at the tall trees surrounding them.

Following her lead, Richard gazed up and noticed the sun's rays peeking through the branches, creating a dazzling display of light and shadow. They chuckled at a squirrel attempting to make a daring leap between branches, only to fall on the one below.

Soon, JP called for a meeting to discuss their next steps. Limited numbers fit inside the cramped old hut, so most of the men stayed outside. Some of the men kept watch, while others took a break in the sheltered and peaceful location.

Remi was the first to speak. "We were lucky this time, and we are ... grateful that Claire made it out alive ... with minimal damage."

JP let out a chuckle, then winced and clutched his wound. Others in the room joined in with cheers and nods of agreement.

"But Mortimer is still out there and he won't give up easily. Our actions may have delayed his plans, but they will also provoke him further." Remi's voice turned serious. "He won't stop until he gets what he wants."

JP spoke next. "We cannot create a plan of action until we unravel the truth behind this chaos, and we all deserve some answers!" The room fell silent as everyone's gaze turned towards the stranger sitting at the end of the table.

The stranger's intense eyes and stark white hair testified to a life of hard–fought battles, yet his confidence and calmness comforted everyone. He cautiously surveyed the small group of people from all walks of life: Gerard and his boys, there to defend an older woman and her niece they'd only recently met; a few brave men who'd risked their lives for a stranger in need. In what seemed like the chaotic abyss of despair, these mixed souls found strength in a unified purpose – saving a young girl. Little did they know the true magnitude of what was at stake. They deserved to know the truth.

"Before I begin, you must all swear that what I'm about to tell you will remain secret, never to be revealed beyond this room," the stranger said, speaking in a strange accent that hinted at far–reaching lands. As the group nodded in agreement, Remi shifted uncomfortably in his seat. It wasn't just the foreignness of this man's speech that made him uneasy; it was the feeling that he was caught up in something far bigger than himself.

"My name is Amir Rafik, Captain of The Serpent Watch. An order that has protected our world for generations."

"Protected it from what?" Pierrick asked.

"To understand our mission and purpose, I must take you back thousands of years to when it all began ..."

His words hung over the group like fine mist. Everyone waited in eager anticipation to hear what would come next.

"Around 2500 B.C., something extraordinary occurred in a small village in modern–day Turkey – a strange creature plummeted from the sky. No one knew where it had come from, but it wasn't of this world. When it crashed to the ground, it was close to death. The three young daughters of a humble fisherman named Morrat discovered it. As its last breath left its body, the creature bestowed an object upon Morrat with two cryptic words: "*Onu koru.*" In the old language, it means *Protect it,* or *Keep it safe.*"

Pierrick's curiosity was piqued again. "What was it?" he asked.

"The object was a powerful cube carved from an unknown material. Ancient texts reveal that the fisherman Morrat formed a telekinetic link to the creature moments before it vanished into a million specks of dust. Thus he was made aware of the immense power and danger of this object. This enigmatic cube has the extraordinary ability to connect deeply with whoever possesses it, altering reality to fulfil their deepest desires and ambitions. The cube hums to life when it senses its owner's ambition and desires, emitting an imperceptible surge of energy. If the intentions are pure, this energy will benefit all who cross paths with the cube's possessor. However, if the intentions are malicious, this unseen force corrupts everything in its wake. This power was not dangerous for Morrat, who only wished to provide a better future for his beloved family, free from the hardships that had plagued them for generations. With the cube's power, he managed to turn the tide of his family's fortunes, ensuring their prosperity and happiness.

"However, Morrat's newfound success and affluence attracted the envious eyes of an elder in his village, a ruthless figure named Eras. Consumed by ambition and greed, Eras devises a scheme to steal the cube from Morrat, believing that with its power, he could amass wealth and influence beyond his wildest dreams.

"Eras convinced all the elders to force Morrat to share the cube with them, under the guise of bringing prosperity to the village. But Eras's intentions were far from generous, and when he activated the cube's powers, his desires manipulated the world around him. His wealth and influence grew rapidly as he accumulated power, land, and possessions, all with the intent of becoming the most powerful figure in the realm.

"With the cube's power amplifying his ambitions, Eras gradually transformed the village into a place of opulence and grandeur with himself as the only ruler. However, his insatiable desires and unchecked ambition led to unintended consequences. The village's harmony and sense of community began to crumble under the weight of his greed.

"Morrat, now without the cube, watched as the village he loved deteriorated. He realized that the cube's power, while capable of fulfilling desires, also came at a great cost to one's humanity and the wellbeing of others. Morrat knew Eras had to be stopped at all costs. He drew upon every resource he could find to raise a small army to battle against the powerful elder. Bloodshed and carnage ensued as many brave souls lost their lives in the struggle. In the end, Morrat emerged victorious, but at great cost, as he sustained a wound that brought his own life to an end.

"Morrat knew the cube's power was too enticing for any mortal to resist. It had to be hidden, or better yet, destroyed entirely. As he took his last breath, Morrat made his eldest daughter, Halina, swear to bury him with the cube at the bottom of the sea. This Halina did. And yet the following day, Halina discovered the cube had mysteriously reappeared in her house. She attempted multiple times to sail far away and sink the cube, only for it to miraculously reappear each time. Halina soon discovered the cube's indestructible nature and ability to resurface no matter where it was hidden.

"In order to protect her loved ones, Halina escaped with a few trusted companions. She traveled far and wide, and the cube became her silent companion, granting her the means to survive and ensure its safety for years. As time passed, her relationship with the cube evolved. What began as a tool for survival slowly revealed itself to be something far more complex. She began to understand that the cube was not merely a relic but a mechanism designed with a purpose. Its powers were vast yet purposeful. As her understanding grew, so did her questions about the cube's true purpose.

As time passed, the relic's memory became mere legend, then myth, until its existence was forgotten – or so Halina thought. Treasonously, one of her trusted friends had succumbed to the temptation of wealth, selling the secret of the cube to a wealthy Merchant. The merchant's greed, ignited by tales of the cube's power, spared no expense. He hired deadly mercenaries and ruthless hunters to pursue Halina and her friends. With their forces overrun, Halina found herself surrounded by enemies, fighting for her life in one final, desperate attempt to protect the cube.

"But then, something incredible happened: as one of the mercenaries approached to deliver the killing blow, Halina clasped the cube close. The cube exploded in a blinding flash of light, bringing down the attackers with a single blast. As the light slowly faded, Halina bent down and reverently retrieved the cube's broken pieces. She could feel its energy course through her fingertips, pulsing with a newfound life that seemed to expand infinitely. Strange patterns materialized within each piece, and a wild cacophony of shapes looped together in an ever–shifting mosaic of power. Clutching the three pieces tightly in her trembling hands, she felt a sudden surge of power run through her. The cube had chosen her as its protector.

"Absorbed by the powerful bond, she connected with the cube's origins, immense power, and terrifying dangers. As she deftly connected and disconnected the pieces, a surge of reverence washed over her at the thought of the cube's untapped potential and limitless might.

"Knowing that hiding the cube was no longer viable since its power would always draw attention, she proposed a different strategy. Instead of concealing it from the world, they would share its power among carefully selected individuals to help the world. Selected people with noble intentions would be entrusted with a fragment. They would grow in power and influence – while ensuring safety for their respective fragment. This decision led to the formation of The Serpent Watch Order, which vowed to protect the cube's secret at all costs, and ensuring each fragment stayed in the hands of the right people. Although there were risks – as its power could corrupt even those with good intentions – this seemed the best course of action if the cube was to remain safe. The never-ending conflict between good and evil would ensure that the power of the cube remained forever in equilibrium, an invisible balance holding the fate of the world in its fragile grasp.

"For eons, the Serpent Watch Order has proved an unyielding sentinel, enabling a select number from all four corners of the world to rise as kings, emperors, heroes, and scientists. However, there were times when the power corrupted and darkened the hearts of the chosen ones, allowing greed and ambition to take over their lives and transforming them into despots and tyrants. Each time this happened, it fell upon the Order to restore balance by returning power to the deserving – a daunting task that was often deadly, yet one that we never shirked from."

"Hold on," Gerard interrupted. "So are you telling us that your Order has had a hand in empowering some of the most powerful people in history? Is this what you're saying?"

"More or less, yes!" came the reply. "Though it often became a matter of choosing the lesser evil. Rulers such as Ramesses II, Julius Caesar, Alexander the Great, Táng Tàizōng, Genghis Khan and many more: notorious figures have all benefited from this power, and in doing so, assisted us in keeping it safe from being discovered by the world at large. At other times, we delegated power to people whose ambitions were limited to the realms of science, psychology, or medicine. Scientists such as Archimedes and Galileo Galilei were no less influential, leaving an everlasting imprint on mankind's progress.

"You see, for some people, morality diminishes as power increases, while others feel a greater responsibility to humankind. That is why our history is filled with good and bad alike – each have their part in shaping the world as it is today. Our mission is not to shape or control history; we don't seek power or influence. We do not get involved in politics or wars.

Eventually, we came to understand that the cube possesses the incredible ability to shift allegiances when the balance of power is threatened. Both forces must coexist, for one cannot exist without the other. The concept of good loses its meaning without the existence of its opposite. This makes the cube an instrument of unparalleled power. It could reshape societies, topple empires, and rewrite the laws of nature. It is a formidable force that works in secret, unseen but always present. Our very existence depends on the cube's power remaining balanced and secure."

A heavy silence descended upon the room as everyone absorbed what had been revealed. Each person searched within themselves for a better solution. But was there one? After a few moments of contemplation, Gerard said: "So, I'm guessing Napoleon has one of the fragments?"

Amir nodded.

"Why isn't he using the cube's power to regain control?" Gerard continued.

"The cube's power isn't magical and won't make one invincible. It amplifies the nature of a person, and any bad choices they make will soon prove their downfall – human nature being flawed. Napoleon's undying ambition for expansion of the empire was also his undoing.

"The Order didn't choose Napoleon either. Napoleon had a keen interest in history, which only intensified when he discovered the legendary Galileo Galilei's diary. Galileo was relentless in his pursuit of knowledge – harnessing the cube's power to expand his knowledge beyond his wildest dreams, dedicating years to exploring its origin. Galileo transcribed all his findings in a detailed diary known as 'The Galileo Codex.' Once Napoleon located Galileo's journal, he learned of the cube's existence, its power, and hints of where Galileo's piece was hidden.

"As I previously stated, the cube has the ability to shift protectors when the balance of power is threatened. Good or bad, Napoleon was necessary to restore stability and balance. It's unclear whether Napoleon stumbled upon the cube through his own efforts, or if the cube intended to be found. However, that detail is insignificant in the grand scheme of things. As Napoleon's influence grew, he became acutely aware of the immense power contained within the cube and the peril of such power if it fell into the wrong hands. The cube would relentlessly seek its guardian to protect it, so Napoleon decided to enlist you, Professor, to craft the safe to keep his piece safe. The secure box you created would safeguard the cube and Galileo's secret diary."

Gerard glanced skeptically at Amir.

"But if the cube's fragment is sealed away inside the safe, how can it possibly work?"

"Galileo discovered that once a connection is made between the cube and its protector, the two remain linked – The cube doesn't have to be physically handled to release its power. All Napoleon needs to do is stay close to the safe to use its power."

Amir took a deep breath. "Mortimer was once a trusted friend of Napoleon, and perhaps, in some twisted way, he still is. Somehow, Mortimer uncovered the safe's hidden secret, and became consumed with the desire to claim it for himself. It could be argued that the cube selected Mortimer specifically to balance its power - in this case, the darker side of its nature."

"Are you saying the cube chose Mortimer?" Gerard asked, surprised.

"In a way, yes. The cube's understanding of good and evil transcends our mortal comprehension. It views these forces not as absolutes but as complementary aspects of a greater whole. For every protector, there must be an opposing force. A counterbalance that seeks to seize its power."

"But how can the cube choose both a protector and a threat?" JP asked, struggling to grasp the concept.

"The cube doesn't adhere to our notions of morality. Its primary function is balance - an equilibrium that must be maintained at all costs. In choosing Napoleon as a protector, the cube simultaneously set in motion the events that would lead Mortimer down his dark path, manifesting the darker side of his twisted nature. It's a cruel irony. Two sides of the same coin, locked in an eternal struggle that transcends good and evil as we understand them.

"Despite our unsuccessful efforts to uncover his true intentions, Mortimer expertly maintained a facade with Napoleon. When he discovered that Anne possessed the pendant gifted to her by Napoleon, Mortimer's unwavering loyalty gave way to his insatiable thirst for power. Mortimer and Napoleon spent years searching for Anne and the pendant, but in time, it all started to feel like a distant memory, buried and forgotten. That is until recently, when you appeared, Claire ... with the missing pendant. To confirm your identity, our comrade Vincenzo skillfully infiltrated the ranks of Mortimer's men.

"With Napoleon ousted from power, Mortimer finally has free reign to get what he wants: the pendant, and Claire as a bargaining chip. He won't rest until he gets what he wants – and with no real authority to stop him, the situation only grows more dangerous by the day."

Claire hung her head low, feeling an immense weight of responsibility for all that had happened – if she wasn't who she was, would any of these people be risking their lives for her? Having learned the truth, she sought out Vincenzo's eyes; he nodded to her ever so slightly. Richard stood behind her and placed a hand on her shoulder, reminding her that she was not alone despite the fear that consumed her. Violet tenderly grasped Claire's hand, softly stroking it.

"Why don't we all take a break? There's still a lot to discuss, and we could all use some fresh air," Amir suggested with a forced smile. They all agreed, eager for a change of scenery. They started filing out of the room. Pierrick grabbed Claire by the hand, wordlessly asking her to join him in search of supplies. Richard chuckled before following them both.

Vincenzo lingered behind, waiting for everybody else to leave, while Amir sat deep in thought.

"Why didn't you tell them the whole story?" Vincenzo asked in a hushed tone laced with urgency.

"I don't know if it is wise. It might endanger them even more ..." Amir trailed off.

"True! But they already know so much, and it's their lives on the line," Vincenzo prodded. Amir silently reflected on his options.

"I'll think about it," he said at last. "Let's get some fresh air." They both joined the others outside.

26

Crackling twigs and birdsong echoed through the trees. Claire looked down, kicking a small pebble on the path. The sky was a vivid blue, melting into the lush green grass. A warm breeze rustled through the trees, and Richard watched Claire's hair dancing in the wind as she moved with effortless grace. He had never known someone so gentle could be so strong.

Richard felt his heart pounding as he stared at her beauty. Claire turned around, feeling his gaze upon her. She smiled at him shyly and asked what was wrong, embarrassed by the thought of him staring at her like that.

"Do I have something on my face?" she asked.

"Oh no, no!" Richard quickly replied, a bit embarrassed. "I was just looking at your ... umm ..."

"My ...?" she giggled.

Richard opened his mouth to speak but stopped short when Pierrick crashed into the scene, breaking the spell and embarrassing them both.

"He likes you!" His voice echoed through the trees, bringing an abrupt end to their moment of bliss.

"You lovebirds need to come inside. Everyone is back in the room," he declared with a smirk, dodging Richard's attempted lunge and running away.

Claire and Richard walked into the cabin, greeted by Violet's piercing glare as she gestured for Claire to sit beside her. Violet had a sudden coughing fit and quickly covered her mouth with her hand. The coughing caused a sharp pain in her chest, and she instinctively placed a hand over her lungs.

"Nana, are you okay?" Claire asked with concern. "I'm fine, just a silly cold," Violet replied dismissively. Richard took the spot by Pierrick, giving him a light nudge on the arm. Pierrick retaliated, but Gerard quickly put an end to their shenanigans.

The eight people in the room fell silent in anticipation of what Amir would say next. Remi jumped up, interrupting the silence.

"Personally, I don't care about this *cube* or the *pendant* or any of it. All I want is to kill that awful man and move on with my life. If you've got a plan to kill Mortimer, count me in. Whatever plans your *secret order* has for our world doesn't concern me. It's all fucked up anyway."

Vincenzo shot a hostile look at his friend, but who could blame him? The hopelessness of the situation weighed heavy on everyone in the room. They felt trapped in a never–ending circle with no way out.

Amir sighed. "I empathize with your feelings. Carrying this weight is not something anyone would willingly choose, especially not those of you who are young and have so much ahead of you. We may never fully understand why life has taken us down this unpredictable path. However, it's the Order's mission to prevent this power from falling into the wrong hands. If any of you want to leave, I completely understand, and no one will blame you. As for me and my men, we will do what we can to keep Mortimer as far away from the cube and you as possible."

"Does that mean you're going to kill him?" Remi asked tentatively.

"It's not up to us to decide who lives or dies," Amir answered, but Remi interrupted. "Just get me close enough," he said firmly. "I'll make that decision for you. I don't owe anyone here any loyalty. That man needs to die."

The atmosphere in the room was tense as Remi continued.

"All I ask is that when the time comes, you won't stand in my way. Promise this, and you can count on me and my men."

Amir nodded silently in agreement, appeasing Remi's fervor.

In a sudden burst of courage, Violet added her voice. "I can't believe I'm actually suggesting this," she said softly, "but what if we brought Claire to Napoleon? Give him the pendant and let him deal with Mortimer."

The suggestion hung in the air as everyone considered it carefully. Amir spoke cautiously.

"It's not a bad plan. However, we must consider how Napoleon will react and whether he will even believe us. Even if he trusts us, can he actually help other than offering you refuge in Elba? Also, journeying safely won't be easy. Mortimer's network spans the entire country, so getting to Elba will take a lot of work. On the one hand, if everything goes according to plan, we could keep Claire safe until Mortimer is dealt with. On the other hand, if things don't go well ... well, it won't end well for any of us."

Remi interjected. "We have over twenty trained men who can accompany Claire to the harbor."

"Do not underestimate Mortimer," Amir warned wisely. "He will strike back when we least expect it."

After much debate, the group reached a consensus and agreed to follow Violet's suggestion. They would brave the journey to meet with Napoleon. They were running out of supplies, and they hut wasn't equipped to shelter so many people. Remaining perpetually on the run was not a viable option for any of them.

***

Napoleon landed in Golfe–Juan with a fierce band of over a thousand loyal soldiers, their spirits high for at the prospect of adventure ahead. With his top generals gathered around him, they quickly began planning their next move. But amidst all the excitement and chaos, one thought kept nagging at Napoleon's mind: the daughter Mortimer claimed he had, Claire. He longed to meet her, but above all else, he needed answers about Anne. Swirling in his mind were a million thoughts he longed to say to her; there were so many things he needed to clarify and explain. Yet, he needed to focus on his ultimate goal of regaining power.

Napoleon singled out General Pierre – a man who had stood by him through thick and thin. Despite being a man of few words, Pierre possessed a brilliant mind and an unbreakable character.

"I have a favor to ask," Napoleon said, inviting Pierre to his tent.

"Anything you need," Pierre responded.

"What I'm about to tell you must remain between us." Napoleon's voice was grave and intense, and Pierre acquiesced without hesitation.

"In his letter, Mortimer disclosed something that took me by surprise. He found something – and someone – that is very important to me, which I only learned about recently."

"What's this?" Pierre asked, curiosity piqued.

"Many years ago, I met a beautiful and wonderful woman – someone I will never forget. We shared a short but intense night and I've spent a long time searching for her, trying to reconnect. Mortimer assisted in the search, but she seemed to have disappeared without a trace." Memories of Anne flooded Napoleon's mind for a moment before he continued. "She bore me a daughter I never knew about until now. I suspect Mortimer is using her as a means to an end, pursuing something that does not concern him. And once he sets his mind on something, it's nearly impossible to reason with him. You know how he loves to play mind games," Napoleon said.

"Do you believe he'll hurt her if his demands aren't met?" Pierre inquired.

"No, no, nothing like that. But it would put my mind at ease if we had some of our men escort him ... and her here. After all, we've already lost so much, and I don't have much family left."

Pierre nodded in understanding.

"What's her name?" he asked.

"Claire," Napoleon replied, a subtle smile playing on his lips.

"I'll assemble a group of reliable soldiers right away," said Pierre. "It would be a perfect opportunity to let him know you're back. I have no doubt he will be eager to serve his country once again."

Napoleon agreed. "Make sure this mission is kept quiet. These are delicate times, and I must focus on reclaiming power."

"Leave it to me, *mon général*," Pierre reassured him. With determination, he quickly organized the chosen men, and a small yet formidable force was secretly dispatched.

27

Claire took a deep breath and pushed open the heavy wooden door, stepping into a lavish ballroom filled with revelers. People danced wildly, while others sat around a long table heaped with decadent dishes. A small band played lively tunes, adding to the heated atmosphere of celebration.

As she walked through the crowd, all eyes turned to her, and cheers erupted. Violet clung to her hand, tears streaming down her cheeks as they approached a man standing at the end of the room with his back turned to them. Claire's heart raced with excitement as she drew closer and closer to him. But just five steps away, she stopped. Violet squeezed her hand tightly, not wanting to go, but Claire smiled gently and pulled away, continuing alone. She was about to get what she wanted, but suddenly, she felt afraid. The man turned to face her, his smile sending terror coursing through her veins as she recognized Mortimer.

"Claire ... CLAIRE!"

She jolted awake, gasping for air. Her grandmother's concerned face hovered inches from hers.

"You were mumbling in your sleep. Are you okay?" Violet asked, placing a hand on her forehead to check for fever.

"I'm fine," Claire replied shakily. "Just another nightmare."

"Is it the same one?"

Claire nodded, still reeling from the vividness of the dream. "But each time, it feels more and more real."

"Don't worry, my child," her grandmother reassured her. "It will never come true. I promise."

Everyone was preparing to leave their latest encampment except for Pierrick, who trudged along like a lifeless lump, clearly unhappy about being awake so early in the morning. Claire quickly tidied herself, smoothing down her hair before joining the others. Richard's smile greeted her.

"Morning, Claire," he said warmly. She smiled shyly in return before turning to help her grandmother. Pierrick rolled his eyes at the two.

"Ugh," he grumbled, but Richard shot him a deadly look. Pierrick couldn't care less – he was already irritated from the early wake–up call and the meager rations they had been given.

"When will we eat a proper meal?" he complained, only to receive the answer that they would stop at a tavern on their journey – a few more hours of patience were required. Pierrick didn't seem pleased with that response.

The long road to Nice port stretched ahead, and they needed to keep moving. The past few days had been exhausting what with riding nonstop, but Claire couldn't shake off the uneasiness feeling they were being followed by Mortimer's men. However, when she looked around at her companions, she felt safe. Vincenzo had been her guardian angel throughout her captivity. Richard and his family had saved her more than once, and now, a small army was escorting them. For a moment, she felt grateful to be the daughter of such an important man, but deep down, she desperately wished for her old life back. How she longed to see the world and experience new things – but perhaps this was all too much, all too soon?

Just then two scouts returned to camp, their horses lathered and panting. They quickly relayed a message to Vincenzo and Remi. The news seemed to shake everyone, including Amir, who joined the group with a grave expression.

"Are you sure about this?" he demanded of the scouts.

"We saw it with our own eyes," they replied grimly. "An army of over thousand men are less than half a day away, and moving closer."

Amir's mind raced as he processed this information. He knew it would change everything. Remi suggested meeting them head–on, but Vincenzo hesitated – was it wise for a group of mercenaries to charge towards such an overwhelming force?

JP had an alternative suggestion – send a messenger to Napoleon directly, tell him of their dire situation and beg for help. He even volunteered himself for the mission.

"You're in no condition to ride alone," Amir pointed out. "I will go with Gerard. I'm sure he would appreciate seeing a familiar face after all these years. He'll also be more likely to believe you,"

The news spread quickly, excitement mixed with unease rippling through their ranks. Claire's emotions ran wild, her heart and mind racing with a million thoughts and questions. She knew she would meet her biological father eventually, but now it seemed that moment was approaching much sooner than anticipated. On the one hand, safety under Napoleon's protection seemed within reach, but on the other hand ... he was Napoleon, the great Napoleon, and she was just a simple farm girl. Her thoughts were interrupted by Richard's words.

"Are you excited to meet him?" he asked eagerly.

Claire snapped out of her thoughts, still grappling with her surreal new circumstances. "Who?" she asked, her voice barely above a whisper.

"Napoleon! Your ... father."

Richard kept talking, trying to provide reassurance, but Claire couldn't shake the feeling that something was about to go terribly wrong.

Meanwhile, Pierrick's stomach growled loudly, a constant reminder of his need for food. He stormed off towards the horses, hungry and frustrated by the long delay. But before he could even rummage through their bags, a knife was pressed against his throat, and a hand clamped over his mouth. His eyes widened in terror as he saw two dead bodies on the ground nearby – it must have been the men on watch.

Armed men emerged from the shadows, slowly advancing towards them. Claire and Richard tried to warn the others, but it was too late. The men surrounded them, guns aimed at their heads. "Down your weapons," the men holding Pierrick demanded. "Or this one goes first."

Gerard pleaded with everyone to obey, terrified for his son's safety. Amir and Remi's men showed no signs of surrendering their weapons, but nobody dared to make a move as Pierrick's life hung in the balance. In an instant, their adversaries opened fire.

Remi's mind raced as he assessed the dire situation, knowing that any attempt to fight back would only result in more bloodshed and certain death for all of them. Reluctantly, he ordered his men to surrender. Amir did the same, knowing they had no chance against their well-armed attackers. Gerard begged for everyone to stay calm while Pierrick quivered, the knife still pressing against his throat. They all stood at gunpoint, defenseless. In a split second, their fate was sealed as the attackers coldly executed every one of Remi and Amir's soldiers.

Helplessly, they watched as their brave fellows fell one by one – their lives snuffed out like candles in a storm. It was a massacre, and there was nothing they could do to stop it. Pierrick was thrown to the ground, his body sliding across the rough surface as he tried to regain his footing. Richard rushed to help his brother, joining the rest of their captured group.

A limping figure appeared from the ranks of their captors, using a cane to prop up his stiff body. Remi's heart sank.

"How is he still alive?" he whispered to himself in horror.

Gaul's sadistic laughter filled the air.

"Well, well, well," he sneered. "So you thought you could escape? How foolish." His words were laced with venom and malice, his eyes glinting with wicked pleasure.

Gaul turned to Claire and motioned for one of his men to grab her. She screamed in terror as Richard lunged forward, only to be knocked down by another attacker. As Claire was dragged away, Gerard pleaded for them to stop, his eyes wide with fear for his son's life. But Gaul seemed to revel in the chaos and violence.

JP leaped onto one of the men who was brutally attacking Richard. Remi joined in, his kicks hitting with calculated precision as he fought to save Richard from certain death. But more of Gaul's men appeared, joining the fight and increasing the odds against them. Gaul's enjoyment grew with each passing moment as he watched the violent scene unfold. He finally raised his gun and fired one shot into the air, commanding everyone to stop fighting.

"That's it! Enough!!" His voice echoed through the chaos, a chilling command that temporarily halted the fierce battle.

"You people just never learn," Gaul scoffed, though his wounds made it difficult for him to stand straight. "There is no escaping Mortimer. There is no escaping me. And now, there is no escaping death ... at least for some of you." He grinned savagely at them, relishing in their desperation.

"You tried to kill me... twice, and yet here I am."

Remi seethed with rage. "Next time, I won't miss," he vowed through gritted teeth. "I'll gut you ..."

But before he could finish his threat, one of Gaul's men struck him with the butt of a rifle, knocking him to his knees.

"Why wait?" Gaul taunted.

With a sly grin, Gaul removed his knife from its sheath and hurled it towards Remi's feet. The blade embedded itself in the ground mere inches from Remi. A devilish glint flashed in Gaul's eyes as he taunted, "Do you feel lucky today, Remi? Or are you too Afraid?"

"Don't fall for his manipulations, Remi. He wants you to play into his trap," JP's voice rang out.

Remi's gaze flickered between Gaul and the knife, his heart racing with adrenaline. If only he could get his hands on that knife ... but he knew JP was right. It wouldn't be a fair fight. Gaul didn't seem to play by any rules.

As Gaul cackled with cruel amusement, Remi stood tall and stared directly into his cold eyes without fear. Gaul stared back at this enigma of a man; he couldn't help but wonder if he was dealing with a fool or a brave warrior. After all, Remi had fooled him twice before. Gaul reached for his gun and pointed it against Remi's head. But instead of quivering, Remi pressed his forehead against the barrel and declared defiantly, "Do it, you sick bastard."

For a moment, Gaul was taken aback by this display of courage and defiance. But then, with a cruel smile tugging at his lips, he pulled the trigger and sent a bullet straight into Remi's skull.

JP struggled to keep his composure as he watched Remi's body collapse in front of him. He knew this was not the time for heroics – Gaul was too dangerous and unpredictable for that. With a cruel glint in his eyes, Gaul ordered his men to seize Vincenzo and beat him: punishment for being a traitor. Blood spurted from Vincenzo's broken nose, and his body contorted in agony as he struggled to stay conscious under the relentless assault. Tears streamed down Claire's face as she turned away from the heartless scene. The beating continued, each blow landing with bone–crushing intensity until Vincenzo was barely clinging to consciousness.

"That's enough ... for now," Gaul sneered. "Leave something for Mortimer."

Gaul's orders were ruthless and unforgiving. "Take the old man and the old lady. Kill everyone else!" he commanded with a sneer, reveling in his control over life and death.

Gerard's heart dropped as he begged for mercy, pleading for his sons' lives. But Gaul showed no remorse, no humanity. Battling his captors, Gerard was desperate to reach his son Richard, who lay motionless on the ground. With adrenaline coursing through his veins, Pierrick seized his chance amid the chaos and lunged for the knife lying on the ground. With trembling hands, he grabbed Gaul from behind, pressing the blade against his throat.

Taken by surprise, Gaul started taunting him as Remi had done, daring him to follow through. But Gaul's taunts only fueled Pierrick's shaky determination. "I just want you to leave us alone," he pleaded, his voice trembling with emotion. "I just want my family and Claire and Violet ..." Pierrick struggled to think of whom he may have forgotten to include on the list of people to save. "...and JP," he added.

One of Gaul's soldiers grabbed Gerard and held a gun to his head, causing Gaul to laugh in amusement.

"So what now? Boy."

Struggling to think clearly, Pierrick eased the pressure of the knife against Gaul's neck as he looked to his father for guidance. But Gaul used this opportunity to strike back, elbowing Pierrick in the stomach and sending him crashing to the ground. Then he snatched his sturdy walking stick and swung it, hitting Pierrick twice, rendering him helpless.

"You people are too ... feisty," Gaul sneered as he looked down at Pierrick. "That's the reason why I can't let you live."

Then his sadistic grin turned into a menacing frown as he locked eyes with JP. "That one," he said, pointing towards JP, whom Gaul's men now dragged away, "I also want alive. It's personal."

JP whirled around.

"Leave the boys alone, Gaul," he pleaded. "They're just kids. You've already won; there's no need to kill them."

His words only seemed to enflame Gaul's sadism. This was a matter of pride for him. They had all humiliated him in front of Mortimer. This was his moment for revenge. He leveled his gun at Pierrick, a cruel smirk twisting his lips. JP grit his teeth and growled, "Don't do it!"

Gaul grimaced at his target, ready to pull the trigger. In a moment of desperation, JP broke free from his captor's grip and lunged at Gaul, knocking him to the ground and causing the shot to miss its mark. He landed several powerful blows on Gaul before being pulled away by Gaul's men, who overpowered JP and beat him to the ground.

Gaul relished the chaos, wiping the blood from his mouth with a brutal smile. He retrieved his pistol and aimed it at Pierrick again, poised to finish what he started. He pulled the trigger. There was a click – no bullets left.

Relief washed over Gerard as he watched his son narrowly escape death. But Gaul only ordered one of his men to give him a loaded gun. As he prepared to take another shot, one of his men yelled, "Soldiers approaching!"

28

Frustrated by the interruption, Gaul barked orders at his men to kill the incoming soldiers while he finished off Pierrick.

"Army approaching!" another yelled.

"What army?" he demanded in confusion.

"Napoleon's army!"

"*Napoleon?* What? Are you drunk?"

The soldiers around Gaul shifted uncomfortably, unsure of what to do. Before he could give any further orders, the small battalion crashed through the trees, commanding them all to drop their weapons. A tense silence fell over the scene as the battalion's commander stepped forward, scanning the group with suspicious eyes.

"What is the meaning of this? Who are you?" he demanded, his voice laced with authority.

Amir and JP exchanged uneasy glances. Gaul knew he had to take control of the situation before it spiraled out of hand; he addressed the commander politely.

"We are employed by Mortimer Du Udille, the Marquis de Rouge. I'm sure you're familiar with him, as he is a close ally of Napoleon's."

The commander nodded in recognition.

"I am aware who he is. But can you explain ..." he gestured towards the bodies scattered around.

"These lowly servants thought they could steal from my master and get away with it," declared Gaul flippantly. "My men were simply following orders to bring them back."

The commander raised an eyebrow incredulously. "These servants managed to overpower your trained men?" he questioned skeptically.

Before Gaul could respond, Amir stepped forward. "We are not thieves, sir. We were bringing Napoleon some crucial intelligence when these men ambushed us."

The commander's eyes narrowed even further as he considered these words. The tension in the air was palpable as everyone held their breaths, waiting for his response.

"What business do you have with Napoleon?"

"I am not at liberty to say," JP interjected firmly.

The commander scoffed. "I won't let you near Napoleon unless you give me a damned good reason."

Amir limped towards the commander and pleaded for a private conference. The commander's expression remained skeptical while they conferred.

"Why would an urgent matter require you to travel with an old woman and a girl?" the commander questioned.

"I understand your skepticism," Amir replied earnestly. "But we must speak with Napoleon only. If he does not believe us, you may take us as prisoners."

"We don't have time for this, and we certainly don't have the resources to take prisoners with us."

Amir gripped the commander's arm, his voice shaking with urgency. "Sir, I must insist. Lives are at stake."

The soldiers aimed their rifles at Amir and his group, ready to fire.

Amir raised his hands in surrender. "We are no threat, please. We only need to speak with Napoleon ... or someone close to him."

"And I've already told you, unless you give me a damned good reason, you won't get near him," the commander growled.

Gerard intervened. "Tell him, Amir."

"Tell me what?" The commander glared at them.

Amir took a deep breath before saying loudly enough for everyone to hear, "I know you won't believe me, but that young girl over there ... she is Napoleon's daughter."

Silence fell over the group as the commander studied Claire.

The unexpected news caught most of the men off guard. Gaul could feel his body tense up as the commander's piercing gaze landed on him, but he remained defiant. He raised a finger to his forehead in a mocking gesture. It was clear that he questioned Amir's sanity.

Finally, the commander spoke. "Yeah, okay. I can see the resemblance."

Relief flooded through Amir as he asked cautiously, "So will you take us to see Napoleon?"

"Will I take you? Will I ...?" The commander sneered and laughed cruelly.

"You are fortunate we have a much more important mission. Under any other circumstance, I would have you all killed for spreading such lies about our Emperor."

With a sly smile, Gaul added, "And yet, the guilty will always weave the most ... *creative* stories to save their skin."

The commander nodded in agreement and shoved Amir back. "There's something not quite right about all of this, but we don't have time to waste on this nonsense." He commanded his battalion to lower the weapons and return with the rest of the army. "Take your business elsewhere; this is no place to settle scores. And send my regards to the Marquis."

Gaul politely nodded and saluted the commander as his men encircled the group again. Amir bowed his head in resignation as a rough shove from one of Gaul's soldiers forced him toward the rest of the group. As the army retreated to a safe distance, Gaul slowly turned towards Amir and the group with a twisted grin, his eyes gleaming with pleasure.

"Move."

Gaul and his men relentlessly pressed forward. Claire could feel the weight of her friends' fate upon her shoulders. Whenever things seemed to be turning for the better, a cruel twist sent her spiraling back into despair. This man, this Gaul, was the most brutal of adversaries. She couldn't help but marvel how darkness seemed to pull in even more darkness: Mortimer had a way of attracting the worst kind of people into his service. Claire refused to accept that evil could win. She clung to the hope that the tide would turn sooner or later and luck would shine again. They just had to hold on and keep moving forward.

Violet clung to Claire's hand, her face white and immobile. Gerard marched with his two sons close behind, followed by JP and Amir. Vincenzo looked over his shoulder to where his friend Remi lay lifeless on the ground. It was because of Remi and his men's sacrifice that they were still alive. But was it worth it?

Gaul's eyes narrowed as he suddenly ordered a halt and closed in on Claire.

"Give it to me!" he demanded.

"What?" Claire asked, her fear palpable.

"The pendant," Gaul growled, coming closer and closer.

"I don't have it. I already told your master," Claire interjected, struggling to maintain her composure.

Gaul's lips curled into a cruel smile. "Oh, but I'm not easily fooled by you." With that, he roughly grabbed Claire's dress and pulled her towards him, his hands groping her body in search of the pendant.

Claire was frozen in horror, too scared to even struggle against him for fear of what he might do.

"Leave her alone, you pig!" Violet's voice rang out as she smacked Gaul and tried to push him away. But it was no use.

Gaul let out a demonic laugh as he brushed off Violet's feeble attempts at defense. "Enough!" he barked, grabbing her arm and delivering a brutal punch that sent her crashing to the ground.

Gerard strained against the men surrounding him, desperate to reach Violet but unable to break free. Meanwhile, Claire knelt to help her grandmother up.

"Are you okay, Nana?" she cried, gasping as she saw the blood dripping from her grandmother's nose.

"I'm ok," Violet responded weakly.

But Gaul wasn't finished yet. He grabbed Claire by the hair and pulled her up cruelly, continuing his intrusive search for the pendant.

"Please stop!" Violet begged, trying to stand up again despite the coughing fit that befell her.

Gaul was preparing to deliver another vicious blow when he saw Violet reaching for something inside her dress. She pulled out a small object – the cursed pendant.

"Here! Take it! Take the damned thing!" Violet spat at Gaul as she held out the prize.

Gaul snatched it from her hand and examined it, disappointment evident on his face. "All of this for a worthless piece of junk? It's not even gold! What is wrong with you people?" he scoffed before ordering his men to move along.

Claire helped Violet to her feet, and they moved forward. Amir closed his eyes in defeat as he watched the pendant move one step closer to Mortimer. Their chances of success had just drastically diminished – perhaps even signaling the end for them all.

Gaul ordered his men to speed up the pace, his fear of encountering another Napoleonic patrol driving him onwards. Napoleon was on the march,
and it was unexpected news. He wondered if Mortimer was aware of it.
Time was of the essence as they strained to reach the safety of Rouen's walls
and regroup. As darkness descended, they discovered an empty house and
chose to take shelter there. Gaul assigned guards and secured their prisoners
before letting his soldiers rest.

JP, Vincenzo, and Amir huddled together, attempting to devise a plan,
but hope seemed far out of reach in the darkness. For now, all they could do
was try to make it through one more night and hold onto the belief that luck
would eventually turn in their favor.

***

Pierrick's bladder ached, and he could no longer contain his urgent need to
relieve himself. He spoke up, his voice straining with discomfort.

"I need to pee."

Claire chimed in with a plea of her own. The guards by the fire growled
at them to be quiet, their indifference towards the prisoners palpable.
Ignoring the warning, Pierrick persisted, hoping one of the guards would
show some humanity. "I really need to go," he said.

"Piss yourself or hold it," came the cold reply from one of the guards.

JP tried to speak up on behalf of the women's modesty, but another
guard turned, irritation etched on his face. "If I have to untie the ladies just
so they can pee, I'll expect something in return. Is that what you want?"

His words were laced with a sinister tone that sent shivers down Claire's
spine. She shook her head vehemently, repulsed by the suggestion.

"We're good," she spat.

"That's what I thought. Now shut the fuck up," the guard snarled, while
his companion chuckled at his dominance over the helpless prisoners.

Violet made an effort to suppress her cough, not wanting to alarm Claire any further about her deteriorating condition. The group huddled close together for warmth as the night air grew chillier. They couldn't shake off the gnawing feeling of hopelessness that took hold as they waited for dawn to break and their fate to be decided.

29

The sound of galloping hooves reverberated across the landscape as Mortimer and his men urged the horses forward, pausing only briefly to let them rest before continuing their journey towards Rouen Castle. The ride had been merciless, with few breaks or moments of reprieve, but after two exhausting days, they'd finally reached their destination.

As they rode through the gates, Mortimer's keen eyes immediately noticed that something was amiss. The castle was eerily quiet, its walls scrubbed clean. New sentinels he didn't recognize patrolled the grounds. Mortimer wasted no time and charged inside, summoning Louis to his study. But instead of seeing his trusted man rushing to meet him, he was met with confusion and incompetence from one of the servants.

"Where is Louis?" Mortimer demanded. The dogs greeted him with joyous barks, but Mortimer could not be bothered by their enthusiasm. He petted them absentmindedly.

The servant stammered and stumbled over her words until a soldier burst in with the news.

"Louis is dead, sir!"

Mortimer reeled with disbelief and anger. "What do you mean he's dead? How? When?"

"He was killed during the attack on the castle ... a few nights ago," the soldier replied.

Mortimer could feel his control slipping as he struggled to make sense of this news. "Why wasn't I told about this?"

"Gaul specifically instructed us not to inform you. He said he would take care of it."

"Where is that idiot?" Mortimer bellowed, his frustration mounting.

"He went after the girl," said the soldier in a trembling voice.

"The girl escaped? You incompetent imbeciles!" he roared. "I leave for a few days and return to utter chaos! Who is in charge of the guard?"

"I am ... sir."

Mortimer took a deep breath and closed his eyes, trying to calm himself. He turned towards the soldier. "Come with me. You will tell me everything." The newly appointed commander nodded, fear etched into his face. He followed Mortimer.

In his study, Mortimer mulled over the information he had just received. Claire's escape had disrupted his plans, and now Gaul's mission was their only hope.

"That idiot Gaul had better succeed, or I'll end him myself. For every soldier we lost, I want ten more to take their place. No cowards or weaklings. We must be ready to fight and defend the castle."

The soldier's voice quivered as he asked, "Sir, who are we fighting? I don't think the mercenaries will return."

Mortimer's reply came filled with unwavering determination. "What is about to come," he said gravely, "is far worse than a group of ragtag mercenaries attacking the castle walls. Do as you're told."

The soldier's eyes narrowed grimly as he nodded to acknowledge Mortimer's instructions. Without a word, he turned and strode off to carry out the order.

Mortimer downed the last drops of his cognac, feeling the warmth spread through his body. He collapsed onto the couch with a heavy sigh. His exhausted limbs giving way beneath him, his eyelids drooped heavily as he slipped into a deep, dreamless sleep by the crackling fireplace.

30

As the sun began to rise in the small harbor of Le Havre, seagulls screeched and circled above the restless sea, their keen eyes scanning for any signs of fish. Nearby, fishermen readied their boats for the day's work as the harbor patrol made their rounds, barely vigilant in their security duties. A massive ship emerged from the morning's shrouded mist. The sailors swiftly tied ropes to secure the ship to the dock while the wooden plank was lowered for disembarkation.

A sudden hush fell over the scene as heavy boots thudded against the wooden plank, signaling someone's descent from the ship. All eyes turned towards the captain, whose distinctive hat was the only feature visible through the dense fog.

The figure set foot on solid ground, reached up and pulled back the scarf that obscured her face. For the enigmatic ship's captain was none other than a woman with fierce features and an air of undeniable power, dressed warmly in garments that seemed to have come from a distant, frozen land. Her piercing gaze swept over her surroundings, then she paused to speak to the formidable bodyguards flanking her on either side. The gathered crowd instinctively parted, creating a path for the imposing entourage as they marched toward the city center.

Le Havre Inn was eerily quiet when the group of mercenaries entered. One of the men quickly spoke with the innkeeper, arranging for horses, food, and water for their journey. They gathered around a table where a man with a dark hood sat waiting for them. Coins exchanged hands, ensuring silence and speed on their quest. As time ticked by, the rest of the crew arrived at the inn, taking their seats with hushed conversations. The captain's gaze swept over her men, ensuring they were all present.

"All is ready, captain," one of the men reported.

She nodded in approval and signaled for her men to move out. As they exited the inn, she turned to the man with the dark hood.

"One last thing. Did you manage to locate her?" she inquired.

The man beside her leaned in and whispered hoarsely, "Last I heard, she was the Marquis du Udille's prisoner in Rouen Castle."

"Then that's where we will go," she declared.

"If I may ... Rouen Castle is impenetrable. It would be nearly impossible to gain entry without an invitation," he warned.

"You worry about the accuracy of your information," she snapped before striding away.

"He's coming with us," she commanded over her shoulder, her tone brooking no argument.

The man's eyes widened in panic. "Oh no. I can't ... I – I have a family and a shop to..." he blabbered nervously to the imposing figures now flanking him. The two burly men made it clear that refusal was not an option. Their meaty hands clamped down on his shoulders, propelling him forward into the unknown.

***

"WAKE UP!"

The prisoners were brutally jolted awake by the boots of Gaul's men, accompanied by vicious insults. The captives scrambled to rouse their fellow inmates, desperate to avoid another round of ruthless blows. But it seemed the soldiers reveled in the unnecessary violence, grinning with pleasure.

Gaul gave orders to one of his lackeys, who reluctantly brought the prisoners a meager amount of dry bread and water. The pitiful scraps were thrown on the ground before them, followed by spittle. Claire felt her stomach turn with disgust at the unfairness and cruelty. She had no appetite and could only think of finding a way out.

Pierrick forced himself to take a few bites of the tasteless bread, but the rest of the group only drank the water – their hunger was overshadowed by despair. After what felt like an eternity, the soldiers commanded them to get up and march towards the waiting horses. Each prisoner was assigned to a soldier.

"Remember," Gaul sneered, "Mortimer only needs the girl, the old man and the old lady. The rest of you are just dead weight, but he may find some use for you yet. One wrong move, and you're as good as dead."

Approaching JP In one swift motion, he delivered a punch straight to his wound, causing JP to stumble and lose his balance. Everyone knew there was no place for heroism or bravery, and Gaul relished his control over the group, sneering at them with a wicked grin.

"Why the long faces?" he taunted. "You're all still breathing ... for now."

With help from one of his men, Gaul mounted his horse and ordered, "We ride non–stop to Rouen! Anyone who tries anything funny, kill him ... except for the girl, of course."

With that, they galloped off towards the north, leaving behind a trail of dust.

The sound of galloping steeds hit Gaul's ears: a group of unfamiliar riders was gaining on them. As he urged his men to drive their horses faster, he made a chilling decision.

Amir was the first to fall, his body rolling off his horse in a cloud of dust, a bullet deep in his skull. All around them, soldiers were pulling out their pistols.

JP's eyes widened in horror as he realized what was happening. "Jump off your horses!" he screamed to the others.

Pierrick was the first to jump off his horse and roll to the ground. Richard wasn't fast enough to avoid a gunshot wound to his side, causing him to fall off his horse.

"Faster!" Gaul bellowed, the walls of Rouen Castle looming into view.

Pierrick scrambled to his feet and rushed towards Richard, who lay bloodied and moaning on the ground. They stumbled over Amir's lifeless body in their attempt to escape the riders hot on the heels of Gaul's men, clutching each other in a panic.

One of the riders slowed and took a sharp turn, circling close to the boys. Pierrick's heart raced as he yelled at Richard to focus and get out of harm's way. But Richard was frozen, his eyes locked on a rider who looked hauntingly familiar. She let out a fierce order in an unknown language, so that two riders broke away and came to trot around Richard and Pierrick. With a fierce howl, she spurred her horse and continued the chase after Gaul. The intensity of the moment sent chills down the boys' spines as they watched the unknown rider disappear into the horizon.

The two riders quickly dismounted from their horses. One man hurried over to help Richard, who was losing a lot of blood and struggling to stay on his feet.

"What happened?" The man's words were slurred with a thick foreign accent that Pierrick struggled to place.

"He is badly hurt. Please, he needs help," Pierrick begged. After examining Richard's injury, the man instructed Pierrick to apply pressure to the wound, which was gushing blood.

"He has lost much blood. We must cauterize the wound before he bleeds out."

The man spoke quickly in a foreign tongue to his companion, then retrieved a backpack. Pierrick watched every move. The other man approached with a leather bottle and forced Richard to drink its contents.

"What is that? What are you giving him?" Pierrick asked anxiously.

The man holding the bottle replied tersely, "For pain. He needs it."

As Richard choked down the potent liquid, the other man poured gunpowder onto his open wound, causing him to scream out in agony.

"Stop it! What are you doing?" Pierrick tried to intervene but was stopped by the firm grip of the other man.

"No," he said firmly. "Nazir saves your friend."

"He's my brother," Pierrick mumbled, torn between trusting these strangers and fearing for Richard's life. But if the strangers wanted them dead, why would they go to all this trouble?

The man called Nazir ignited the powder with a dazzling display of sparks, effectively cauterizing the wound and halting the bleeding. Richard screamed again and passed out.

"What happened? Is he alright?" Pierrick clutched his brother's limp hand, panic rising in his chest.

"He will be fine. He fainted from shock," Nazir replied calmly as he applied a strange green cream to the wound. Next, he produced a small bottle and waved it under Richard's nose, causing him to wake up instantly.

Pierrick was stunned. What kind of sorcery was this?

"Richard, are you okay?" Pierrick asked with concern.

Richard slowly regained his senses. He blinked and smiled weakly.

"He needs water and rest. He has lost a lot of blood," Nazir stated.

"Thank you ... Nazir," Pierrick said, with sincere gratitude in his voice. "I'm Pierrick, and this is my brother Richard."

Nazir nodded wordlessly as he packed up his tools. His long, raven-black hair cascaded past his shoulders. Pierrick observed his skin, a warm, rich hue resembling sun-baked soil, and his eyes, deep and dark like a moonless night. The two men helped Pierrick move Richard under a nearby tree.

"Now we wait," Nazir declared, resting against the tree trunk. Meanwhile, his companion took a swig of the remaining liquor and kept a sharp lookout for any potential threats.

"Pierrick, did you see that woman?" Richard whispered weakly to his brother.

"What woman? There are no women here," Pierrick replied dismissively.

"The woman on horseback, the one who gave the order," Richard insisted, struggling to speak through his pain.

"There was no woman, Richard. You must be delusional from the injury. Try to rest."

But Richard was insistent. "No, Pierrick ... I saw her ... she looked ... so familiar ... her eyes ..." His words trailed off as exhaustion overcame him.

"You mean our captain?" Nazir interjected, overhearing their conversation despite Richard's quiet tone.

But Richard had fallen asleep.

***

Gaul and his men raced against time, desperate to reach the borders of Rouen. As their pursuers closed in, Gaul's men fired shots in an attempt to hold them off. It was futile: one by one, they fell at the hands of their more skilled attackers.

Amidst the chaos, JP galloped towards Violet. "Give me your hand and jump! Trust me!"

Adrenaline coursing through her veins, Violet grabbed JP's hand and landed safely on the back of his horse.

They rode away from the bloody battle, Gaul's men falling all around them.

"Gerard!" JP waved for the professor to join them. Meanwhile, Vincenzo spurred his horse towards the action, searching for Claire, who was flanked by two guards.

He approached the man riding on the right side and forcefully yanked his jacket, causing him to fall off his horse. Vincenzo then shouted at Claire to jump off her horse. The other man quickly pulled out a gun and fired at Vincenzo, but he ducked and avoided the bullet. Meanwhile, Claire was struggling to control her frantic horse as it bolted from the chaos and gunfire.

"Claire, give me your hand!" Vincenzo shouted.

With fear pulsing through her veins, Claire took one hand off the reins and reached for Vincenzo's hand. She let go of the reins and allowed him to pull her towards him as she landed safely in front of him. The sudden impact caused Claire's head to bump into Vincenzo's chest, which she held tightly to avoid falling from the horse.

Gaul was horrified at this dreadful turn of events. He urged his horse on with all his might, casting frantic glances at his relentless pursuers and desperately firing shots, though all his shots missed their mark. His luck was running out. Just as he reached the border, a lasso snaked around his neck, yanking him off his horse with breathtaking force. He tumbled to the ground, feeling bones crack and wounds reopen as he fought for breath. His anger burned hotter than the pain as he struggled against the rope that dragged him mercilessly across the ground.

He let out a primal scream.

31

Vincenzo and Claire caught up with the rest of the group. The horse stopped abruptly, and Claire released her grip on Vincenzo. Vincenzo helped her off the horse, and she thanked him gratefully. Her heart was still racing from the adrenaline rush as she watched from downfall of their captors from a safe distance. Once again, they had been rescued by an enigmatic gang shrouded in mystery. Who were these saviors? She pushed those questions aside for now – she and her friends were no longer under Mortimer's control, and most of them were still alive. Looking towards the commotion she'd just fled, she saw a regal, horse-backed rider dragging a squirming man by a rope. It was Gaul and the mysterious captain. Claire's breath quickened. That man had caused her and her friends unspeakable suffering. She wanted him dead.

The rider dragging Gaul threw the rope to the ground, so that Gaul managed to free himself and stumble to his feet. He was drenched in blood and teetering like a drunk. The rider bore down on him. He rubbed his eyes, trying to regain focus, but the haunting sight remained the same.

"What the hell is this?" Gaul gasped, staggering back and glancing around wildly. "Who the fuck are you?"

He reached for his gun, only to discover he no longer had it. Desperately searching his body, he found a knife tucked into his belt. With trembling hands, he unsheathed it and threatened, "Stay back, or I will gut you!"

The captain just laughed an enchanting, musical laugh, and jumped off her horse.

Gaul lunged forward with all his might, but she dodged his attack with remarkable agility. Again and again, he tried, each time with increasing anguish, but she always managed to outmaneuver him. As if tiring of the charade, the captain closed in, disarmed him in two swift moves, and sent him toppling to the ground. Gaul couldn't believe it – Knocked down by a woman? This must be hell.

The small group watching from the trees saw the captain signal to one of her men. He quickly rode towards the group, dismounted, and approached Claire with a gun. JP and Vincenzo rushed to shield her, fearing the worst, but to their surprise, the man raised his hands in a peaceful gesture and explained that the gun was for Claire to use against Gaul. Claire's heart raced as she grasped the gun in trembling hands, torn between the rival thoughts rushing through her mind. Could she take a life? As she hesitated, Violet's hand on hers trying to talk her out of it, the sight of Gaul's head thrown back in mocking laughter spurred her forward. She broke free from her grandmother's grip and walked towards her tormentor with determined steps.

Face to face with him at last, Claire raised the gun to his forehead. Her hands were shaking uncontrollably.

"You could *never* shoot me," gurgled Gaul with dark mirth.

The captain walked behind her and gently took hold of her hand, stopping the tremors. Gaul's laughter ceased as he witnessed what looked like some sort of witchcraft.

"It's alright," came a whisper in Claire's ear as they both pulled the trigger, sending a bullet straight into Gaul's skull and silencing his laughter forever.

Claire's fingers trembled as she loosened her grip on the cold steel. The deafening gunshot still echoed in her ears. It was over. The end of a chapter written in blood and gunpowder. But the weight of the act, the finality of it, pressed against her chest like a physical force. She took a shaky breath, trying to process what had just happened. As she slowly turned, her heart pounding in an erratic rhythm, confusion clouded her vision. Behind her stood a figure shrouded in mystery, a presence both menacing and oddly comforting. The voice that had spoken moments ago was achingly familiar yet wholly impossible. A whirlwind of emotions washed over Claire as she struggled to comprehend this unexpected turn of events.

"Hello, sister."

32

The words hung in the air, heavy with meaning and laden with questions that clawed at the edges of Claire's consciousness. She watched, almost in slow motion, as the woman before her unwound the scarf obscuring her features. It fell away like the last veil of mist at dawn, revealing a face mirroring her own in ways that defied explanation.

Claire's mind reeled with implications, each thought colliding with the next. The resemblance was uncanny, a reflection gazing back at her through the looking glass of reality.

She had a sister? A *twin* sister?

Claire tried to form words, but all that came out was a weak "Hi." The stranger in front of her smiled, introducing herself as Elena. Elena raised an eyebrow, expecting Claire to introduce herself in return. But no words came.

Finally, Elena spoke again. "If I'm not mistaken, you are Claire. Right?"

At the mention of her name, something primal within Claire responded. A numb nod was her only confirmation, her body acting on instinct while her mind lagged behind, trapped in a web of shock.

Elena's lips curved into a knowing smile, and she stepped closer, bridging the gap that fate had carved between them. Her movements were graceful, betraying an innate confidence.

"Words seem to have abandoned you," Elena observed, her tone soft. "That's alright. We've been strangers until today; take your time."

With that, Claire shook off her daze and exclaimed, "You have to meet my ... *our* grandmother!"

Pierrick was the first to spot his father and JP approaching on horseback, accompanied by two others. Gerard's heart swelled with relief as he embraced his two sons tightly. He wasted no time checking on Richard's condition while Pierrick recounted the events – especially the part about how the strangers had used some kind of sorcery to patch Richard up. Grateful and relieved, Gerard thanked the two men for saving his sons' lives.

"We are forever in your debt," he pledged.

Vincenzo gestured toward Amir's lifeless body. "We can't leave him lying there on the ground. Help me move him under the tree."

With assistance from the riders, they gently lay Amir beneath the broad oak tree. Vincenzo knelt beside him and closed his friend's eyes. The weight of all the lives lost in this conflict weighed heavily on his heart. He softly whispered, "May you find peace in the next life, my dear friend."

"Can you ride?" Gerard asked Richard, who nodded despite his injuries. Together, they rode back to rejoin the rest of the group, grateful to still have each other amidst the chaos and death surrounding them.

***

"Grandmother," Elena whispered.

As soon as Violet saw Elena, her face turned ghostly pale, and she froze in her tracks. Was this real or a dream? The air seemed to vibrate with the unsaid, with questions and revelations that hung heavy between them. Claire watched, her own emotions a tumultuous sea threatening to spill over. This was more than a simple reunion; it was the collision of past and present.

Elena stepped forward with a resolve that belied the uncertainty reflected in her eyes. And in that step, the spell broke, giving way to a new chapter in their shared history reborn from the ashes of secrecy. Violet clung to Elena like a lifeline; tears cascaded down her cheeks as she whispered, "Is it really you? I never thought I would see this day."

Elena and Claire exchanged worried glances.

"Nana, please let her go ..." Claire said, feeling a little embarrassed by the dramatic display of affection. Violet heaved a great shuddering breath, loosening her grip on Elena. She stepped back, her hands trembling as she tried to compose herself, wiping her cheeks in a vain attempt to erase the evidence of her vulnerability.

Elena, her expression a mixture of confusion and concern, nodded to one of her men, who stood at a respectful distance.

"Prepare for our departure," she commanded, her voice slicing through the thick tension, decisive and urgent. "We can talk more later. Right now, we need to get out of here. It's not safe."

She stepped forward, placing a gentle kiss on Violet's forehead – a silent promise of discussions to come. Then, turning to Claire, she offered a reassuring pat on the shoulder, the corners of her lips tilting upward in a small, hopeful smile. Claire opened her mouth, a torrent of questions ready to spill forth. She needed answers – about Elena, about their past, about what all this meant for their future. But before a single word could escape her, two of Elena's men materialized at their sides.

"Madame, please," one said, extending his hand to assist Violet onto the back of a waiting horse. His companion offered the same courtesy to Claire, who hesitated only for a moment before accepting, her mind still reeling from the revelations and the sudden urgency of their departure. She had no choice but to trust in the enigmatic sister she'd just discovered. Claire felt exhilaration. Was this her life now – an unscripted adventure?

JP dismounted his horse and approached Gaul's corpse. Even in death, he seemed to exude a malevolent aura, a final echo of the wickedness that had defined his life. While JP ordinarily believed every life held value, the sight of Gaul's spirit stilled in death gave him a resounding feeling of justice done. He nudged the body with his foot, causing it to roll onto its side. He reached into Gaul's pocket and retrieved the pendant. Using his fingers to wipe off the dirt and the blood, JP turned and walked towards Claire, who sat atop her horse, her eyes fixed on him. He held the pendant out to her, but Claire's hand remained at her side, hesitation clear in her eyes. The pendant, once a symbol of her heritage, now seemed tainted by the strife it had brought into her life.

Sensing Claire's reluctance, JP spoke softly. "In the end, what matters is not the world's darkness, but how we choose to cherish the memories of those who have come and gone."

A gentle smile played on his lips as he patiently waited, the pendant still extended towards Claire.

Elena, observing her sister's uncertainty, intervened. "Jean-Philippe, give it to me," she instructed, her voice calm but firm. JP complied, placing the pendant in Elena's outstretched hand. She examined the pendant before tucking it away in her pocket.

The moment was broken by the calls of Elena's men, urging the group to move forward. As one, the company began to ride, leaving behind the treacherous land of Rouen and the dark chapter it represented in their lives.

33

Mortimer paced the length of his grand chamber, footsteps echoing off the stone walls with the cadence of a metronome gone mad. The noise disturbed the peaceful rest of the hounds. Sensing their owner's agitation, they moved to a quieter spot, leaving Mortimer alone. For the hundredth time, he checked the ornate clock perched above the mantelpiece, its hands inching forward ever so slowly, mocking him with each tick.

"Where in the devil's name is Gaul?" he muttered, his patience worn thin.

Mortimer stopped mid–stride and turned to gaze out the open window, the fresh air brushing against his sallow cheeks, doing nothing to soothe the rising storm within him. A gust of wind slammed the shutters shut, causing him to flinch, but a sudden urgent rapping at the door drew his piercing gaze away from the horizon.

"Enter," he commanded, his voice sharp.

The door swung open, revealing a disheveled messenger, panting heavily, his eyes wide with dread. "My Lord," he gasped, "there's been ... it's about Gaul."

"Speak!" Mortimer snapped, his fingers curling into fists.

"He and his men were ... found dead just a few miles from here. Ambushed, it seems."

Mortimer towered over the quivering figure.

"Dead? Ambushed?" his voice lowered to a growl. "By whom?"

"We are still gathering information. They were discovered by a local farmer ..."

Mortimer's rage exploded. "I am surrounded by imbeciles!"

He slammed his fist down on the table, causing maps and scrolls to scatter in all directions.

"What is the status of our defensive preparations?" he demanded.

"All men are on high alert at their posts. In addition, we have recruited fifty more men to strengthen the castle's defenses," the soldier responded anxiously.

"Fifty? That's not enough!" Mortimer seethed, paranoia consuming him. "I want more men. Double it, no – triple it!"

Mortimer's master plan was falling apart at an alarming pace. Without Claire, things could spiral out of control quickly. Keeping her alive was a mistake. With Louis and Gaul dead and lacking crucial information as to why, he could not strategize effectively. Time was running out, especially with news of Napoleon breaking free from exile. Mortimer despised loose ends, and Claire was now one of them - a dangerous one that could expose his entire facade.

Sentinels' shouts shattered the silence around the castle as a small army of thirty soldiers marched towards the gates, their banners emblazoned with Napoleon's insignia.

"Open up in the name of the emperor!"

A shiver shot down Mortimer's back as he considered the worst possible outcome. What if Napoleon had found out about how he mistreated Claire? But how could he have found out so quickly? Meanwhile, the captain of the guards stood frozen in indecision. It was a test: should he prove his loyalty to Mortimer and keep the gates shut, or submit to Napoleon and open them?

"Open in the name of your emperor! I will not ask twice. Failure to obey will be seen as an act of treason!"

In the nick of time, the order to comply came straight from the gasping mouth of Mortimer's messenger. The commander signaled to unlock the gates and allow Napoleon's soldiers to enter. They stormed through the fortress walls.

Mortimer stood on the parapet, his piercing gaze locked on the small army entering his fortress. The dull echo of hooves against the cobblestone courtyard sliced through the tense silence that had settled over Rouen Castle like a thick fog. The banners they bore fluttered in the wind – a sea of blue, white, and red that spoke of their allegiance to Napoleon Bonaparte.

The contingent came to a halt. A man of commanding presence dismounted, his uniform adorned with rank embellishments. He glanced around, surveying the towering walls of the fortress as he confidently walked towards the castle's main door and requested an audience with Mortimer.

"Marquis de Rouge," the commander began, "I bear orders directly from Emperor Napoleon. He summons you into his presence."

"Does he now?" Mortimer's tone was laced with a dangerous edge, yet his expression remained calm. "As far as I know, he is not emperor anymore."

"Your loyalty to France is not in question, surely?" the officer challenged, narrowing his eyes.

"Nor is my commitment to my safety," Mortimer countered smoothly. "Given recent ... events, I am reluctant to leave my stronghold. I'm sure you'll understand."

"Nevertheless," the man insisted, "the Emperor expects your immediate compliance." He extended a sealed letter bearing Napoleon's insignia.

Mortimer's lips twisted into a sinister smirk as he gently took the letter, breaking the seal and scanning its contents with a practiced eye for any hint that his standing was in jeopardy. To his relief, Napoleon was merely asking for his assistance in reclaiming power. The letter expressed gratitude to Mortimer for finding Claire, and offered him men to escort them back to Paris. Mortimer knew compliance with this suggestion was no longer possible, but he had no intention of explaining why not. He needed time to devise a plan that would maintain his facade and keep his secrets hidden.

"Tell the Emperor we will come," Mortimer replied, folding the letter.

"The orders are to accompany you myself," the commander insisted.

Mortimer's face lit up with a smile.

"I am deeply obliged, Commander, and I would accept without hesitation under normal circumstances. However," he said, his voice dropping to a whisper, "I fear for your safety within these walls. You see, there are rumors of traitors among us."

"Traitors, Marquis? Where?" the commander asked in confusion, but before he could utter another word, a sharp blade severed his jugular. Mortimer's brand-new commander stepped away from the bleeding body.

"Well done," said Mortimer dryly. 'Though I believe I told you to await my signal."

"Apologies sir. I thought –"

Mortimer calmly stroked his eyebrow and gave a subtle nod. With a thunderous creak, the heavy gates sealed shut behind the unsuspecting visitors, trapping them inside.

"*That* was the signal," he said. Pouring himself a measure of cognac, he added, "Kill them all. Not a single soul leaves this castle alive."

His soldiers sprang into action, their movements swift and precise. Mortimer watched from his window. There would be no audience with Napoleon today, only a message delivered through absence.

"Form up! Shield wall!" a voice commanded from within the ranks of the besieged. Arrows rained down, finding their marks with deadly precision, and the shield wall of thirty men crumbled under the relentless assault. Steel clashed against steel, bullets echoing through the stone corridors of Rouen Castle as the massacre continued. The walls, once the proud ramparts of

Mortimer's ancestors, were splattered with crimson, each droplet a testament to his brutality.

A haunting silence settled over Rouen Castle as the flagstones ran red with the blood of Napoleon's men, their bodies strewn about like broken dolls discarded by a petulant child. Breathing heavily, Mortimer surveyed the carnage, his steely gaze taking in the result of his grim work. This castle, his legacy, would not fall today – not to Napoleon, and not to any who dared challenge him.

"Time to clean up!" Mortimer commanded, his voice echoing off the blood–stained walls. "Burn the dead. Let no trace of them remain. This never happened!"

34

Elena's command to halt their journey echoed through the weary group, bringing a momentary respite. Claire sagged with relief. Her muscles ached from hours in the saddle, but her mind was still buzzing with unanswered questions. The forest around them seemed to close in, its shadows deepening as the sun dipped lower on the horizon. As she watched the men tend to the horses and prepare a fire for dinner, she noticed Pierrick and JP helping Richard off his horse. They settled him against the gnarled trunk of an ancient oak, its sprawling branches offering a semblance of shelter.

Claire's gaze lingered on Richard, her heart constricting at the sight of his makeshift bandages now stained with blood. The events of their narrow escape played on repeat in her mind, each flash of memory bringing fresh waves of anxiety. A rumble from Claire's stomach broke through her reverie, reminding her of more mundane concerns. The aroma of dried meat and herbs began to permeate the air as someone – she couldn't tell who in the growing darkness – began preparing their meager rations.

As if sensing her turmoil, Elena's eyes met Claire's across the makeshift campsite. There was a softness there, a flicker of understanding that momentarily soothed Claire's frayed nerves. She took a deep breath, inhaling the scent of pine and woodsmoke, and squared her shoulders. There would be time for questions later. For now, they needed to focus on survival. With renewed purpose, she moved towards Richard, intent on offering what aid she could.

"How are you feeling?" Claire asked Richard.

"I'm okay. Just a scratch," he replied, wincing in pain as Pierrick helped him find a more comfortable position.

"Do you need anything?" Claire asked, genuinely concerned.

"A kiss?" Pierrick suggested.

Overhearing this, Gerard scowled.

"What? What did I say?"

Pierrick shrugged as Claire smiled awkwardly and quickly gave Richard a peck on the cheek before walking away.

It wasn't long before she found her grandmother. Sitting beside Violet, Claire felt confused and unsure of what to say. It was unlike Violet to be silent and distracted, and it only added to Claire's inner turmoil. She desperately tried to organize her thoughts, but before she could speak, one of the men interrupted with bread and cheese. Grateful for the distraction, Claire accepted with a gentle smile and a thank you.

"Do you want some water?" Violet asked, breaking her silence.

Claire realized then how thirsty she was and eagerly accepted.

"You might need something stronger than that."

Elena stood over them and offered a wineskin, which Claire grasped in both hands. She immediately regretted it when the strong liquor burned her throat.

"How can you drink this?" Claire handed the wineskin back to Elena, who laughed at her sister's reaction.

"You get used to it," Elena replied with a smirk as Claire continued coughing. Her eyes shifted uneasily from Claire to Violet.

"So, how are you feeling, Grandmother? Gosh, it feels so strange to even speak that word. It was never part of my vocabulary ... until now," Elena rambled, coming to sit beside them.

Violet smiled and reached out a hand to tenderly caress Elena's cheeks. Claire, on the other hand, could handle the mystery no longer.

"Why are you acting so strange, Nana? And why did you say, 'Is it really you?' Did you know I had a twin?"

Violet leaned back, closing her eyes as if trying to contain an emotional storm. Elena grasped Claire's hand and tried to ease her nerves. She then turned to Violet and gave her hand a reassuring squeeze.

"Whenever you're ready, we'll listen," Elena said calmly, almost as if she knew something that Claire didn't. Emotions were running high for Claire. Violet seemed to resign herself to telling the story.

"When your mother gave birth ..." Violet paused and took a sip of water. "Maybe I need to go back even further."

"Tell me," Claire begged.

"Many years ago, we owned a small tavern far from here. It wasn't unusual for us to host soldiers and commanders, but that one night when Napoleon came ... something in your mother changed." Violet's voice filled with regret. She went on. "They were both young and lost in themselves. I never understood what she saw in him. I tried to warn her as any mother would, but she wouldn't listen. She ... she ... your mother was a stubborn woman."

Violet smiled sadly, taking a deep breath.

"Anyway, when we found out she was pregnant, we tried to keep it a secret. It wasn't good for a young, unmarried woman to be with child. You know how people talk. But she never lost hope that one day Napoleon would come for her. How naive." Violet's voice trailed off as she shook her head in disbelief and sadness.

"One night, our very same JP arrived with an urgent message from Napoleon himself. He handed Anne a letter and a pouch of money. In the letter, Napoleon professed his undying love for her amidst the delicate and dangerous times of his rise to power. He spoke of enemies and danger, but his main concern was for the return of the pendant he had given her. Napoleon gave the pendant to your mother as a symbol of his promise to return, and she treasured it in hopes that he would keep his word. But when JP saw Anne was pregnant, he feared for your mother's safety and the secret she carried, and convinced us to leave immediately. But our escape was short–lived as we soon realized we were being followed. JP risked everything to protect us, and for all I knew, he died that night to save us. It wasn't until a month ago, when he reappeared at the château, that I learned of his fate.

"Your mother and I rode through the night and for days on end until she could no longer bear the journey. In our darkest hour, fate brought us to a kind stranger. He was a doctor, and he offered us a safe place to stay during Anne's pregnancy. With his help, our new life became a lot easier. But as the time grew closer for her to give birth, it became clear that something was wrong, and despite his skill and knowledge, the doctor couldn't save her.

"It was the worst day of my life. I had thought I was prepared to raise a baby and be a grandmother, but in just moments, I lost my only daughter. The responsibility of two newborns seemed too much. Yes, two. My heart shattered into a million pieces as I held your mother's lifeless body in my arms."

Violet's clutched her heart as she revealed the truth to her granddaughters. She could sense their hurt, but couldn't bear to keep this secret any longer. The memory of that fateful night when she lost Anne still haunted her, and she struggled to hold back tears.

"The doctor let me stay a little longer. However, I wasn't strong enough to handle everything on my own. He would talk about how he longed for a child of his own, but his wife passed away before they could have one. So, in my most vulnerable moment, I resolved to give one of you to him to raise as his own, but I was mistaken. I deeply regret it, girls, and I am so, so sorry."

Violet looked deep into Claire's eyes, which had clouded with anger.

"Why didn't you tell me?" Claire cried, her voice trembling. "All these secrets! You had no right to keep this from me. Do you even realize how my life, MY LIFE, has been completely upended because of ... your lies? I've lost count of the times I could have been raped or killed, all because you kept me in the dark. You couldn't even protect me from any of this!"

Claire's tears flowed, unstoppable now that she had let go of her facade of strength. Violet reached out to comfort her, but Claire pushed her away.

"No. No!" she cried. "You had no right!" She stormed away, unable to bear being near her grandmother any longer.

"Claire. .." Violet called after her, but Elena stopped her from following.

"It's okay. She needs some space to process everything," Elena reassured her.

Violet coughed a few times before allowing this was true.

"Let me get something for your cough, Nana. You've been coughing for a while now," said Elena, her eyes full of concern. She glanced toward Nazir, who seemed to have already guessed her intentions.

"I'll be fine, dear. Just a cold from the rough journey," Violet replied, trying to brush off any worries. She didn't want anyone to be concerned about her when more pressing matters were at hand. Just as she spoke, Nazir interrupted with a small cup of green liquid for Violet to drink. She took it gratefully, but couldn't help coughing more at the bitter taste. She thanked Nazir, and Elena held her hand in support.

"Much better," Violet said, forcing a smile. In a sorrowful voice, she asked, "Why are you not angry with me too?"

Elena gave a small smile.

"Well, for starters, I'm one minute older than Claire, and my father told me the truth long ago," she admitted with a hint of bitterness. "I've come to terms it and have moved on."

Violet nodded, grateful for Elena's understanding and support. Elena's expression softened.

"Please tell me about my mother. What was she like?"

As they talked, Violet felt years' worth of secrets and regrets unburdening. It was both liberating and heartbreaking. Elena gently prodded Violet with simple questions about her mother – what she liked to wear, her favorite foods – anything that would keep Violet from recalling more painful memories.

35

Richard watched from afar as Claire stormed away, tears streaming down her face. The men sitting around the fire looked at each other with confusion. She walked quickly, searching for a quiet place, longing for privacy. She found solace under a large oak tree at a safe distance. Elena's men stood guard, giving her space while also watching for potential threats. Richard called out to Pierrick for help getting up, but Gerard warned him to leave Claire alone. Ignoring the warning, Richard heaved himself up. He found Claire with her head doubled over between her legs, sobbing uncontrollably.

Approaching cautiously, Richard stood by her side, not knowing what to do or say.

"I promise I'll be okay," he tried to joke. "You don't need to cry this much for me."

Surprised by his attempt at humor, Claire stopped sobbing and managed a weak laugh.

"That makes me feel better," she said, wiping away her tears and trying to compose herself.

"So ...what a day, huh?"

Claire simply nodded in response.

"Dare I say, you're handling all of this very ... uhh ..." Richard struggled to find the right words.

"Very what?"

"Very well," he quickly clarified. "I honestly don't know how I would ..."

"Are you mocking me?"

"No, no, Claire. Never," Richard backpedaled. "I was just trying to ..."

Claire laughed bitterly.

"I'm teasing you," she admitted. "It's just a lot to take in."

"Yeah ..." Richard sat close to her. "Do you want to talk about it?"

Claire launched into a tirade about how her world had been shattered in the past month.

"Weeks ago, I was just Claire. Now? I'm a walking target in a power play and, apparently, royalty?" She paused, her breath coming in short, angry bursts.

"I've stared death in the face more times than I can count. I've felt hands on me that had no right to be there. And for what? Because my father – the man I thought was a nobody – turns out to be the fucking emperor?"

Claire's laugh was bitter. "And let's not forget a twin sister – and I never knew she existed. All because *grandmother* decided to play... God with our lives."

"I mean, I get that my grandmother wanted to protect me," Claire fumed, "but not even telling me I have a sister? That's just cruel."

Richard tried to offer some semblance of understanding.

"You're right," he said, but Claire's anger wasn't so easily abated.

"Yes, I am," she snapped back, still seething.

After a moment of tense silence, Richard cautiously spoke up.

"But ... what if ... this was meant to happen?"

Claire turned to him with disbelief and anger written all over her face.

"What do you mean?" she demanded.

"I mean, life can be unfair and throw us these horrible challenges," Richard explained, "But maybe things had to happen this way for a reason."

Claire was not convinced or comforted by this perspective. But Richard continued.

"I'm not comparing our situations because yours is undoubtedly much, much harder," he said earnestly, "But my dad also kept a ton of secrets about our mother and his old life from us. And while I may not agree with his decisions, I have to believe he did what he did out of love and wanting to protect us."

Claire listened begrudgingly as he went on.

"And your grandmother loves you more than anything," Richard added. "She would go to war with the entire world for you. Maybe keeping these secrets from you wasn't fair or right, but in the end, she did it out of love."

Claire's eyes softened at this realization.

"Look at everything that's happened to us in just two weeks," Richard said. "Our lives have been turned upside down, and we don't even know if we'll make it through the rest of today alive. I mean look at me, I'm barely alive right now." They shared a laugh. "Do you really want to spend more precious time dwelling on an unfair past, or do you want to spend it on making new memories ... with your grandmother and your sister?"

Claire was overcome with gratitude, and tears filled her eyes again. His brown eyes met hers and he reached to wipe away a stray tear. Time seemed to stand still as a gentle breeze brushed Claire's face. In that moment, she felt more than just gratitude; she felt something deeper, something new she had never felt before. Claire hugged Richard tightly, causing him to yelp in pain.

"Oh, I'm sorry," she gasped, releasing her hold.

"It's okay." Richard smiled before encouraging her to go to her family.

"Thank you, Richard," she said sincerely.

As she stood to return to her loved ones, Claire paused, looking at the young man who had put everything on the line for her. Now, his wisdom had pulled her out of emotional chaos. Before she could second-guess herself, Claire found herself kneeling before him. Her heart raced, its thunderous beat drowning out all other sounds.

"What are you doing?" Richard's voice was soft, tinged with confusion and something else – anticipation?

Claire's mind was a battlefield of desire and doubt. Was this right? Was this wise?

"Right now..." she began, her voice barely above a whisper, "I'm creating a new memory."

Claire leaned in before reason could reassert itself and pressed her lips to Richard's. The kiss was electric and passionate, a release of pent-up emotions and unspoken longings. For a blissful moment, the world fell away. There was no conspiracy, no hidden identities, no looming danger – just two people finding solace in each other.

Claire's eyes fluttered open as they parted to meet Richard's gaze. A bittersweet smile tugged at her lips as reality began to seep back in. This moment, beautiful as it was, couldn't last. They both knew it.

With a final, lingering look, Claire tore herself away. She ran to rejoin her sister and grandmother, her heart pounding with exhilaration and a tinge of regret. Behind her, she left Richard in a daze of newfound happiness, his world irrevocably changed by that single, stolen moment.

He barely had time to process what had happened before Pierrick's voice cut through his reverie, dragging him back to the harsh realities they faced.

"Finally, one of you had the courage to take the first step," he declared, plopping down next to his brother. "Only, it wasn't you. What a disappointment!"

Richard couldn't help but laugh at his brother's audacity, but deep down, he was grateful for his family. Joining his sons, Gerard placed a comforting hand on Richard's shoulder as they sat together, enjoying the rare gift of being a family.

36

The flickering flames of the fire cast a warm glow over the group as they sat around, sharing a meal and some well–deserved relaxation. Elena had strategically placed a few of her men as sentinels to ensure their safety throughout the night. The rich aroma of roasted meat and vegetables wafted through the air, tempting Pierrick to offer unsolicited cooking advice to the designated cook, Byron. However, Byron was not pleased with constant suggestions and muttered for Pierrick to take over the task. Pierrick happily accepted the challenge without hesitation, convinced that Byron was ruining the dish. Gerard and Richard chuckled at Pierrick's boldness while Byron waited for Pierrick to *improve* his creation. In no time, Pierrick added the finishing touches and had the cook taste it. Byron tried to find something wrong, but it was undeniably better.

"Fine, fine. You win. Now you get to help me serve everyone," he said, playfully bumping Pierrick as they filled plates and mingled with the group – laughing, telling stories, and sharing toasts for fallen comrades and friends.

All night, Richard kept stealing glances at Claire. Noticing this, Elena asked Claire whether anything had happened between them and Claire, blushing, confessed in vivid detail.

"Looks like you're in love, sister," Elena remarked.

Claire hesitated. "Maybe ... I don't know. I've never been in love."

"Well, he seems like a nice guy, and he's willing to risk his life for you. That's hard to find these days," Elena said, genuinely happy for her.

"And what about you, Grandmother? What about that Gerard? He seems to like you," Elena boldly asked Violet.

"Oh goodness, child, at my age? Oh no!" Violet exclaimed in surprise.

"Why not, Nana? He's perfect for you. Handsome and ... single," Claire chimed in, joining forces with her sister.

Violet tried to brush off their teasing, but their giggles caught the attention of Gerard and his companions. He shared a smile with Violet, causing Claire and Elena to exchange knowing looks and tease their grandmother further. The teasing banter was interrupted by Pierrick's boisterous voice from across the fire.

"So, Elena, how did you end up with this small army of men?"

"Pierrick, why do you always have to be like this?" Richard scolded him.

"What did I say? It's a fair question. Aren't you curious? I mean, just look at her; she looks like a ..." Pierrick trailed off as he noticed all eyes were now on him. He tried to backtrack and hide in silence, but Elena pressed on.

"What do I look like, Pierrick?"

"I ... I don't know," he stammered, trying to save face.

"A pirate? Is that the word you were looking for?" Elena finished for him, her voice laced with amusement.

Two of Elena's men stepped forward with menacing expressions, causing Pierrick to shrink back and mumble something incoherent. After a few interminable seconds of silence, the whole crew erupted into boisterous laughter. Pierrick, feeling a little disoriented, sat in silence, disappointed. Elena's laughter only added to his confusion.

"Come on, Pierrick," she said, sensing his discomfort. "Don't be such a grump. We're just having some fun."

Pierrick remained silent, not appreciating being the target of their amusement.

"Come closer so I don't have to speak so loudly," Elena beckoned, ready to tell her story. "As you all know by now, I am Claire's *secret* sister."

"Yeah, you two do have some similarities," Richard teased with a wink.

Elena's eyes sparkled with nostalgia and pride as she recounted her extraordinary childhood.

"My father," she continued, "was no ordinary doctor. He was a seeker of knowledge, a healer who believed that wisdom knew no borders."

She described how her father's insatiable curiosity led them from the bustling markets of Marrakech to the serene temples of Kyoto, from the icy fjords of Norway to the lush rainforests of the Amazon. In each place, he would immerse himself in the local healing traditions, learning ancient remedies and cutting-edge techniques alike.

"He had this… gift," Elena continued, gesturing animatedly. "He could walk into a village where no one spoke his language, and within days, he'd be trading jokes with the local healer and discussing the medicinal properties of plants I couldn't even pronounce."

His reputation grew with each life he saved, where grateful maharajas showered him with gifts and days in humble villages where their payment was nothing more than a warm meal and heartfelt blessings.

"But it was never about the money for him," she said, her voice softening. "The real treasure was the knowledge he gained, the lives he touched."

As their travels continued, her father's dream of owning a ship began to take shape. With the funds from his more affluent patients, he purchased a modest vessel, christening it *The Hippocrates* in honor of the father of medicine. But it wasn't long before *The Hippocrates* became more than just a medical ship.

"He had this… fire in him," she said, "Any injustice, any cruelty he witnessed was like a physical pain to him. He couldn't stand by and watch the strong prey on the weak."

Whether it was standing up to corrupt officials, rescuing enslaved people from brutal captors, or protecting villages from marauding bandits, he never hesitated to act. "It wasn't always the smart thing to do," Elena admitted with a rueful smile. "But it was always the right thing. And people noticed."

Those he saved, inspired by his courage and kindness, often chose to stay with us. A motley crew of formerly enslaved people, reformed criminals, and grateful patients began to form around her father, each bringing their own skills and stories to the ship's growing legend. "We became a floating sanctuary and... a small army."

"As the years passed," Elena continued, "our crew grew larger, and so did my father's ambition to right the wrongs of the world. He shifted our focus to trading. Trading became our cover and our means. We'd sail into a port ostensibly to barter goods, but our real mission was to right the wrongs we encountered. My father's legacy wasn't just the lives he saved or the injustices he corrected – it was this family he created"

"So, are you traders or pirates then?" Pierrick interjected, feeling confused.

"If you want to simplify it, I suppose you could say we are '*good pirates*.' We only target those who have wronged others and we never harm innocent people. It's shocking to see the extent to which wealth has been stolen from innocent people, the families torn apart due to humanity's insatiable desire for power and riches. We simply try to level the playing field."

"But aren't you afraid of getting caught by the law?" Richard asked with concern.

"What law?" Elena scoffed. "We don't belong to any government or country. We are a self–sufficient group, and that makes us both dangerous and invisible. My father was a wise man who had a deep understanding of humanity. He firmly believed that with good fortune comes a responsibility to give back. He found his unique way of making a positive impact. Never mistake my father's kind heart for naivety: he was just as ruthless as he was compassionate."

Elena paused, her gaze distant as she continued her story.

"As we traveled around the world, we heard many stories – legends, prophecies, tall tales. But now and then, one would turn out to be true. Such was the case when we stumbled upon Nazir. His entire battalion and their families had been slaughtered while escorting a powerful stone for their king. They paid with their lives for the knowledge they possessed."

Elena's voice grew softer, almost sorrowful. "Nazir had barely managed to escape with his life when we found him being pursued by a small army."

Richard and Pierrick turned towards Nazir, who remained motionless as he listened to his story, head bowed.

"Nazir told us he'd been transporting a powerful stone with the ability to manipulate reality according to one's desires. My father recognized that if such a power were real, it could be a formidable weapon in correcting injustices. He decided to investigate further. Throughout our journeys all around the globe, we encountered tales of bizarre occurrences and inexplicable happenings, all seemingly connected to this powerful stone. As we delved deeper, he started to believe that more than just one stone was involved in these events. However, every tale we encountered that revolved around this *force* ended in death and destruction. Despite this, my father's curiosity only intensified. We spent years searching for answers, even up till his dying day. I found it all a little hard to believe, but I would've done anything to make my father happy.

"Before he passed, my father revealed to me that I had a sister – a part of the story he had always left out. He knew me well enough to know I wouldn't rest until I found her. The only knowledge he had of her whereabouts was that she resided in France. When he died, I took over the family business and started to search for Claire. We planted informants in every tavern and brothel we could find. Eventually, we caught wind of a young girl who matched my sister's description being held captive in the north of France by a powerful man. We followed the trail and learned of her escape with the help of some friends."

Elena turned to address Claire directly.

"At the time, I didn't know for sure it was you, but something urged me to continue pursuing the trail – it was simply unjust what was happening to you. I also had a feeling that your destiny was tied to mine, and it all had something to do with those mysterious stones. So, we set off for the nearest port and followed our latest lead. We trailed behind until at last we spotted your group. We rode as fast as we could once I was certain it was you. The rest, you know."

Silence followed Elena's words as everyone took this in.

"The series of events that have brought us to the present day feel so unreal," remarked Gerard, giving voice to the group's astonishment." It's as if we are merely pieces on a game board controlled by someone else. It's both astonishing and jarring at the same time."

"Don't underestimate the cube's influence," Vincenzo said gravely. He was a man of few words, so when he spoke, everyone listened intently.

"What do you mean? What cube?" Elena asked.

"That magical stone your father was searching for was only one piece of a broken cube more powerful than you can imagine. It is sentient, and it has the ability to swerve things around to rebalance power," Vincenzo explained.

"But none of us possesses a portion of the cube or have been exposed to it. How could it affect us? We don't hold any status or ... power." Gerard said, confused.

"Ah, but that's where you're wrong, my friend," chuckled Vincenzo. "The cube feeds on the desires of its protector, yes, but it also has a will of its own. Anyone can become entangled in its power, and some of you have been exposed to it in some way, directly or indirectly. In our Order, we call this phenomenon the 'Shadows of Power'. It's as impressive as it is terrifying."

"Shadows of Power," Gerard repeated under his breath.

" I can't bring myself to believe that it's true, and I refuse to let a... *piece of rock* dictate my choices," Elena mused.

Others in the group concurred with resounding "Ayes". The idea they were but pawns in an invisible game was overwhelming for them to consider.

"Rather than battling the *if*, I suggest we focus on understanding the *why*," Vincenzo interjected.

"What do you mean by that?" Elena inquired. "Are you suggesting we try to understand why things happened in the past and stop debating whether the cube is actually in control or not?"

"That's precisely what I mean. Once we have an answer to that question, we can either regain control of our lives or, at the very least, gain a better understanding. Something we could all use right now. The extent of coincidences occurring here is quite alarming," Vincenzo stated, his voice serious. "All signs seem to lead to one conclusion: we are all in the cube's spotlight."

Gerard and JP both nodded, comprehension dawning. They could feel something bigger than themselves at play, something they couldn't fully comprehend, and they wanted answers. Gerard couldn't help but reflect on his past actions and how they led him and his family to this moment. His connection to the cube was through Napoleon, and as exciting as this adventure was for him, he couldn't help but regret that his involvement had put his sons' lives in danger.

"Perhaps this is the reason I'm still breathing. Maybe I still have a part to play in some greater scheme," JP pondered.

"I do not have the same level of knowledge as Amir," Vincenzo continued, "but I've been a part of the Order for ten years. And one thing I can tell you is that denying the reality of the cube's power will only hinder your understanding of reality."

Elena shook her head in disbelief. It was hard for her to accept that an unseen force had been shaping all their lives from the beginning. But she also remembered her father's ultimate wish, and thought about the vast impact this force could have in the right hands.

"The big question is: do we want to continue pushing forward into the unknown in hopes of finding answers?" Elena asked, struggling with her doubts.

Pierrick and Richard were captivated by the stories unfolding before them. To them, it all felt like an incredible fairy tale come to life. They listened intently, eager for anyone to divulge more information about the cube's wonders – they wanted to know everything.

Claire, however, shared her sister's concerns. Was she willing to risk her life again? What about the lives of her friends? The past month had been traumatizing; she longed for peace and quiet. But something inside her remained curious and longed to understand the "why." She couldn't help but wonder if her mother and Napoleon had been destined to meet.

37

Violet started to cough.

"Are you okay, Nana?" Claire asked with concern. "You've been coughing a lot lately."

Violet waved off her worries and assured the group she was okay.

"Just something in my throat," she explained, covering her mouth as she coughed again and again. When she removed her hand, there were tiny dots of blood on it.

"Nana, you have blood on your mouth ... and your hands. What happened?" Claire exclaimed, growing more concerned by the second.

Elena reached out a hand to feel her grandmother's forehead and confirmed her fears – Violet had a high fever. Calling for Nazir, Elena asked him to treat her grandmother, who was once again coughing harshly. Despite all her efforts to downplay it, Violet could no longer deny that this was more than just a simple cough.

"How long have you been coughing like this?" Nazir asked as he checked Violet's pulse.

"I don't remember exactly ..." Violet continued to cough until suddenly, she fainted.

"Nana! Oh my God, Nana!" Claire cried out, frantically trying to revive her.

The rest of the group gathered closer to see what was happening, but Elena urged them to give Nazir space to work.

"She's unconscious. Her heartbeat is weak, and she needs rest," Nazir assured Claire, causing her to release a breath she didn't know she was holding. Locking eyes with the sorrowful Nazir, she understood that her grandmother's condition was advanced.

Gently placing a hand on Claire's shoulder, Elena invited her to let go of their grandmother's hand and allow Nazir to care for her. Nazir instructed some men to bring soft covers to make the ground more comfortable for Violet. He carefully opened her mouth and administered some medicine before gently closing her mouth again.

Claire's eyes were tearing up as she asked her sister, "What's wrong? Will she be okay?"

Elena hugged Claire tightly. "Claire, I'm not sure how ... to say this," she whispered.

Confused, Claire released herself from her sister's embrace and asked, "Say what?"

Taking a deep breath, Elena explained, "I know something of medicine myself, my father taught me well. Our grandmother has pneumonia, and it's in an advanced stage."

"What does that mean? Is she going to die?" Claire pleaded.

Elena struggled to find the right words, but was interrupted by Violet coughing softly in the background.

"Nana!" Claire ran to Violet's side and knelt beside her.

Violet smiled weakly at Claire, almost as if she knew her time was near.

***

The hours that followed were the most heartbreaking time of Claire's life. She clung to her grandmother, praying for a miracle. Claire's mind raced

— afternoons spent baking in the sun-drenched kitchen, nights curled up listening to Violet's fantastical stories, the comforting scent of lavender that always clung to her grandmother's clothes. Each memory was a dagger to her heart, a stark reminder of what she stood to lose. Gerard wanted to comfort Claire, but he knew it was best to give her and Elena as much time as possible with their beloved grandmother. He instructed his sons to give them space and pray for a miracle. However, deep down, he understood that Violet's condition was a death sentence, especially considering all the emotional and physical turmoil she had endured in the past weeks.

Elena turned to Nazir, hoping his knowledge and expertise could buy them more time.

"How much time do you think she has? Is there any way we can bring her with us on the ship?" she asked beseechingly.

Nazir looked at Elena, trying to think of a solution.

"I know this is not what you want to hear, but I don't think she will make it through the night. Not at her age. Not after everything she's been through," he replied gently.

Elena felt a wave of sadness and anger. She couldn't accept losing her grandmother like this, with no control over the situation and so soon after finding her. All she could do was spend whatever precious time Violet had left at her side. Nazir prepared a potion to ease Violet's pain, which Elena brought to her. Elena's men had made a comfortable bed for Violet under the stars.

Taking a deep breath and wiping away her tears, Elena joined Violet and Claire. "Hey there, how are you feeling?" she asked gently.

Violet looked at the small glass in Elena's hand.

"Is that for me?" she asked weakly.

Elena nodded and handed her the liquid, helping her drink it with Claire's assistance.

"It will help with the pain," Elena assured her.

"Thank you, my dear."

The heavy silence weighed down on them all, causing Claire to break down in tears while Elena tried to remain strong for both of them.

"I can't lose you, Nana. How would I handle this life if you're not here?" Claire sobbed, her heart breaking.

"My darling, I will always be with you. In every story you write, and every challenge you face. I will be there watching over you."

Claire's grip tightened on Violet's frail hand as her grandmother's words hung in the air, each syllable a precious gift. The fire's soft glow cast long shadows across the grass. Violet's eyes sparkled with an inner light as she gazed at Claire.

"My darling girl," she said, in a voice barely above a whisper, "I thought the weight of the truth ... it was mine to bear. I thought by keeping it from you, I could shield you from the pain, the responsibility. But I see now that was my mistake. You are stronger than I ever gave you credit for. You have always been destined for greatness. From the moment you took your first steps, tottering across every room, I knew you would leave your mark on the world. I'm so proud of you. So, so proud."

Claire choked back a sob as memories of her life with her grandmother flooded her mind: the farmhouse, Willy, Monsieur Émile ...

"Elena, my dear Elena."

Violet's frail hand reached out, trembling slightly as she cupped Elena's cheek.

"Being able to see you again, even for a brief moment, is a blessing beyond words. You have grown into a remarkable and resilient woman, and I am so proud of you. But remember this: true strength lies not in building impenetrable walls around our hearts, but in having the courage to be vulnerable. Allow yourself to feel, to hurt, and to love."

At this, the dam Elena had built around her heart ever since her father's death began to crack. She had always been the pillar of strength, the one who held everything together when the world seemed to be falling apart. Tears, hot and unrestrained, streamed down Elena's cheeks. She let out a sob that seemed to come from the very depths of her soul. It was a release of all the pain, fear, and uncertainty she had bottled up for so long. At that moment, she wasn't just crying for the impending loss of her grandmother, but for every moment she had denied herself the luxury of vulnerability.

Violet's eyes sparkled with unshed tears as she watched the two young women before her.

"I see so much of your mother in both of you," she said, her gaze moving back and forth from Elena to Claire. "Her spirit lives on in you, in your kindness, your resilience, and your care for others. Promise me ... that you will always take care of each other."

"I promise," Claire whispered, her voice thick with emotion. Elena nodded, unable to form words through her tears.

Violet's lips curved into a soft smile and she breathed her last: "I ... love ... you!"

At that moment, time stopped. A gentle breeze swept through the air, as if carrying away Violet's soul. The two sisters clung to each other, their sobs echoing in the suddenly empty space. The void left by Violet's departure was palpable; a physical ache resonated through their bodies. Yet, amid their grief was a thread of comfort – the knowledge that Violet's love would forever be a part of them, guiding them through the darkest times.

38

As the first rays of morning began to warm the desolate fields, Gerard and Pierrick dug a grave beneath an ancient, gnarled oak, its branches reaching out like protective arms. With heavy hearts and tear-filled eyes, they laid Violet's body to rest and covered it with dirt. Each handful of earth felt like another goodbye. Everyone stood silently, the weight of their loss palpable in the crisp morning air.

Amidst the solemn silence, Pierrick sang a sweet melody in honor of Violet's memory. In that bittersweet moment, his gentle voice became their only solace. They mourned the passing of a remarkable woman whose absence forever left an irreplaceable void in their lives.

The wind carries notes of sorrow,
One of the flowers is no more
The rain will bring us the memory,
Reminding us we are but dust
But the night will have a new star,
It will show our path in the dark.
The wind carries notes of sorrow,
To gift us a new tomorrow.

An overwhelming sense of gratitude filled the stillness.

"Thank you, Pierrick. That was beautiful." Gerard's words hung in the air, tenderly acknowledging the shared pain and love that bound them all together.

"I can't believe she's gone," Claire whispered. The world around her felt alien and intimidating. "What will I do without her?"

"Claire, I am here." Elena's voice was soft yet firm, her warm and steady hands held Claire's cold, trembling ones.

"Where is here? I don't belong in your world," she protested.

Elena's eyes softened, filled with a mixture of empathy and determination. She reached out, her touch gentle as she cupped Claire's face.

"We don't need to figure this out right now," Elena murmured, her thumb gently wiping away a tear. " But know that I will take care of you. You are my family. My family!"

Elena pulled Claire into a warm embrace, and in that moment, Claire felt a flicker of something beyond grief – a sense of belonging. Claire nodded, her head nestled in the crook of Elena's neck. She inhaled deeply. It wasn't closure, not yet, but it was a start. In Elena's arms, in this moment of quiet understanding, she found a glimmer of strength to face the uncertain future.

***

All morning, Richard struggled with the urge to comfort Claire in her time of need. He wanted to wrap his arms around her and remind her that he was there for her. But every time he went to approach her, it never seemed like the right moment. Claire sat quietly by Violet's grave, deep in contemplation. The ancient oak tree was an oasis of shade under the warm sun.

Meanwhile, Elena's men were packing up camp and getting ready to depart. Elena settled beside her sister, the fresh grass fragrant beneath them.

"Claire," Elena began, her voice soft yet firm, "there's something important we need to do before we can move forward."

Claire turned to Elena. "What do you mean?" she asked.

Elena took a deep breath, choosing her words carefully.

"We need to meet with Napoleon," she said.

Claire's brow furrowed, her eyes wide with surprise.

"Why?" she asked, her voice stronger now and tinged with a note of defiance.

Elena reached out, gently taking Claire's hand in hers.

"Think of it as the final chapter of your old life before we start writing a new one. Meeting Napoleon face-to-face will allow you to address the years of absence and unanswered questions. It's a chance to look him in the eye and show him the strong women we've become without him. Finally, by revealing the truth about Mortimer, we can ensure our safety moving forward. Napoleon has the power to neutralize that threat, giving us the freedom to start anew without looking over our shoulders.

"Claire, no matter how this meeting goes, it will provide a sense of resolution. Also, remember what Nana said? Napoleon spent years searching for our mother, and, she did love him and hoped to see him again. In a way, by meeting with him, we're honoring her memory."

As Elena spoke, Claire's expression softened. The tension in her shoulders eased slightly. Elena continued, her voice gentler. "I know it's daunting, Claire. But remember, we're doing this together. You're not facing him alone."

Claire sat quietly for a moment, processing Elena's words. When she finally spoke, her voice was quiet but resolute.

"You're right," she admitted. "As much as I'd like to sail away and forget everything, I know we can't truly move on until we do this."

Elena squeezed her sister's hand, a small smile on her lips. "That's my brave little sister," she said, her voice filled with pride and affection.

"You were born just one minute before me."

"That makes me one minute wiser," Elena shot back.

"Ok, so what's the plan, big sis?" Claire playfully retorted.

"Jean-Philippe left a few hours ago with some of my men. They could return at any moment," Elena explained.

"Here? How?" Claire's nerves frayed at the thought of facing Napoleon without time to prepare.

"Napoleon's army is camped nearby. Jean-Philippe knows Napoleon, and he brought your pendant with him. That pendant carries his seal. He will come."

39

Decades had passed since JP had failed in his task, but the sight of the imperial tents stirred a potent mixture of fear and determination within him. Each step felt like a journey through time, bringing him closer to a moment of reckoning he had both dreaded and longed for.

Pierre, Napoleon's trusted general, recognized JP instantly. His eyes widened with a mixture of shock and disbelief, as if he were seeing a ghost materialize from the mists of the past. He ushered JP towards the heart of the camp, where the general awaited.

The moment JP stood before Napoleon, time seemed to stand still. His piercing gaze, still as sharp and commanding as JP remembered, bore into him with an intensity that threatened to unravel the carefully constructed narrative he had prepared. As he began to speak, sharing the fruits of his long absence, he felt the threads of fate tightening around them all.

Napoleon listened with an eerie calmness, his face an inscrutable mask. When JP mentioned Claire, a flicker of emotion passed across his features. A deep, haunting sadness. The revelation of Elena's existence truly surprised him.

Yet the true test lay ahead. As JP steeled himself to reveal Mortimer's betrayal, the air in the tent grew thick with tension. He could almost see the gears turning behind Napoleon's eyes, recalculating alliances, reevaluating past events in light of this new information.

"Lies and deceit," he muttered, his voice low and dangerous. "All these years..."

Though decades delayed, JP knew that his mission was finally nearing completion. But as they drew closer to the camp where Claire and Elena waited, he wondered if fate had one last role for him to play in this grand, terrible drama. He couldn't shake the feeling that this was not an end, but a beginning.

***

The sound of hooves pounding against the ground grew louder. A sharp whistle signaled the return of Elena's emissaries, spreading an ominous tension throughout the camp.

"You ready?" Elena whispered to Claire.

Her fingers moved swiftly, tucking stray hairs into place. Claire mirrored her actions, her heart pounding. The sisters stood side by side, their shoulders barely touching, as they faced the approaching cavalcade. The thundering of hooves grew louder, and a cloud of dust rose on the horizon, heralding the arrival of a small army. As the dust began to settle, a sea of uniformed men surrounded the camp, their presence both intimidating and awe-inspiring.

Amidst the commotion, one figure stood out – a rider atop a magnificent white stallion. The horse moved with grace and power, its coat gleaming in the sunlight as it slowed to a stop mere feet from where Elena and Claire stood. Atop this majestic beast sat Napoleon Bonaparte himself.

The camp fell into a stunned silence, all eyes drawn to the imposing figure of the former emperor. Even at the ebb of his power and influence, his presence was overwhelming. He sat solidly in the saddle, his piercing gaze sweeping across the assembled crowd before settling on the two young women before him. Napoleon's eyes, sharp and calculating, moved from Elena to Claire and back again. His expression was unreadable, a mask of imperial composure that gave no hint of the emotions churning beneath the surface. The sisters, in turn, studied the face of the man they had only known through stories – their father. They watched him dismount his horse.

"Claire ...?" Napoleon asked, his voice carrying the hint of a question.

"That's me," Claire confirmed, struggled to contain her emotional turmoil.

Napoleon's gaze moved to Elena, who stood stiffly, projecting an unimpressed air.

"...and Elena," he said, his tone almost guarded.

Napoleon's imperial mask slipped for a moment, and a genuine smile spread across his face.

"Claire and Elena," he repeated, as if savoring the names. "It's so great to... meet you both."

The words came out haltingly, a far cry from the eloquent speeches he was renowned for. The great emperor, conqueror of nations, seemed at a loss for words in the presence of his long-lost daughters. The sisters exchanged glances, both surprised and somewhat disarmed by Napoleon's apparent discomfiture. It was a side of him they had never imagined, let alone expected. However, the moment of warmth was fleeting. As quickly as it had appeared, Napoleon's smile faded. He drew a deep breath, squaring his shoulders as if preparing for battle.

"Let's talk, shall we?" His tone having regained its confidence and authority, the words came out not as a question but as a statement.

Claire felt a mixture of anticipation and dread coil in her stomach. This was the moment they had been waiting for, yet she felt woefully unprepared now that it was here. She glanced at Elena, drawing strength from her sister's steadfastness.

In a secluded area by the large tree where Violet had been buried, Napoleon motioned for Claire and Elena to sit on a fallen log. His gaze scanned the freshly disturbed soil.

"Someone died?" he asked abruptly.

Claire's eyes immediately welled up with tears, the grief still raw. Napoleon noticed her reaction.

"I'm sorry; I didn't mean to revive any pain," he said, his voice softening with genuine remorse.

"Our grandmother died last night," Claire said softly.

Napoleon took this in.

"I remember her," he said. "She wasn't too fond of me, but she loved your mother very much. I'm sorry for your loss."

His gaze once again scanned both girls.

"You both resemble Anne so much," he said.

Claire wiped away her tears.

"We never had the chance to meet our mother. She died giving birth to us."

Napoleon turned his back to them for a moment and bowed his head.

"I am very sorry to hear that," he said, his voice heavy with regret.

Elena, her patience wearing thin, interjected harshly, "Stop apologizing. We don't need your sympathy."

Napoleon paused, visibly taken aback by Elena's bold response. It was clear he wasn't accustomed to being addressed in such a manner. A flicker of imperial indignation crossed his face for a moment, but he quickly suppressed it.

"Alright," he said, his tone measured. "Then I'll get straight to it."

"We're listening," Claire said, giving Elena a subtle glance. Elena's posture remained tense, but she offered a barely perceptible nod.

Napoleon's eyes softened as he began to speak, his usual commanding presence giving way to the vulnerable demeanor they'd glimpsed when he first laid eyes on them.

"I don't know what you've been told or what you believe about me, but I am not the heartless and ruthless man people often portray me as. I did care for your mother. Very much," he admitted, a hint of sadness coloring his voice.

He paused, his gaze distant as if lost in memory. "She was ... she was a force of nature. A ray of light in this dark world. She made me believe there was hope for someone like me – that I could be normal and loved."

His voice grew quieter, tinged with regret. "I searched for her for a long time after she disappeared, to no avail. I should have kept looking, but I was burdened with ..." He trailed off, overcome with emotion. "As you are aware, I placed great trust in someone I thought was a friend, only to be betrayed by him. I now understand this is why I was never able to find your mother."

Napoleon's expression contorted with anger at the thought of Mortimer's betrayal. Taking a deep breath, he continued, his voice regaining some of its strength.

"I don't intend to justify or explain my actions to you, but even in my absence, know that I cared. I had no knowledge of you ... I certainly didn't know there were two of you."

His eyes moved between Claire and Elena.

"When I learned I had a daughter, I found a new purpose. It gave me the strength to escape my exile and fight back. The world may see my actions as a quest for power and perhaps it is, but the bigger motivation was finding you, and ... I was hoping to see your mother as well."

Claire looked into his eyes, searching for truth in his words. To her surprise, she saw kindness and sincerity there. A small smile formed on her lips.

"I'm starting to understand why my mother fell for you despite my grandmother's discouragement," she chuckled softly.

Napoleon's face lit up with a genuine smile.

"She didn't approve of me, I know," he said, a touch of amusement in his voice.

His expression grew serious once more. "We don't have much time. There are still things I must see through to the end, not just for myself, but for France. It may be hard to comprehend, but many lives depend on what I do next. And as much as I would love nothing more than to leave everything and spend time with you both ... I can't."

The weight of his words hung in the air, a reminder of what else they needed from him.

"We understand more than you realize," Claire said, glancing at her sister for confirmation. Elena remained silent but attentive, her eyes fixed on Napoleon, willing to listen to his perspective despite her reservations. Napoleon's hand disappeared into his pocket, emerging with the pendant that had caused so much turmoil.

"There is something about this pendant that you should know," Napoleon began, his voice taking on a softer tone. "When I gave it to your mother, I was in a different stage of my life and truly planned on returning for her. But fate had other plans."

His fingers traced the contours of the pendant. "This pendant belies its modest appearance; it's more important than either of you could ever imagine."

"We are aware of what it is protecting," Elena interjected, her voice sharp and clear. Napoleon's eyebrows shot up in surprise.

"You do? How?" he asked, taken aback.

Claire took a deep breath, her eyes meeting Elena's. Her sister gave her a reassuring look, encouraging her to speak. Claire's words slowly began to form, flowing with emotion and newfound wisdom.

"I'm led to believe destiny has a plan for all of us, and we must follow the path it sets out for us. These past few months have been a journey of discovery. My entire life has been turned upside down. Everything I thought was true turned out to be a lie." She paused, her eyes distant as she recalled the harrowing events. "I've experienced pain and fear unlike anything before. I've encountered pure evil, the kind you only fear in nightmares. I've faced hunger, thirst, and chill. I've almost been raped and killed more times than I can count. And all because of ..." her voice trailed off, and Napoleon tensed, anticipating her following words.

"All because of you. A father I never knew existed."

Napoleon's face fell, a look of utter powerlessness washing over him – an expression unfamiliar on the face of the once-great emperor. He opened his mouth to speak, but Claire continued, her voice growing stronger.

"But on this journey, I've also traveled further than most people do in a lifetime. I've met the most selfless and courageous people. I've made new friends. I found out about my sister, Elena, whom I never knew existed either." She turned to Elena, taking her hand with a warm smile. Elena squeezed back, a silent show of support. "... and I found love."

Napoleon's expression shifted from guilt to pride. He saw in his daughter the strength and resilience that had once defined him. He felt compelled to offer her guidance.

"Claire," he began, his voice conveying the weight of his years and experiences, "let me tell you this. Don't let anyone dictate how you should live your life or what destiny has in store for you. You are the master of your fate." His eyes blazed with intensity as he continued. "Yes, a path may be laid out for us, but it is blurry and full of grey areas. Think of it as a map leading towards your destiny. How you get there is entirely up to you, and no one else's opinions matter."

Claire's eyes were fixed on the pendant in Napoleon's hand. "Speaking of paths and destinies, each time we attempt to distance ourselves from the power protected by that pendant, strange occurrences bring us back to its orbit. We're connected in ways beyond our understanding."

She glanced at Elena, a small smile tugging at her lips. "That's how I met a sister I never knew I had."

Elena returned the smile. Claire's gaze returned to Napoleon, her expression growing more serious.

"We didn't choose to be born into this dangerous game of power, but here we are."

Napoleon listened intently, his face a mask of concentration as he absorbed every word.

"I'm grateful for the chance to meet you and share whatever this is," Claire continued, her eyes hardening as she came to the crux of her speech. "But all we need is that you take care of Mortimer, the monster who brought so much suffering into our lives."

The mention of Mortimer's name sent a visible ripple through the group. Napoleon's eyes narrowed.

"Mortimer," Napoleon repeated, his voice low and dangerous. "I give you my word that Mortimer will be dealt with."

Just then, a rustle announced the arrival of his trusted general, Pierre: "*Mon général*, I'm sorry to interrupt, but we must leave soon."

"Just a moment," Napoleon said, his tone brooking no argument. His hand quivered as he held out the pendant. "I believe this belongs to you," he said, his voice thick with emotion as he extended it towards Claire and Elena.

Claire's voice was tinged with bitterness as she asked, "Weren't you searching for it all these years?"

"I was. But that was a long time ago. Before I knew ..." Napoleon's voice trailed off, unable to finish the thought.

Elena's sharp tone cut through the air. "Knew what?"

Napoleon sighed heavily.

"It doesn't matter now," he said. "This pendant is more than just a reminder of the past. It's a key to something greater."

"We know it unlocks a safe protecting a powerful stone," Elena said, her voice steady.

"Powerful ..." mused Napoleon. "Yes, I was once drawn to this stone because of its powerful potential. Once it became mine, I believed I would conquer the world, and I almost did. Then I met your mother, and at first, I thought it was just a coincidence. But our connection was undeniable – like two magnets. It wasn't until later that I understood why. The stone wanted us to meet."

Claire, confused, asked, "What do you mean by that?"

Napoleon reached into his jacket, retrieving a leather package. Taking a deep breath, he said: "This was meant for your mother, and now it's yours. Please keep it safe. I wanted to give it to her, knowing she would do better than me."

"Better than you at what?" Elena demanded. "What is this?"

"My encounter with your mother was part of a larger design I cannot fathom. This force of power connects everything ... Everything you need to know is inside here, trust me."

With that, he handed over the leather package. Claire's eyes lingered on her grandmother's grave.

"It sounds dangerous," she said. "The last time you gave something to our mother, her world fell apart."

Napoleon's eyes gleamed. "You've seen firsthand how ruthless and destructive people can be when they have power. Imagine what good you could do if power was yours, and don't be afraid."

As Claire grappled with her conflicting emotions, Elena felt a strong connection to her father's last wish. Despite her confusion, she sensed a greater purpose and was determined to uncover the truth.

"I am not asking for your forgiveness or sympathy," Napoleon went on. "I cannot change anything about the past. But this was meant for your mother, and now it's yours. You are my blood, whether you like it or not. All I ask is that you take this. I know, in time, you will understand."

After exchanging a look with Claire, Elena reached out and took the gift from Napoleon. He nodded and smiled, visibly relieved.

"When you decide to open it, remember this: You are my blood."

Elena gave him a curious expression. "Yeah, I think we already knew that part."

"Unfortunately, the future of this country still rests in my hands. And you both need to leave France for a while. I'm about to shake things up one more time," he chuckled. " I truly hope to see you again, although I'm not sure I will be so lucky."

His smile did little to ease the tension.

"We will leave today," Elena replied, her face expressing steely resolve.

"I notice you have a lot of protection. Do you need more men?" Napoleon offered.

"We're good. We can take care of ourselves," Elena stated.

"I'm sure you can."

Napoleon's gaze softened as he looked at his daughters, his eyes shimmering with pride, regret, and newfound wonder. In Elena, he saw a reflection of his younger self – the fire, determination, and unyielding spirit that had once conquered nations. A bittersweet smile tugged at his lips as he recognized the strength that flowed through her veins, a strength he had unknowingly passed on. Claire, on the other hand, radiated a gentle warmth that pierced through Napoleon's hardened exterior. In her kind eyes and compassionate demeanor, he saw Anne – the woman who had once shown him a different kind of conquest, one of the heart. Claire's presence was a poignant reminder of the love he had let slip through his fingers, a love now reborn in his daughter's gentle spirit.

As he stood before them, Napoleon felt a surge of emotion he had long thought himself incapable of experiencing. These two young women, burnished by adversity, now shone with the perfect balance of his ambition and his lost lover's compassion. They were living testaments to a legacy that transcended his military conquests. His voice, usually commanding and assured, now quivered slightly with emotion.

"For what it's worth, I feel very proud of both of you."

In the silence that followed, the air seemed to vibrate with unspoken emotions. Elena's stoic facade cracked slightly, a flicker of vulnerability crossing her face at her father's unexpected praise. Claire's heart was torn between the joy of hearing these words and the pain of all the years they went unspoken.

For a brief moment, the three of them stood connected by an invisible thread of shared blood and destiny. The past, present, and future converged in that single, precious instant –a family fractured by history, now standing on the precipice of a new beginning. As the seconds stretched on, Napoleon realized that in his daughters, he had found a victory greater than any he had ever achieved on the battlefield. In their eyes, he saw not just his legacy but his redemption.

Turning around for one final glance, his eyes lingering on his daughters. Finally, he strode back to his entourage. In doing so, his gaze met Gerard's, and he paused, a flood of memories washing over him.

"You've gotten old, my friend," Napoleon said, his voice warm with affection as he embraced Gerard tightly.

Gerard chuckled, his eyes twinkling with mirth. "Not so much as you," he retorted good-naturedly.

Their laughter, rich with shared history, filled the air. Gerard introduced his two sons. Pierrick and Richard, visibly nervous, mumbled greetings as they shook hands with the legendary emperor, their awe palpable.

Napoleon's general, ever-mindful of their pressing schedule, urged him to move on. With a nod of acknowledgment, Napoleon turned to Jean Phillipe, his expression softening.

"You know, you could come back with me," Napoleon offered, his tone sincere. "I am truly grateful for everything you've done."

Jean-Philippe's response was measured, his words careful. "*Mon général*, I will always be your loyal servant. But with your permission, I think I have found the best way to serve you."

Napoleon's face broke into a genuine smile.

"I couldn't ask for more," he said, touching Jean-Philippe's shoulder. "I leave them in good hands."

In one swift motion, Napoleon mounted his horse, his posture straightening as he assumed the mantle of leadership again. All eyes followed as he and his army rode off, his presence still commanding respect and a hint of fear.

For a fleeting moment, as the distance between him and his newfound family grew, Napoleon felt a pang of regret for all he had sacrificed in the name of his country. The weight of his choices, the loves lost, and the paths not taken pressed heavily upon him. Was it worth it? The question echoed in his mind, unanswered. Only time would tell, he mused, as he led his men towards an uncertain future, leaving behind a legacy more precious than any empire – his daughters.

As Napoleon's silhouette faded into the distance, Claire's gaze remained fixed on the horizon. Elena, meanwhile, wasted no breath on sentiment. Her sharp and decisive voice cut through the air.

"We move now!" she commanded, her words galvanizing the group into action.

The sisters stood before Violet's grave one last time, their silence a testament to all that had been lost and gained. Elena's hand found her sister's shoulder, a silent promise of protection and unity.

As they mounted their horses, the air thrummed with anticipation. Leather creaked and hooves pawed at the ground, eager to carry them towards their destiny. Claire's eyes met Richard's, a flicker of understanding passing between them. Jean-Philippe nodded solemnly to Elena, ready to follow her lead as they rode not just away from danger but towards something greater – a destiny unwritten.

40

The ride to Le Havre was a race against time as Elena pushed the horses to their limits, determined to avoid any incidents with Mortimer's goons. The sharp cries of seagulls and the pungent smell of fish welcomed the group as they arrived. It was a new and unfamiliar world for Claire, Richard, and Pierrick.

Orders were given, and the men swiftly carried them out. Some headed to the harbor, while others tended to the exhausted horses. Elena led the rest to a nearby tavern which hummed with activity; wooden floorboards creaked under their feet, and the warm glow of oil lamps cast dancing shadows on the rough-hewn walls. The air was thick with the aroma of roasted meats, freshly baked bread, and the pungent scent of ale.

JP's eyes darted nervously around the room. He leaned in close to Elena, his voice barely above a whisper. "Are you certain this is safe? We're exposed here."

Elena's lips curved into a reassuring smile, her eyes gleaming confidently.

"Relax, JP. My men have the entire harbor under surveillance." She gestured to a large table in the corner, partially hidden by a wooden partition. "Besides, sometimes hiding in plain sight is the best strategy."

As they settled into their seats, the tavern keeper approached. He was a portly man with a ruddy face and a welcoming grin. "What can I get for you, fine folks?" he asked, wiping his hands on a stained apron.

"Your best ale," Elena replied, "and whatever hot food you have ready. We've had a long journey."

Pierrick could barely contain his excitement, his eyes wide as he took in the lively atmosphere of the tavern. It was far from the tense, silent ride they had endured for days.

"This is incredible!" he exclaimed, his voice filled with wonder. "I've never been in a place like this before."

Despite his lingering concerns; JP couldn't help but smile at the young man's enthusiasm. He watched as Pierrick's gaze darted from the group of grizzled sailors arm-wrestling at a nearby table to the bard tuning his lute in the corner. As steaming bowls of hearty stew and crusty bread were placed before them, Elena raised her tankard. "To safe arrivals and new beginnings," she toasted, her voice low but filled with warmth.

Amidst the convivial atmosphere, Claire sat motionless, her food untouched, her gaze fixed on some distant point only she could see. Elena, ever observant, noticed Claire's distress. She gently set down her tankard and placed a comforting hand on Claire's shoulder.

"There will be time to grieve," she whispered, her voice low and soothing. The words seemed to break Claire's trance, and she turned to meet Elena's gaze. "But right now, you need to eat something. You've been through so much, and your body needs energy to process everything. We'll take things one step at a time, one day at a time. And I will be here for you every step of the way."

Claire's eyes, brimming with unshed tears, searched Elena's face.

"Promise?" she choked out, her voice barely audible over the tavern's ambient noise.

"Promise," Elena replied, her smile warm and reassuring. The simple word seemed to carry the weight of an unbreakable vow.

Slowly, as if awakening from a deep slumber, Claire reached for a piece of bread. She took a small bite, the warmth of it spreading across her tongue. She took another bite, then another, her body suddenly remembering its hunger. Elena watched with quiet satisfaction as Claire ate.

As the night wore on, the tavern's atmosphere grew more subdued. The bard in the corner strummed a gentle melody, soothing notes weaving through the air. Having finished most of her meal, Claire leaned slightly against Elena's shoulder. Pierrick, his initial excitement tempered by exhaustion, stifled a yawn.

Claire closed the door to her small bedroom and allowed herself to succumb to her exhaustion. The room was dimly lit by a single candle, its flickering light casting long shadows on the walls. Silence enveloped her, a stark contrast to the bustling tavern below. For a moment, she stood there, her forehead pressed against the rough wooden door, as if it were the only thing keeping her upright. Finally, her legs gave way, and she stumbled towards the bed. The mattress creaked as she sat heavily upon it, her body sagging with the weight of exhaustion and grief.

For a brief moment, Claire closed her eyes, relishing the quiet. She took a deep breath, then another, feeling the tension in her shoulders start to ease. But as her defenses lowered, the memories she had held at bay came rushing back. Her grandmother's face, peaceful in death, flashed before her eyes.

A lump formed in Claire's throat as she remembered the hugs she had rushed through, and all the things she'd left unsaid. A simple "thank you" for the countless times her grandmother had been there for her. For the warm meals that always awaited her after a long day, for the gentle wisdom imparted over steaming cups of tea. Tears welled up in her eyes as she thought of all the "I love yous " left unspoken – the depth of her affection, the gratitude for a lifetime of unconditional love and support – all the things she had always assumed there would be time to express. Time lost all meaning as Claire wept. Eventually, exhaustion overtook her, and she fell into a fitful sleep, her face still damp with tears.

***

"Claire!"

Claire groggily opened her eyes and looked up at Elena.

"What? Where?" she mumbled, disoriented. "How long have I been asleep?"

Elena's lips curved into a gentle smile. "You slept through the night," she replied, her voice low and soothing. "It's time to leave."

Claire nodded, her body aching from the awkward position she had slept in. She ran her fingers through her tangled hair, took a deep breath, and stood up. Elena left the room, and Claire took a few moments to gather herself before joining the group downstairs.

The tavern was abuzz with quiet activity as the group prepared for departure. Everyone seemed alert and ready to move, their bags packed and weapons ready. Everyone except for Richard, who stood awkwardly off to the side, unsure of how to approach Claire after the tragedy they had all witnessed. His heart ached to offer comfort, but fear of intruding on her grief held him back.

As Claire descended the stairs, Richard mustered his courage.

"Good morning, Claire," he said, offering a hesitant smile. His voice was soft, almost lost in the tavern's ambient noise.

Claire's eyes met his briefly. She returned the smile. Without a word, she went across the room to sit beside Elena, who immediately placed a protective arm around her shoulders. Richard watched her go, his heart sinking. He couldn't help but steal glances at Claire, noting the dark circles under her eyes.

"Richard!" Gerard's sharp voice cut through the air, startling him from his reverie. But before Richard could respond, a sudden, sharp pain shot through his ankle.

"Ow!" he yelped, stumbling slightly. Pierrick stood nearby, a mischievous glint in his eye.

Gerard's brow furrowed as he looked at his younger son. "Pierrick," he said, his tone a clear reprimand.

Pierrick shrugged, unrepentant.

"He wasn't listening," he said matter-of-factly.

Richard lowered himself into a nearby chair, wincing as he massaged his throbbing ankle. He shot a glare at Pierrick.

"Why did you kick me, moron?" he grumbled, his earlier melancholy replaced by irritation.

"Enough, both of you," Gerard interjected, his voice carrying the weight of authority. He turned to Richard, his expression softening slightly. "Richard, this is a delicate moment for Claire. She is in great hands now, and we've already done everything we could."

Richard's gaze drifted back to Claire, who was now engaged in quiet conversation with Elena. He nodded slowly, understanding Gerard's words but unable to shake the helplessness that had settled over him.

Gerard took a deep breath, knowing his sons would not be pleased with what he was about to say.

"I think it's time for us to return home," he announced.

"What? Home? Why?" Pierrick and Richard's voices collided in a cacophony of indignation.

"Hold on, boys," Gerard said, raising his hands, "I understand your disappointment, but this is no longer just our adventure. We need to be prepared for ... well, to return to our normal lives."

Pierrick and Richard stood there, arms crossed, looking like two disgruntled statues. JP decided to lighten the mood.

"Why the sad face, Pierrick? Not enough food to keep you happy?" JP quipped.

"Ha ha," Pierrick replied sarcastically.

"Father wants us to leave," Richard complained bitterly.

JP raised his eyebrows.

"Well, boys, this isn't up to us anymore," he finally said.

"You too, JP?" Pierrick cut him off. "After all we've been through to-gether, we're just going to be tossed aside like garbage? Like we don't matter anymore?"

"No one is treating anyone like garbage. All I'm saying is –" Gerard began, before Pierrick's whiny voice interrupted.

"That it's time for us to go home," he mocked childishly. "We're not kids anymore. It's unfair, and I don't want to go home."

"What's not fair?" Elena suddenly appeared, her presence catching the group off guard.

Gerard calmly explained the situation to her. She responded with a thoughtful nod.

"Your father is right, boys," she agreed, looking at them sternly. Both Pierrick and Richard were disappointed by her statement. "However, we must consider that your lives may be in danger now. Mortimer will surely seek revenge for all the trouble you've caused him."

The boys looked worried.

"And you did help save my sister," Elena continued, "so and it wouldn't be fair for us to leave you on your own when you may need our protection."

Richard and Pierrick's hope began to flicker back to life.

"I'll assign five of my best men to escort you back."

The boys slumped in defeat.

Elena looked at them seriously before breaking out into a grin and play-fully hitting Pierrick on the shoulder.

"I'm just kidding," she chuckled. "You should come with us ... if you want to, of course."

The boys' faces lit up with excitement, their eyes wide.

"Are you serious?" Richard asked, unable to contain his excitement. Elena nodded slyly. JP couldn't help but grin.

"Of course we would love to!" they chorused. The boys were ecstatic and immediately began proposing tasks they could handle on the ship. But Elena quickly silenced them with a stern warning.

"You will earn your keep on my ship. Now go get ready; we leave soon." With that, she walked away to finish preparations.

Richard's attention suddenly shifted. His eyes locked onto Claire's as she gracefully approached the tavern's exit. Time seemed to slow as he watched the way the morning light caught her hair. With a smooth gesture, Vincenzo held the door open for her to enter first. Richard watched with growing unease as Vincenzo leaned close to Claire, murmuring something lost in the tavern's din. Whatever Vincenzo said, it had the desired effect. A smile bloomed across Claire's face, lighting up her features. Despite his admiration of her beauty, Richard couldn't ignore the twinge of jealousy that gripped him. He knew his reaction was unfounded. Claire was free to talk to whomever she pleased, and Vincenzo had given him no real reason for concern. Richard grappled with his emotions as Claire and Vincenzo disappeared through the doorway, still deep in animated conversation. He was so entranced that he didn't notice Pierrick sneaking up behind him.

"Earth to Richard!" Pierrick bellowed directly into his ear, causing Richard to jump a foot in the air. "Stop mooning over Claire, and let's move!"

Richard's face flushed crimson. "I wasn't – I mean, I was just –" he stammered, but Pierrick was already attempting to stuff an alarming amount of bread and cheese into his bag.

JP appeared at his elbow, eyebrows raised in amusement. "Planning on feeding an army, are we?"

Pierrick looked up, his cheeks bulging with a mouthful of purloined cheese. "You never know when we might need emergency rations!" he protested.

JP chuckled, gently prying a loaf of bread from Pierrick's grasp. "Trust me, lad. There's plenty of food on board."

Pierrick's eyes widened. "Really? Like, how much food are we talking about?"

Before JP could answer, Gerard's voice cut through the chaos. "Alright, boys! Time to move out. The ship won't wait forever."

As the group approached the gangplank, the ship loomed before them. Pierrick released a low whistle of appreciation while Richard's eyes widened in awe. The deck bustled with activity as the crew made their final preparations for departure.

Gerard placed a hand on each of his son's shoulders. "Remember, boys. This isn't a game. We're entering a new world of adventure, danger, and uncertainty."

Pierrick and Richard nodded solemnly as they took their first steps onto the ship. They were embarking on the adventure of a lifetime, and nothing – not danger, not uncertainty, and definitely not their father's well-intentioned warnings – could dampen their spirits.

Gerard watched his sons scamper off to explore every nook and cranny of their new floating home. He couldn't help but feel a swell of pride tinged with nostalgia for his youthful adventures. Whatever lay ahead, he knew one thing for sure - it would be one hell of a journey.

41

The large ship, christened "The Flame," slowly pulled away from the bustling harbor of Le Havre. The salty sea breeze whipped through the air, carrying with it the promise of adventure and the faint scent of danger. The wooden deck creaked beneath the crew's feet as they scurried about, securing ropes and adjusting sails.

Richard and Pierrick stood at the railing, their eyes wide with excitement as they watched the shoreline gradually recede. The reality of their situation was finally sinking in – they were embarking on a grand adventure far beyond anything they had ever imagined.

"All hands to stations!" Elena's voice rang out across the deck. The crew responded efficiently, each person moving to their designated post.

Richard and Pierrick found themselves momentarily lost as The Flame picked up speed, cutting through the waves with purpose. They exchanged uncertain glances, unsure where they fit in this well-oiled machine. JP appeared beside them, a knowing smile on his weathered face.

"Come on," he said, clapping them both on the shoulder. "Shall we explore?"

They followed JP eagerly, climbing the steps to the elevated platform where Elena stood, her keen eyes surveying the horizon. Richard noticed Claire standing alone in the corner of the deck, tears glistening in her eyes as she looked out at the water. He walked over to her, his heart aching for the pain she was still going through.

"How are you holding up?" he asked gently.

She didn't reply but simply shook her head.

"I'm so sorry, Claire. There are no words," he murmured, the phrase feeling hollow even as it left his lips. He felt useless and powerless in the face of her grief.

Claire leaned closer to him, resting her head on his shoulder; Richard's heart quickened, a flutter of nervousness mingling with a deep-seated desire to protect and comfort. Hesitantly, he wrapped his arm around her, drawing her closer. The gesture felt as natural as breathing, as if the universe had conspired to bring them to this moment.

As they stood entwined, the world seemed to fall away. The crash of waves against the ship's hull became a distant melody, the salty breeze a gentle caress. Claire found a moment of respite from the tempest of her grief in the cocoon of their embrace. She released her pain to the sea, letting the endless waters carry it away on their eternal journey.

Claire's thoughts turned to the mysterious package Napoleon had given to her and Elena.

"Part of me wants to see what's inside," she confessed to Richard. "But I'm afraid of what I might find. If one pendant can shake my world so much, I don't know if I can handle something new. I wish I were stronger, like Elena or my mother ... but I'm not."

With infinite tenderness, Richard brushed a wayward strand of hair from her eyes, his touch lingering. "You are not weak, Claire. You are the strongest person I know. And you are not alone."

As Claire looked into his intense brown eyes, she felt herself falling deeper, not just in love, but into a profound connection that seemed to transcend time and circumstance. This man, who saw strength in her when she couldn't see it in herself, was becoming her anchor in a storm-tossed world.

"Maybe it's because you keep saving me," she teased, a hint of playfulness breaking through her melancholy as she took hold of his hands.

Richard's smile was soft, tinged with an emotion too complex to name. "Or maybe it's you who is saving me," he whispered, his face inching closer to hers.

"Saving you? From what?" she asked, curiosity piqued.

"Pierrick, to start with," Richard quipped.

Claire's laughter, though brief, was like music. "Oh, hush. Your brother is a darling," she chided gently, nestling deeper into his embrace.

"From the boring life I had," Richard continued, his tone growing more serious.

"Well, boring right now sounds kind of fun…and safe." Claire retorted with a wry smile, eliciting a chuckle from both of them. But as their laughter faded, Richard's expression became earnest, his gaze intense as he gently tucked a stray lock of hair behind her ear.

"If I had to do it all over again just to be here, right now with you, I would – one thousand times," he whispered.

"You have no idea what you're getting into," Claire warned, her tone playful but her eyes betraying a hint of vulnerability.

Before she could say more, Richard's hand cupped her face, his touch as gentle as a summer breeze. Time seemed to slow as he leaned in, his lips meeting hers in a tender and passionate kiss. The world fell away at that moment, leaving only the two of them suspended in a perfect instant of connection and possibility.

Richard's eyes fluttered open as their lips parted, the world slowly coming back into focus. His moment of bliss was abruptly interrupted by the sight of Pierrick standing nearby, his face contorted in an exaggerated expression of disgust.

"How much is enough for you two?"

Richard and Claire exchanged amused glances as they turned to Pierrick with mock irritation, struggling to suppress their smiles.

Pierrick rolled his eyes dramatically. "Anyway, when you're done doing whatever this is, there's food if you're hungry." He turned on his heel, clearly annoyed at having been delegated the role of dinner herald.

"Thank you," Richard called out, reaching out to pat his brother on the back.

Pierrick shrugged off the gesture. "Thank Elena. I didn't want to come all the way over here."

Claire, her eyes twinkling with mischief, stepped forward. "Thank you, Pierrick," she said sweetly, planting a quick peck on his cheek.

"Eagh!" Pierrick exclaimed, wiping his cheek with exaggerated disgust. Despite his protests, a small smile tugged at the corners of his mouth. The three of them went to the ship canteen amidst jokes and laughter.

As they entered the canteen, they were greeted by the warm glow of lanterns and the inviting aroma of a hearty meal. The long table was laden with various dishes, steam rising from bowls of savory stew and platters of freshly baked bread. Gerard and JP sat at one end of the table; their faces relaxed for the first time in what felt like ages. The constant vigilance of the past weeks had taken its toll, and this moment of peace was a welcome respite. Elena presided over the gathering, her usual stern demeanor softened by the joy of having found a sister. She watched Claire with a mixture of protectiveness and pride, occasionally catching her eye and sharing a silent moment of understanding.

Stories flowed as freely as the wine, and Pierrick regaled the group with increasingly outlandish tales of his "heroic" exploits, much to everyone's amusement. Richard and Claire found their gazes continually drawn to one another. A shared glance, a secret smile, a lingering look – each interaction seemed to heighten the intensity of their feelings. Claire felt her heart race every time their eyes met. The warmth of Richard's gaze seemed to envelop her, making her acutely aware of every inch of space between them. As the night wore on, the laughter and chatter of the canteen faded into a distant hum as Claire's thoughts centered on Richard. All she wanted was to be in his arms again, to lose herself in his embrace and forget the world outside. She watched how his eyes crinkled when he smiled, how his hands moved animatedly as he spoke, and how his lips curved gently while listening intently to others. Each detail only served to deepen her longing. Their eyes met across the table again, and a silent understanding passed between them. The night was still young, and the ship was full of quiet corners where two people might steal a moment alone.

Claire practically leaped into his arms when they met behind a barrel, kissing him with all the pent–up desire she had been holding back.

"Ouch," Richard winced in pain; his wound was still hurting.

"I'm sorry," Claire said with a remorseful expression. "I'll be more careful."

She flashed him an apologetic smile. Richard slowly led her below deck to the storage room. He opened the door and they stumbled inside, Richard falling onto the floor with Claire on top of him. They laughed together before Claire closed the door behind them and walked towards Richard, her hands fumbling to unlace the back of her dress. As she stood before him in nothing but her undergarments, Richard couldn't help but feel like the luckiest man in the world. Without a word, he stood up and pulled her close to him, his hands uncovering every inch of her body as passion consumed them both. Their clothing fell to the ground in tattered shreds, torn away by their intense passion. They lay on a pile of flour sacks. The crashing waves served as a primal beat to their frenzied kisses, fueling the fire burning between them. Richard's hands greedily explored every inch of Claire's body, committing it to memory with each touch. He traced his lips down her neck, savoring the taste of her skin before moving lower to her nipple, teasing it with slow, deliberate kisses.

Claire's hands tangled in Richard's hair, pulling him closer as he ravished her body. Their excitement reached new heights as she sat up and grabbed his face, kissing him deeply and igniting a new level of desire within them both. They lost themselves in each other's touch, letting their bodies take over and surrendering to overwhelming pleasure. As they reached their peak together, cries of ecstasy echoed through the storage room until, finally, they collapsed in a state of utter satisfaction. Laughter bubbled from their lips as they basked in the aftermath of their intimate moment.

Their perfect moment was shattered when the cook, Byron, barged into the storage room. They scrambled to cover themselves, faces flushed with embarrassment as Byron ignored them, nonchalantly filling ale jars. As they hastily dressed and tried to regain their composure, another crew member came in looking for the cheese. Though they were now fully clothed, Claire's hair was still messy, and her cheeks were flushed with post–coital glow. The crew member merely smirked at them before leaving. Realizing that more crew members could show up, Richard suggested that they return to the canteen before anyone else stumbled upon them.

42

Claire and Richard re-entered the canteen, their attempts at noncha-
lance betrayed by their disheveled appearance. Claire's hair was
charmingly tousled, and both their faces bore the telltale flush of recent
exertion. Elena raised a single eyebrow, a knowing smirk playing at the corners of her lips.

"I think it's time we open what Napoleon gave us," Claire said to Elena.

Elena turned to her, surprised. "Now?" She noticed that Claire had
a new energy, a spark of determination.

Claire leaned in closer, a sly challenge in her tone.

"The night is still young," she replied, her eyes glinting excitedly. "Unless
you have other plans?"

Elena hesitated, her gaze flickering between Claire and the rest of
the group.

"Very well," she said, her voice barely above a whisper. She stood up, addressing the room with the authoritative tone of a captain. "If you'll excuse
us, gentlemen, there's a matter that requires our attention."

Elena's hand rested on the door handle, but she didn't immediately open
it. She turned to Claire, her expression serious.

"Are you sure about this?" she asked, giving her sister one last chance to reconsider.

Claire nodded. "We've come too far to turn back now," she said firmly. "Whatever secrets, we face them together."

The two sisters stepped into the captain's quarters, the door closing behind them with a soft click.

The leather pouch was precisely where Elena had left it, tucked away in the bottom drawer of her desk. She placed it on the large wooden table, and they both stared at it. The creaking of the ship on the water seemed louder than usual. Without speaking, Claire opened the package and carefully removed a pack of letters that had been sealed and wrapped in ribbon. On top of the letters, a second pendant glinted in the dim light. They both gasped.

"What are all these letters?" Claire asked as her fingers twitched to tear them open.

"I don't know," cried Elena. "Open them, let's find out."

Claire meticulously unwrapped the lace and unsealed the first letter.

Dear Anne,

My heart aches with the passing of each day. I long to see you again, to hold you tight and never let go. But despite exhausting all my resources and contacts, there is no trace of you. It's as if you vanished into thin air. My trusted friend Mortimer joins in the search, driven by his unwavering determination to bring you back to me. I pray he can succeed where others have failed.

I will never stop searching for you, my dear Anne.

Yours forever.

N

"How could he be so foolish as to trust that despicable man, Mortimer?" Claire burst out.

They opened more letters, searching for something interesting.

"Oh, this one is cute. Listen!" Elena started reading.

My dear Anne,

Every moment I spent with you was a treasure that fills my heart with joy. I replay your laughter in my mind, and it is like a melody that echoes in my mind, lifting my spirits and making even the darkest days brighter. I cling to hope, but sometimes, it feels like a fragile thread in the storm, threatening to snap at any moment. In my darkest moments, doubt creeps in like a thief in the night. Was what we had real? Did I imagine the depth of our connection? But then I remember how your eyes lit up when you smiled at me, the warmth of your hand in mine, and I know that what we shared was genuine and precious beyond measure.

You inspire me to be a better person.

Forever yours.

N

Napoleon's words were a storm of emotions. Some letters dripped with declarations of love and hope, while others were filled with despair. These were not just simple love letters, but windows into Napoleon's soul; his innermost thoughts and feelings were laid bare as if speaking to a diary. But in this case, the recipient was not just any ordinary confidant – it was the twins' mother.

As they sat together, reading each letter for hours on end, it was as if they were meeting their mother through Napoleon's words.

"Claire, look at this one," Elena interrupted. "I think he's speaking of the stone."

"My dearest Anne ... blah blah blah." Elena trailed off, scanning the page until her eyes widened. "Here!"

For years, I've guarded a secret deep within my soul and hidden from the world – a power that has furnished the driving force behind my success. Now, I realize that it was never meant for me. It's hard to put this into words, but I feel it with every part of my being. I must find you before anyone else does.

As I write this letter, my hand trembles with the weight of the truth I'm about to reveal. The power I speak of is not merely metaphorical but tangible and extraordinary. It has shaped the course of history, guided my decisions, and led me to victories that seemed impossible. But with each passing day, I've grown more certain that I am merely its temporary guardian, not its rightful owner. This power was meant for you, and I will do whatever it takes to keep it safe.

You, my dear Anne, are the one for whom this power has been waiting. I've seen it in my dreams, over and over, and I feel it in the air around me when I think of you. It's as if the universe is conspiring to bring this power to you, the true heir. However, I must warn you that great power comes with great danger. There are those who would stop at nothing to possess what I've protected all these years. Dark forces lurk in the shadows. They do not yet know of you, but I fear it's only a matter of time before they discover the truth.

That is why I must find you. Not only to pass on this legacy that is rightfully yours, but also to protect you from those who seek to harm you. The burden I've carried all these years is heavy, but the thought of you in danger is unbearable.

Our paths will cross soon, of that I am certain.
With all my love,
N

Confusion was etched onto Claire's face. She furrowed her brow.

"Why would Napoleon want to give Mother the source of his power?"

Elena shook her head, equally perplexed. "I don't know ... maybe there's more in the letters." She reached for another letter from the stack, only to find it was the last one.

Claire gestured for Elena to open it.

My Dearest Anne,

I am sitting here, lost in a sea of uncertainty and heartache. Each day feels heavier than the last, weighed down by the worry and longing that seem to consume my every thought. I'm searching for you, but the search often feels futile, like grasping at shadows in the fading light.

The world around me continues to turn, oblivious to the void your absence has created. Where are you, Anne? Where are you, my love? With every passing moment, I worry that I may never find you again.

I must be cautious with what I divulge in this letter, as I fear it could lead to disastrous consequences if it falls into the wrong hands. Trust your instincts, for they are more powerful than you know. The pendant I gave you is more than just a family heirloom – it's the key to unlocking your destiny. Guard it well, for it will guide you to the truth of your heritage. Time grows short, and I fear my enemies draw ever closer. But know this, my dear Anne: whatever happens, whatever challenges you may face, you are not alone. This power is greater than any force that stands against you. I will continue to search, holding onto the hope that one day I will find you again.

With all my heart,

N

The sisters stood before each other, silently contemplating the final letter. It was a bittersweet moment, filled with pain and regret for what could have been. For a brief second, Elena's heart softened as she thought about the man who had searched tirelessly for their mother, now reduced to a mere memory in a faded letter.

"I almost feel sorry for him," she murmured.

Claire nodded, understanding.

"I almost wish… I could give him a hug," she confessed, surprising herself with the sudden surge of empathy.

Elena laughed at the thought. "A bit too much for me," she quipped.

Elena picked up the pendant and examined it closely. It looked like Claire's pendant, but she quickly rejected the idea of wearing it.

"It's not my style," she scoffed, placing it back on the table.

Curiosity getting the better of her, Claire reached for the small box still wrapped up in leather. It was heavy, roughly the size of her palm, and exquisitely crafted, with intricate designs adorning its surface. It was made of a material Claire couldn't quite identify – not entirely gold nor silver, but something in between that seemed to shimmer and change in the flickering candlelight of the captain's quarters. As her fingers brushed against the cool metal, she felt a subtle vibration, as if the box was alive.

"Open it," Elena urged.

Claire shook the box, intensely curious. She felt a magnetic pull toward its contents. She and Elena inspected every inch but found no clasp, no way to open it except for a small hole on the top that seemed to be watching them. A sense of foreboding washed over them as they held the box, as though a dark force was trying to seep into their minds. They quickly dismissed the feeling and placed the box on the table.

"Well, that was disappointing," Elena said with a sigh.

"I still can't wrap my head around why our father would want to give this to our mother. And why did he call it our inheritance?" Elena questioned out loud.

"I think he's referring to the cube's power," Claire replied.

"That mysterious cube again ..."

"You didn't hear Amir's tale!' Claire suddenly remembered.

She sat on the bed and began recounting everything.

"So in the end, according to him, Napoleon found one piece of the cube from a man named ... Galolei, or something." Claire tried to remember.

"Galileo Galilei? The renowned scientist?" Elena asked incredulously.

"Yes, I think that's him. Do you know him?"

"Not personally, but I do know who he is. He's quite famous and long dead, actually."

"Ah, okay. Well, anyway, that could be the same power that Father ... um, Napoleon, is referring to. But what I don't understand is why he would say it belonged to her," Claire mused.

Elena leaned back in her chair, her brow furrowed in contemplation. The soft glow of the oil lamp cast dancing shadows across her face, accentuating the thoughtful lines etched there.

"It's as if... as if these events were etched into our lives long before we were born, and I fear we've stumbled into something far bigger than ourselves."

Claire nodded slowly, her eyes distant as she recalled the seemingly impossible coincidences that had led them to this point.

"I know what you mean," she replied. "Everyone we've met or who has helped us somehow has been tied to this story. It's as if invisible threads have been pulling us all together." She paused, her gaze meeting Elena's. "I wonder if Napoleon was right, and this was all meant to happen."

Elena's fingers drummed a restless rhythm on the table as she considered her sister's words.

"We may never know for sure," she finally said, her voice tinged with frustration and wonder. "But one thing's certain: we have many questions and very few answers."

She sighed deeply, the sound loud in the quiet cabin.

The sisters sat silently for a moment, each lost in their thoughts. Claire felt the exhaustion of the day's events settling into her bones. The excitement of discovery had given way to a bone-deep weariness that threatened to overwhelm her. She stifled a yawn, her eyelids growing heavy.

"It's getting late," she said, stretching her arms above her head. "We should get some rest." Elena nodded in agreement, but her eyes remained fixed on the box.

The gentle sound of the boat rocking back and forth was soothing, and the sisters lay in bed, sharing fond childhood memories and getting to know each other better. These moments of peace and bonding were something they both treasured. As they drifted off into a deep slumber, their minds still buzzed with unanswered questions.

43

Elena's eyes snapped open as a blinding ray of light shone directly onto her face. She squinted and rubbed at her tired eyes, still groggy from sleep. Claire was snoring peacefully beside her. Memories from their late–night adventure flooded back to her as she took in dozens of scattered letters strewn across the bed. Both sisters were still holding a letter each in their hands, tightly grasping onto the last remnants of their bond with their mother and father. The mysterious box sat on the table, its secrets still locked away.

Feeling a warm sense of connection to Claire, Elena couldn't help but smile. She gently shook Claire awake.

"Claire. Claire," she urged, her voice low but insistent.

Grumbling incomprehensibly, Claire rolled over. Elena smiled and got ready for her duties as captain, letting Claire sleep in a little longer. The cabin reverberated with the sounds of the ship coming to life – cracking wood, splashing waves, and the crew bustling about as they fulfilled their duties. When Claire finally woke up, Elena was gone but the pile of letters on the bed reminded her of their conversation from the night before. She quickly began picking them up and reading bits and pieces from each one. Some words brought a smile to her face. As she sorted through the letters,

Claire's eyes fell upon the box on the table. Something inside tugged at her relentlessly, urging her to try opening it again. Nothing worked. Frustrated, she threw the box onto the bed with a growl.

Just then, her stomach grumbled insistently. She was hungry, but her mind was a whirlwind centered on one person: Richard. The memory of the previous night together, a vivid tableau of tender touches and passionate embraces, repeated in her mind. She could almost feel the warmth of his hands on her skin, the soft press of his lips against hers. A smile tugged at the corners of her mouth, unbidden but impossible to suppress. The intensity of her feelings thrilled and frightened her. In the midst of danger and uncertainty, she had found something precious and unexpected. But was it wrong to think about Richard at a time like this? She needed air, space to think, to breathe. With a decisive motion, she pushed open the door.

Richard was also torn, debating whether to knock on Claire's door or wait for her to come out. Richard leaned against the wall, closing his eyes; he didn't want to seem too eager, but he couldn't deny his desire to see her. Just as passed Elena's quarters, the door opened and Claire unexpectly emerged.

"I was coming to look for you," she said, flustered.

"Well, I'm here now." Richard replied with a charming smile, leaning in for a quick kiss. "I missed you."

"Did you?" she teased back, unable to hide her happiness.

"You left with your sister, and I didn't see you again after that."

"Oh yes! Come. Look." Claire beckoned him inside the room and pushed him onto the bed.

"My father ... Napoleon ... left us a bag full of letters he had written to our mother. Some are filled with love and affection, while others mention intriguing and peculiar things. He spent so much time searching for her. Unfortunately, his trust in Mortimer turned out to be his biggest mistake. But here's the interesting part: He insists that his power source was, in fact, intended for my mother. He wrote: *'the universe is conspiring to bring this power to you, the true heir.'* Quite odd, don't you think?"

Richard furrowed his brow.

"Interesting. Do you know why?"

"Nope. That's what we are wondering as well." Claire shook her head in frustration.

"He truly loved her," she breathed, her voice filled with wonder and a touch of reverence. "Some of these letters are incredibly poetic."

She paused, her chest rising and falling as she caught her breath. The brief silence was electric, charged with the weight of history and emotions stirred by long-lost words of love. Claire resumed speaking, and Richard found himself utterly mesmerized. Her voice, rich with passion and intelligence, wove a spell around him. Each word she uttered seemed to paint vivid pictures in the air. He watched, entranced, as her lips moved, shaping each syllable with care and precision.

"Anyway, we've been trying to open this box but we can't figure it out." Claire handed Richard the box from the bed.

He sat up quickly, visibly shaking with excitement.

"Claire, I think this is the safe my father made for Napoleon!"

"I remember you mentioning your father knew Napoleon too! Sorry, I wasn't paying much attention. Do you know how to open it?" Claire asked eagerly.

"I do not. But I remember what my father said ... Two pendants locked together are the key to opening the safe," Richard replied confidently.

Claire retrieved the second pendant from the table and unclasped hers, offering both to Richard. He carefully aligned them and locked them into one pendant key, revealing Napoleon's initials carved into the whole pendant. But when he attempted to use it on the box, there was no visible lock except for a small circle.

"You see? No keyhole," Claire sighed in disappointment.

Just then there came the clatter of the door opening.

"I brought breakfast ... Oh. Hello."

"Good morning, Elena," Richard said awkwardly, standing up from the bed.

"We're trying to open the box. Richard managed to lock the pendants together," Claire explained, inviting Elena to join their quest.

"The pendants get locked together?" Elena said, curiosity drawing her closer. She placed the breakfast tray on the table and climbed onto the bed.

"And guess what? Gerard made this safe specifically for Napoleon."

Claire was very excited. She leapt up and selected a pastry from the tray, absently nibbling.

"My father said two pendants would create a master key to open the box. He didn't mention anything else. And we have the master key now ... unless this is the wrong box?" Richard tried to recall his father's words. Claire looked at Richard in disbelief.

"No way. This has to be it. It's the right box," Claire exclaimed, her mouth full.

"Why would Napoleon entrust us with something important without giving us the means to unlock it? There must be something we're missing," Elena mused.

Suddenly, Claire gasped and exclaimed, "Remember what he said when you accepted the package?"

"That we are his blood?" Elena replied with confusion. "But what does that mean in this context? Unless his blood is somehow... the key to opening the safe? I've heard of this before – safes that require blood to unlock."

Richard chimed in. "Father did mention an additional safeguard added to the box, but I don't think he ever knew what it was. Too bad Napoleon didn't also give you a vial of his blood."

There was a pause, and then Elena said, a spark in her eye, "What about our blood? We are his daughters, after all."

Richard's doubtful expression turned to amazement as he considered the possibility. "Could that work?"

Without hesitation, Claire picked up a small bread knife and grazed her finger. She hissed at the stab of pain, and squeezed out a drop of blood.

Richard quickly moved the box closer, so that Claire's blood fell into the small hole atop the box. They all held their breaths as they waited for something miraculous to happen. But nothing did. Claire tried to squeeze out another drop of blood, but it seemed futile.

"Well, that's a shame," Elena said, disappointment evident in her voice.

Suddenly, Richard exclaimed, "Wait! Listen!"

A mechanism clicked into place, and the small hole in the box widened to reveal a keyhole. The trio stood in awe as they realized their plan was working. Richard wasted no time inserting the master key into the lock and trying different movements until it clicked and the mechanism inside began to move. With a sense of wonder and disbelief, they watched as the small box opened.

Without hesitation, Richard handed the box to Elena without even glancing inside. Claire moved closer to her sister, eager to see.

A thin beam of light shone from inside, gradually growing brighter until it was almost blinding. The three of them shielded their eyes, the intensity of the light far surpassing anything they could've ever expected. As their eyes adjusted to the searing brightness, a small object materialized before them, hovering inches above the open box. It was a piece of a rock, no larger than a fist, but unlike any stone they had ever seen. Its surface swirled in an endless kaleidoscope of colors, shifting and changing as if alive. Reds bled into deep purples, electric blues pulsed with veins of gold, and shimmering greens danced across the surface. The effect mesmerized them, drawing Elena and Claire closer and beckoning them with a hypnotic pull.

"Do you hear it?" Claire's voice was barely a whisper, her eyes wide with wonder and a touch of fear.

Elena nodded, her gaze fixed on the pulsating stone.

"I do," she breathed.

Richard looked between the two women and the floating rock, his brow furrowed in confusion.

"Hear what? All I see is a lot of light and a weird-looking stone," he replied.

"You don't hear anything?" Claire's voice quivered, and her eyes widened even further.

Richard shook his head, a growing sense of unease settling in his stomach. "No, I don't hear anything. Why? What do you hear?" But Claire and Elena seemed lost in their own world, their eyes glazing over as they stared at the stone.

"It's ... whispering," Elena murmured, her voice distant and dreamy. "Ancient battles ... stories ... secrets ..."

As Claire's fingertips grazed the surface of the small, iridescent rock, an invisible force seized her, rooting her to the spot. Her eyes widened, pupils dilating as if trying to absorb something beyond human comprehension. Without hesitation, Elena lunged forward, her hand closing around the stone in an attempt to break the connection. Instead, she, too, was instantly ensnared by its otherworldly power.

The air around them shimmered and distorted, reality seeming to bend and warp. At that moment, Claire and Elena ceased to exist in the present. Their consciousnesses hurtled through a kaleidoscopic tunnel of space and time, witnessing flashes of history so vivid and intense it defied description. Empires rose and fell in the blink of an eye, great leaders wielded unimaginable power, and civilizations beyond human reckoning revealed themselves in fleeting glimpses.

They saw the rock – no, the cube – pass through countless hands throughout the ages. Kings and conquerors, prophets and scientists, all touched by its power, all irrevocably changed. But this was more than a passive view of history. Claire and Elena absorbed knowledge with each vision, understanding dawning with each passing millisecond. The cube unveiled its origins, which were not of this Earth, but something far more ancient and profound. Its purpose, shrouded in cosmic mystery, began to take shape in their minds. And with this revelation came an undeniable truth: they were now part of something far greater than themselves, chosen by a force beyond mortal comprehension.

As abruptly as it had begun, the connection severed. Claire and Elena gasped in unison, stumbling backwards as if released from an invisible grip. The rock – the cube – pulsed once with a light that seemed to bend around the edges of reality before settling. It now looked completely innocuous.

"Claire! Elena! Are you alright? What happened?" Richard cried frantically.

But the two sisters could only stare at each other, a silent understanding passing between them. Though their eyes returned to normal, they conveyed new depths – the weight of millennia of cosmic truths too vast for words. Claire opened her mouth to speak but found she couldn't. How could one describe touching the fabric of time itself? Instead, she said, "We now ... understand."

Elena nodded solemnly, her gaze fixed on the seemingly innocent rock. "It's chosen us," she whispered. "And there's no going back."

Richard looked between them, confusion and worry etched on his face. "Chosen you? For what?"

But Claire and Elena remained silent, the significance of their new purpose settling over them like a mantle. They were now guardians of a power beyond imagining, bearers of a responsibility that spanned the cosmos itself.

And somewhere in space and time, ancient forces stirred, aware that the next chapter in an eons-old saga had begun.

"How long were we gone?" Claire whispered, her voice quivering with an ethereal resonance.

Richard's brow furrowed in confusion. "Gone? You never left. You both just touched the rock, and ... froze. But it was only for a brief moment."

Elena was confused. "Impossible. We were ... elsewhere. Everywhen. The cube showed us ... everything."

"Eons of history," Claire murmured, her gaze distant. "Every thread of fate, every seemingly random encounter ..."

"All of it intricately woven," Elena finished, "into a tapestry beyond comprehension."

The air in the room grew dense. Richard's skin prickled with an electricity he couldn't explain, his mind reeling as he tried to grasp the magnitude of their words. But Claire and Elena knew what they had experienced was far beyond Richard's comprehension. The cube wasn't just an object; it was a sentient entity, ancient and unfathomable, that had chosen them for a purpose that spanned the cosmos.

"Richard," Claire began with gravity, "what we experienced ... it wasn't just visions or memories. The cube is alive."

Elena nodded. "It's been waiting. For millennia. Choosing its guardians, guiding events, all leading to this moment."

The air in the room grew thick with energy as Claire and Elena revealed the cube's true nature.

"This cube is not just a source of power," Elena began, her voice resonating with an eerie timbre. "It's an entity older than our world, created millennia ago for a purpose ... far more insidious than we could have imagined."

Elena continued, her words weaving a tapestry of cosmic intrigue. "Its true purpose is not to bestow power. It connects to its guardian, manipulating reality while it watches and learns."

"Learns what?" Richard asked, his voice barely above a whisper, both awed and terrified.

Claire's gaze seemed to pierce through him. "Everything. Our deepest desires, our fears, our loves, our vulnerabilities, our ambitions, our hates. It moves in the shadows, unseen, weaving itself into the very fabric of our existence."

"But why?" Richard pressed, his mind reeling.

"To control and dominate all of creation," Elena replied heavily. "But not through force. It seeks control freely given, making it infinitely more dangerous. Any forceful takeover is bound to face resistance. Still, when the control is ingrained into one's existence, hidden in the shadows as mere coincidences, fate, or free will, it becomes truly unstoppable."

The air around them shimmered as they spoke, reality seeming to bend and warp.

"So someone, somewhere outside of our world, created this cube to control us?" Richard asked, his voice trembling.

Claire nodded solemnly. "We still have many questions, but we know where to start. The other fragments are calling to us. We must find them and reunite them."

Richard's face contorted in confusion and dismay. "Why would you help put together something meant to dominate humanity?"

"Because when Halina decided to protect the cube from falling into the wrong hands, something unprecedented happened. The cube experienced something more powerful than itself. Something that is ingrained in humans, although very rare to find."

"What was that?" Richard asked.

"Selfless sacrifice," Claire replied. "The cube was created as a tool of domination, a means to control and manipulate. It understood power, desire, and fear – all the base emotions that drive sentient beings across the universe."

"But it had never encountered true selflessness," Elena added. "When Halina chose to protect the cube, knowing full well the consequences she would face, she introduced a variable the cube had never calculated before. Imagine an entity older than our civilization, suddenly confronted with the concept of putting others before oneself. Of willingly embracing pain and suffering for the greater good. It was ... transformative."

"The cube's purpose was thrown into chaos," Claire continued. "Its understanding of domination and submission suddenly had to contend with this new factor – self-sacrifice."

Elena nodded solemnly. "It fractured not just physically but philosophically. The good and evil within it, once in perfect balance, now warred with one another. The concept of altruism vs. selfishness conflicted with its architecture. The cube sees good and evil as two sides of the same coin – both capable of being manipulated to achieve its ends. It could inspire great acts of heroism or unspeakable atrocities with equal ease, understanding that both served its overall purpose of domination. The cube's self-imposed fragmentation was no mere malfunction but a calculated evolution—a strategic move to comprehend human nature's intricacies better while formulating the ultimate dominion strategy. And that's why it's so crucial that we be the ones to reunite it."

"Why you?" Richard asked.

Claire's eyes blazed with determination.

"Because we are descended from Halina through our mother. We can put the cube together and tip the scales."

Richard's mind reeled as he tried to grasp what they were saying. "So when you reunite the cube ..."

"We have a chance to redefine its purpose," Elena finished. "To take an instrument of cosmic domination and transform it into something that could uplift civilizations rather than subjugate them."

"But it's a race against time," Claire warned. "The cube's creators are out there. If they reunite it first ..."

"So you see, Richard," Elena continued, "this isn't just about power or control. It's about the very nature of existence."

As if in response to her words, the cube fragment pulsed with a soft, warm light. For a brief moment, Richard felt a surge of something indescribable. He looked at Claire and Elena, no longer seeing two sisters, but the inheritors of a legacy standing at the crossroads of existence itself. Their task was monumental, their burden unimaginable, but in their eyes burned a determination that could move worlds.

Richard understood that he was witnessing the start of a journey that would have far-reaching consequences – a quest that would challenge not just humanity's fate, but the very fabric of reality.

To be continued...

EPILOGUE

The clock ticked ominously, each second stretching into eternity. Mortimer's pulse quickened, a wild rhythm in the stillness of the night. Amidst the chaos of his thoughts, a glimmer of hope flickered; Napoleon had yet to appear. Perhaps, just perhaps, there was still room for a cunning maneuver, a shrewd gambit that could alter his fortunes.

As Mortimer opened the door to his studio, the dimly lit space seemed to pulse with a life of its own, shadows flickering across the walls as if whispering secrets only they knew.

Mortimer stopped abruptly, his heart pounding in his chest. A cloaked figure loomed at his meticulously arranged desk—a stranger in his sacred space. A tense silence enveloped the room until the figure slowly lifted its hood, revealing a face Mortimer knew all too well. Very few things could unsettle Mortimer, but the specter from his past sitting before him was one of them, dredging up memories he had long tried to forget. Catching his breath, he furrowed his brow.

"Gilles?" Mortimer's voice tinged with shock and disbelief. With the barest hint of emotion crossing his face, Gilles leaned forward.

"Hello, brother!"

Acknowledgments

The journey from designer to author has been transformative, pushing me to grow in ways I never anticipated. I am grateful to the good folks who generously shared their ears, time, wisdom, and insights throughout this process. Your support and constructive feedback have been instrumental in refining this book.

Special thanks to Sydney and Ashley for their invaluable assistance.

About the Author

For as long as I can remember, I have had an insatiable passion for creating new, exciting, and unique things. The path to becoming an author was far from smooth. I grappled with self-doubt, fearing that my words wouldn't do justice to the stories in my head.

The journey from designer to author has been transformative, pushing me to grow in ways I never anticipated. I can proudly say that I am now a writer, and this is my first book – a tangible manifestation of my creative spirit and a testament to the power of pursuing one's passions.

This book represents more than just a collection of words on pages. It's a piece of my soul, a window into my imagination, and the culmination of a lifelong dream. As readers dive into its pages, I hope they'll feel the same sense of wonder and excitement that I experienced while creating it. This first book is just the beginning of a new creative adventure, and I can't wait to see where it leads next.

www.stefanoblackwood.com

Made in the USA
Middletown, DE
02 April 2025

73652411R00173